THE

All American

BOOKS BY SUSIE FINKBEINER

All Manner of Things
Stories That Bind Us
The Nature of Small Birds
The All-American

THE
All
American

A Novel

SUSIE
FINKBEINER

Revell

a division of Baker Publishing Group
Grand Rapids, Michigan

© 2023 by Susan Finkbeiner

Published by Revell
a division of Baker Publishing Group
Grand Rapids, Michigan
www.revellbooks.com

Printed in the United States of America

Library of Congress Cataloging-in-Publication Data
Names: Finkbeiner, Susie, author.
Title: The all-American / Susie Finkbeiner.
Description: Grand Rapids, Michigan : Revell, a division of Baker Publishing Group, [2023]
Identifiers: LCCN 2022050952 | ISBN 9780800739362 (paperback) | ISBN 9780800741532 (casebound) | ISBN 9781493436293 (ebook)
Subjects: LCGFT: Historical fiction. | Novels.
Classification: LCC PS3606.I552 A795 2023 | DDC 813/.6—dc23/eng/20221028
LC record available at https://lccn.loc.gov/2022050952

Scripture used in this book, whether quoted or paraphrased by the characters, is taken from the King James Version of the Bible.

Baker Publishing Group publications use paper produced from sustainable forestry practices and post-consumer waste whenever possible.

23 24 25 26 27 28 29   7 6 5 4 3 2 1

For my dearest niece Gwen.
When I wrote the part about the daisies,
I thought of you.

Part One

The first thaw always tricked us into thinking we'd come to the end of winter. We never should have believed it.

From *This Working-Day World*
by William S. Harding

one

According to Mrs. Higginbottom—home economics teacher at Bonaventure Park High School—there were certain skills that the average girl needed to master in order to secure for herself a good husband, live in a nice home, raise clean-cut children, and serve her country. Those skills included, in no particular order:

1. Keeping a spick-and-span house.
2. The wherewithal to put supper on the table at the exact time her husband wanted it.
3. The coordination to wear pumps while chasing toddlers and the grace to maintain her perfectly set hair while scrubbing the tub.

Et cetera, et cetera.

To make an exhaustive list would have only, well, exhausted me. Suffice to say, she believed that the All-American girl was at her best when living a life of married domesticity.

Also according to Mrs. Higginbottom, I, Bertha R. Harding, was doomed to spinsterhood.

Not that she'd ever said as much. She didn't have to. I saw it in her eyes every time I left streaks on the floor I was meant to be mopping, or when a sock I'd darned ended up more hideous than Frankenstein's monster.

It was all right by me, not being at the top of that class. As for my mother, well, she was a little less enthused.

Mam worried that my lack of domestic talents would reflect poorly on her. But the fault wasn't hers. It was completely mine. No matter how much effort I put into that doggone class, I couldn't manage to do much of anything right.

At the start of class that day, Mrs. Higginbottom told all of us girls that making a crust was as easy as pie—to which half of the girls laughed as if they'd never heard anything funnier in their lives.

I, however, had been dubious, remembering my many past failures with all things doughy.

I knew I'd been right to doubt when Mrs. Higginbottom said, "Young house makers, study the recipe on the board. Commit it to memory."

And then, only minutes later, erased all the instructions.

I had not, it turned out, committed it to memory, as was evidenced by the glob of goo that oozed at the edges on the counter in front of me.

All around me the other girls worked happily at rolling their crusts and dusting flour and being utterly and completely girlish.

Then there was me, sweating like a hog and unable to wipe my brow because every inch of my hands was covered in tacky, lumpy, unappetizing pie dough.

I was a mess, the crust was a bust, and I had no idea how to fix any of it.

"Ladies," Mrs. Higginbottom called, clapping her hands twice to get our attention.

Mrs. Higginbottom—sometimes referred to as Old Wigglebottom, but only when she wasn't around to hear it—looked like she was fresh out of a Norman Rockwell painting. Soft and round and in possession of the sweetest smile.

Mrs. Higginbottom really was a nice person. A nice person who—if school gossip could be believed—had a bit of a drinking problem.

"I have business to attend to," Mrs. Higginbottom said.

A few girls in the class exchanged knowing glances.

"Keep working," Mrs. Higginbottom went on. "I expect to see beautiful crusts from each of you when I return."

And with that, she slung her purse over her shoulder and stepped out of the classroom, the door thudding closed behind her.

Glancing up at the clock, I saw that I had just enough time left in class to give it another go. That was, as long as I suddenly remembered the recipe. And if I got started right away. I scooped up what I could of the first crust and dumped it in the trash can. It made the most horrible splatting sound when it hit the bottom.

This was hopeless.

I moaned. It came out louder than I'd meant for it to, and Violet—the poor, long-suffering soul forced to share a workspace with me—cleared her throat.

"Do you mind?" she said, glaring at me.

"Sorry," I said, cringing.

No one—but *no one*—took pie making as seriously as Violet Lancaster. And she had the blue ribbons to prove it. Four years in a row she'd won first place for her apple pie at the county fair. I had no doubt that she could have made a pie in her sleep if she needed to. With one hand tied behind her back.

"You used too much Crisco," Violet said, working the edge of her crust into crimps using thumbs and pointer finger.

"I did?" I asked. "How do you do that?"

She paused and glanced up at me.

"You have to be able to get the recipe right first," she said.

"Right." I sighed, wiping my hands on my apron.

"It's two cups flour, one cup shortening, by the way."

I wrinkled my nose, trying to figure out how I could have messed that up.

"Isn't that what I did?" I asked.

"No. I watched you. You got them switched."

"Oops," I said. "What about the water? One cup, right?"

Violet closed her eyes and exhaled through her nose, pushing her lips closed tight.

"Half," she said through clenched teeth. "Just half a cup."

"Boy, did I ever get it wrong." I chuckled. "You know, Vi, sometimes I wonder why they made you take this class at all."

She looked up from her pie, giving me a look like I had a rat sitting on top of my head.

"Why's that?" she asked.

"Well, it seems you know everything about being a wife already." I put my hands in the pockets of my flannel skirt and turned back toward my side of the counter. "Keep up the good work, sister."

"The water has to be cold, by the way," she called after me. "Ice cold."

I lifted my hand to give her a thumbs-up.

Violet was the kind of girl who planned to get married right after high school. I wouldn't have been surprised if she dreamed of having a late June wedding. She was the type to know just what sort of dress she wanted to wear and who she'd ask to be her maid of honor.

All she needed was for a suitable boy to propose.

As far as I knew, she'd have her pick of the litter when the time came around.

She'd make the perfect wife.

Good for her.

I really meant that.

I let the tap water run, hoping that would get it icy cold like Violet said it should be.

While I waited, I looked at the posters that had been on the far wall for so long I was sure they were stuck there permanently. "Plant a Garden for Victory!" or "Missing Him Won't Bring Him Home Sooner: Get a War Job!" or "Mend, Don't Spend! Save the New for the Boys!"

One poster had a very blond woman—a very young and pretty woman—with a pie balancing on her hands.

"I know how to welcome him home," she said via comic-book bubble suspended over her head. "A homemade apple pie for my own homegrown hero."

I rolled my eyes at that very blond, very pretty girl and measured out a cup of water, hoping that was how much I needed.

Violet watched as I pried the top off the can of Crisco. She crossed her arms while I spooned globs of gunk into the measuring cup.

If I was ever going to get married, I'd need to find a man who didn't have much of a sweet tooth. Either that or a house that was close to a bakery.

two

FLOSSIE

I couldn't have known from personal experience—I'd never been sent to the office before—but rumor had it that Principal Braun kept a paddle that he used on very naughty children. I'd even heard that it had holes drilled into it so it would leave welts.

There was a story that one boy was so scared that he wet his pants right when Mr. Braun lifted the paddle. Then, from what I heard, he got another smack because he'd made a mess of the principal's slacks.

I wasn't sure if any of that was true. Still, I'd made a stop at the little girls' room just in case.

A girl couldn't be too careful.

I stood just outside the office, biting my lower lip so I'd remember not to let it tremble, and I told myself over and over in my head that I was *not* going to cry. Not even if I got the paddle. Not even if Mr. Braun said he would have to call my mother.

Holding my chin up, I walked into the office—well, wobbled might've been the better word for it. I still wasn't used to wearing high heels. I handed Mrs. DeYoung—the school secretary—the note from my teacher, Miss Lange.

Miss Lange hated me.

"Florence," Mrs. DeYoung said, clutching her pearls and looking me up one way and down the other. "Oh my."

I grabbed the sides of my skirt and twisted the cotton between my fingers. I couldn't tell if "oh my" was said in awe or pity.

"I'm supposed to see Mr. Braun," I said with the smallest little bit of a shake in my voice. "Please."

"Okay." She got up from her chair and smoothed her skirt, the teacher's note still folded in her hand.

She hadn't even read it.

While she was gone in the principal's office, I looked down, noticing that the two rolled-up wads of toilet paper I'd stuffed in my undershirt had gone a little cockeyed. Making sure nobody was looking, I did my best to adjust them.

"Florence." Mrs. DeYoung glanced down at my blouse and cleared her throat.

"Yes," I said, dropping my hands.

"Principal Braun will see you," she said.

The lip I'd tried to remind to keep still started to tremble.

"Here, dear," Mrs. DeYoung whispered. Then she used her own hanky to wipe under my mouth. "Your lipstick is just a bit smudged."

"It's my sister's," I whispered back.

"Is that so?"

"Yes."

"Well, it's a very pretty color." She dabbed a spot near the corner of my lips. "I think it might've gotten away from you a little."

"Thank you," I said.

"You've never gotten in trouble at school before, have you?"

I shook my head.

"And you're scared?" she asked.

I nodded.

"Well."

That was all she said. Then she took me by the shoulders and turned me, pushing me into the principal's office.

Mr. Braun was at his desk reading what I guessed was the note my teacher had sent me with. He didn't look up when I stepped in.

"Miss Harding," he said. "Have a seat."

I did. And while I waited for him to read the note—honestly,

15

how much had Miss Lange written?—I searched the room for the paddle and decided he must have it hidden somewhere behind his desk because it wasn't in plain sight.

He took off his reading glasses before looking up at me.

"Oh," he said.

It was like I'd tossed confetti and yelled "Surprise!"

I guessed he'd never seen an eleven-year-old girl with a full face of makeup before. And a shirt full of wadded-up toilet paper. If only he could have seen the high heels on my feet—also full of wadded-up toilet paper. A girl had to make up for her lack somehow.

"Miss Harding . . ."

"Do you have a paddle?" I asked, the words out before I could even think about them.

"Excuse me?"

"Do you have a paddle?" I folded my hands together in my lap. "With holes drilled into it so it gives kids welts?"

"Well, that isn't why there are holes . . ."

"Because if you're going to paddle me with it, I have a right to know."

I pushed my lips into a thin line and squeezed my hands together all the harder.

"Miss Harding, in my twenty years as a principal, I have never paddled a little girl," he said. "Now, would you like to tell me why Miss Lange sent you to my office today?"

"As a matter of fact," I said, "I'd rather not."

"I must insist that you do." He cleared his throat. "How about we start with you telling me why you came to school dressed like that."

"I didn't come to school like this."

"Beg your pardon?"

"Well, of course my mother wouldn't have let me leave the house like this," I said. "I changed in the girls' room before the first bell."

"I see."

He scratched the top of his head, which made me think he definitely didn't understand. That was fine. He was a man so he didn't need to.

"Next you'll want to know why I changed," I said. "Is that correct?"

He nodded.

"I wanted to look older. A little more mature." I crossed my ankles. "Being the smallest in my class is the pits, you know."

"I'm sure it is." He glanced at Miss Lange's note. "Now, if you will, tell me about what happened with Iris Markowitz."

I bit the inside of my cheek because I really didn't want to tell him about that.

Iris Markowitz was the prettiest, best dressed, most well-liked girl in our class. She thought that she was the smartest, but she was wrong.

It was me. I was the smartest.

Bertha had warned me not to brag about it, though, saying that nobody liked a know-it-all teacher's pet.

Well, I wasn't there to make friends. At least that was what I told myself when I ate lunch all alone or heard girls talk about the slumber party I hadn't been invited to.

"Miss Harding?" Mr. Braun said. "What happened between you and Iris?"

"She made fun of me," I answered.

The year before the kids in my class had made up a song about me, which wasn't nice in the least. It was called "Little Baby Bumpkin."

They'd made up scads of verses that had me living in a pumpkin and marrying a munchkin.

My big brother Chippy had told me not to let it get to me, that those kids were just trying to get my goat.

Most days I could ignore them, keeping my nose firmly planted in a book.

But that day Iris had gone too far.

She'd pointed out my toilet paper bosom and sang—under her breath but loud enough for most of the class to hear—a brand-new verse of the Baby Bumpkin song.

"Little Baby Bumpkin, sucking on her thumb-kin," she'd sang. "Never adored cause she's flat as a board."

That was it. I couldn't take it another second.

"What happened then?" Principal Braun asked.

"I slapped her across her stupid face," I said.

He blinked a couple times real slowly, like he didn't quite believe what he'd just heard.

"That's all," I said. "Are you going to paddle me now?"

He squinted at me before shaking his head.

"No, Miss Harding, I am not," he said.

What a relief.

"But," he said, "I do believe I'll have to talk with your mother."

Oh no.

"You do not need to talk to my mother," I said.

"Florence—"

"You may call me Flossie," I interrupted.

"Flossie, I've heard that you're a good student." He pushed his lips together, hard, and it made the corners of his mouth turn down into a frown. "But . . ."

"I make good grades," I said, not pointing out that I had the best grades in my entire class. That would have been arrogant.

"School is about more than good grades."

What a thing for the principal of a school to say!

"Your teacher seems to think you haven't tried very hard to make friends." He held up the letter from Miss Lange, waving it in front of me. "Don't you have any friends at all?"

"Of course I do," I said.

It wasn't a fib. Not entirely.

I had plenty of friends if the characters from books counted. Besides, Chippy was my friend and sometimes Bertha too.

"How about friends in your class?" Mr. Braun asked.

"Oh no," I answered, shaking my head. "They don't like me at all."

"Why do you think that is?"

"I couldn't tell ya."

"Would it hurt to put forth a little effort?" he asked. "To make nice with them?"

The tip-tops of my ears felt like they were on fire, and that was the first sure sign that I was about to lose my temper.

I had tried, honest Abe I had. I'd done everything I could think of to make Iris and them be my friends.

Earlier in the year when all the girls in the class were wearing their hair in ponytails, I started having Mam put mine up in the morning. And when they all added ribbons to their hair, I found a pretty red one in Mam's sewing basket. Then when they all cut their bangs, I did too.

Never mind that Mam had the hardest time trying to get them even after the job I'd done with her sewing shears.

Also—I wasn't proud of it—but I'd even done Iris's homework a time or two.

It hadn't mattered at all in the end. She was mean to me anyway.

"I'll bet Iris wants to be your friend," Mr. Braun said. "She's a very nice girl, don't you think?"

"No, I do not," I answered. "She's horrible."

"Now, why would you say that?"

I reminded him, as respectfully as I could, of the Baby Bumpkin song.

"Just good-natured teasing," he said. "After all, 'sticks and stones may break my bones . . .'"

He lifted his hand like he wanted me to finish the silly little rhyme. But I wouldn't do it. I bit my lips between my front teeth and shook my head.

"Come now, Florence."

I made a "mmm-hmm" sound without opening my mouth.

"Surely you *want* to have friends," he said.

I did. More than anything else in the world.

So much that I couldn't help but burst out into loud, heaving, messy tears just thinking about it. I didn't have a single friend in all the world.

"Now, there, there," Mr. Braun said, pushing a box of tissues across the desk toward me.

I didn't want his pity or his stupid tissues.

I looked him right in the eye and reached down my shirt, grabbing both wads of toilet paper, and used those instead.

His jaw tensed and he cleared his throat before telling me that I was dismissed.

I took off Mam's shoes and walked down the hallway in just my bobby socks.

three

BERTHA

We hadn't always lived in Bonaventure Park. When I was very small, we rented rooms in a house in Corktown. I didn't remember a whole lot about that place or its close proximity to Navin Field where the Tigers played—I was too young and hadn't yet fallen in love with baseball. What a pity. But I did know that the curtains in the kitchen had tiny daisies all over them. Whenever Mam talked about that time, she said that we were all very happy and packed in like sardines.

We didn't even own a car back then. Dad took the streetcar to the Ford factory where he worked, and there was a park that Mam walked my big brother Chip and me to when the weather was nice.

I didn't realize we were poor until I was a bit older and Mam mentioned something about making ends meet and how, most of the time, Dad's paychecks ran out before the days of the month did. Then again, it was the Depression. Practically everyone was in the same boat as us. Either that or a much worse one with a leaky bottom.

We remained, through those lean years, happy sardines in our tiny apartment.

Then we moved out to the suburbs and grew into the big house Dad had bought by adding Flossie, a cat, and a whole bunch of mismatched furniture.

Bonaventure Park was the sort of place where the neighbors

knew each other by name, the grass of every yard was well tended, and there was an American flag waving over every house.

It was also the sort of town where nobody threw any kind of fit when the neighborhood boys took over an old, abandoned plot of land behind Richmond's Department Store and turned it into a sandlot.

Whenever the weather was nice—and sometimes even when it wasn't—the boys of Bonaventure Park picked teams and played themselves a game of baseball.

I guess I was about seven years old when I first got up the nerve to join them, the ball glove I'd gotten from Uncle Matthew at Christmas on my hand in the hopes that they'd let me play. They didn't. And on the next game day, I got there to find a sign nailed to the makeshift backstop that said, "NO GIRLS ALOUD!"

Not being one to correct someone else, I didn't point out the spelling error. But I did come back for the next game and then the next until, one day, they were short a player—Stinky Simon had the flu—and they had no choice other than to put me in the outfield.

The next time I came out to play, there was a second sign nailed below the first.

"ACCEPT BERTHA!"

I sure hoped the teachers wouldn't stop by and realize how terribly they had failed one of their students.

That afternoon, word had gotten around school that we'd play a game as soon as the last class was dismissed for the day. Well, I tried my best to hurry out to the sandlot, but I couldn't very well sprint while carrying the apple pie in my hands.

So, I took it nice and easy all the way.

By the time I got there, they were already in the bottom half of the second inning. They'd started without me. Doggone it.

Aside from that, there was a cluster of girls standing along the third baseline, giggling and making eyes at the boys. When they saw me walking up, they smiled and made room for me to stand with them.

It was nice of them, honestly it was. But the last thing I wanted was for the boys I'd chummed around with for the last nine years to tease me for hanging out with the gaggle of girls. I hesitated until Emily Perez—a girl a year behind me at school—nodded at my hands and asked, "Did you make that in home ec?"

"The pie?" I asked. "Yeah."

"Did you drop it or something?" She wrinkled her nose.

"Well, not exactly." I shrugged and looked down at my pie.

I could see why she might have thought that some tragedy had befallen the poor, homely thing. Lopsided crust, clumsy looking crimps, boiled-over filling, that pie wasn't going to win any beauty pageants.

"I'll bet it tastes all right anyhow," Emily said.

"Gosh. That's nice of you to say." I gave her a smile. "Mrs. Higginbottom gave me a C−."

"That's too bad," she said.

"No. I'm thrilled." I took a step toward the girls. "It's ugly, but I don't think it's poisonous."

Emily looked at the pie like it might bite her.

"It's not," I said. "I was just kidding."

The girls made room for me in their huddle, and it felt nice—strange, but nice—to be included.

But just as soon as I joined them, I heard my name called from the pitcher's mound.

"Bert!" It was Bobbo Gomez. "Quit messin' around. You're at bat."

"Oh!" I smiled at Emily. "Do you mind holding this a second?"

I handed her the pie and got to work on the button of my skirt so I could shimmy it off my hips.

"Geez Louise!" she said.

"Don't worry," I said. "I've got Levi's on under."

"Oh."

I stepped out of the skirt and threw it over my arm. Then I took the pie back, with thanks to Emily for holding it, and turned toward home plate.

"Wait," Emily said. "What are you doing?"

"Playing ball," I answered, looking at her over my shoulder.

23

"With boys?"

"Mmm-hmm."

"Golly."

I marched over to the dugout—nothing more than a bench for the boys to sit on, waiting for their turn at bat. Stinky Simon Abrams eyeballed the pie, and I made it known that it was *not* for him.

"Aw, come on, Bert," he whined. "Just one bite?"

"No such luck for you," I said, placing the pie down, ever so carefully, on the bench.

"Come on!" a kid yelled from the outfield. "What's the holdup? She puttin' on makeup or somethin'?"

"Keep your pants on," I yelled, grabbing the Louisville Slugger and making my way to the plate.

Most of the boys had a ritual they performed before batting. They'd wiggle their behinds or spit to one side or the other. A few of them did special stretches and others tapped their toes with the end of the bat.

Not me. I was content to stand at the plate and get into position.

"Ready?" Bobbo asked. "Want I should take it easy on ya? Toss a nice slow one at ya?"

"Nope," I said, not showing my annoyance.

"I wouldn't want ya to mess up your hair or nothing."

He was trying to get my goat, that was all. I wouldn't let him.

"Just pitch, Bob," I said, calm as I could.

The first was out of my strike zone, and I let it go without flinching. The second was just inside and I should have swung for it. But the third was my pitch. I knew as soon as it left Bobbo's hand.

Somehow my body knew exactly how to move, my muscles knew when to flex and relax, my lungs knew when to hold a breath and when to let it go. I didn't have to think about it at all.

Natural as a heartbeat.

The swing felt exactly as it should have. I felt the connection of bat and ball all the way through my hands, wrists, up through my elbows and into my shoulders. The crack was one of the most satisfying sounds that meant only one thing.

I needed to run.

It ended up being a double, and I took a breather on second while Stinky Simon got himself ready to bat.

He was one who went through an extensive batting ritual, so I had time to rest a minute.

"Nice hit," Leo Schmidt said.

Leo always, but always, played second base. He said it was the most perfect position for a big guy like him.

"Thanks." I kept my eye on Stinky so I wouldn't miss it if I needed to make a break for third.

Leo kept his eye on me because he knew how much I liked stealing bases.

"There's lots of girls here today, huh?" he asked.

"Yup." I licked my lips.

"Probably fishing for a date to the dance."

"Maybe."

Oh, that doggone dance. It was all anybody at school had wanted to talk about. Who was going with whom. What dresses were on display at Richmond's Department Store. And on and on and on. I was already sick of hearing about it, and there was still a couple weeks before it would finally be over.

Then they'd all get started talking about the junior and senior prom.

Merciful heavens, these girls absolutely lived for that sort of thing.

"Say," Leo said, "were you thinking of going?"

Stinky was about halfway through his routine and nobody rushed him for fear that he'd want to start all over again from the beginning.

"To third?" I asked. "Why would I tell you that?"

"The sock hop."

"Oh, that?" I shrugged, then inched away from the base, getting ready to sprint. "Probably not."

"Well, would you want to be my date?" Leo asked.

"Uh . . ." I started.

But I didn't get to give him an answer because Bobbo sent a

curveball to Stinky, who hit it deep into the outfield. I didn't know if it dropped, but I wasn't sticking around second base to find out. I ran like a cougar was at my heels, rounding third like it was nothing.

"Go, go, go!" Stinky yelled from behind me.

How he'd caught up to me so fast, I'd never figure out. But I knew that if I didn't speed up, he was going to run right over me.

But when I was halfway to home, I saw Otis Piles—the kid playing catcher on that particular day—blocking the plate. That meant one thing and one thing only.

I was going to have to slide if I ever had any hope of making it.

I ran harder, faster, and didn't even care that I was sliding all over in the dirt. When I was nearly there, I dropped into a slide, feet aimed right at Otis to kick him out of the way so both me and Stinky could get a run for our team.

Before I knew what was happening, I was on top of Otis and Stinky was on top of me, a cloud of dust puffed up around all three of us.

"Safe! We're both safe!" Stinky yelled, using my shoulder to push himself up. "We made it."

"You all right, Bert?" Otis asked.

"Yeah," I said, not entirely sure I was okay. "I think so. You?"

"You sure knocked the wind outta me." He rolled over onto his back and rubbed his left side. "I think I have a dent the shape of your foot in my ribs."

"Oof. Sorry about that, pal."

He didn't wince too badly when I helped him up, so I figured he hadn't broken anything. At least I hoped not. I'd have a few bruises and maybe a strawberry but wasn't too worse for wear.

On days like those, we only played four innings. Five if we were going through hitters fast. If we played any more, we'd run out of daylight and—even worse—be late for supper.

A few of the girls were still gathered on the sidelines, hoping, I supposed, to be noticed by a boy or two. Luckily for them, a couple of boys were making their way to them. The boys were Stinky Simon, Bobbo, and Otis, so it was up to those ladies to decide if that was good or not.

I grabbed my things—most notably the pie that made it through the game in better shape than I had—and headed in the direction for home. Leo hollered after me to wait up.

He jogged up to me, big old silly grin on his face.

"That was some good playing," he said. "Can I walk you home?"

The boy had been walking home with me every day after school for as long as I'd lived in the neighborhood. He'd never bothered to ask permission before.

First, asking me to the dance. Next wanting to escort me home? What in the world had gotten into him?

"Sure," I said. "I guess so."

He reached for my books, and I snorted and shook my head.

"I'm plenty strong enough," I said.

"I know you are." He sighed. "I'm *trying* to be a gentleman."

"Fine." I let him take them.

We talked about the game while we went the two blocks to the alley behind our row of houses and all the way to my backyard gate.

"So, what do you think?" he asked, turning toward me. "Will you let me take you to the dance?"

I gulped.

Mrs. Higginbottom would have been appalled. A lady wasn't supposed to gulp when a boy asked her out on a date, even if it was Leo Schmidt who was asking.

"Are you sure you wouldn't rather go with Violet?" I asked. "Or . . . or somebody like her?"

"Nah." He closed one eye. "You're more fun than any of the other girls at school."

"Yeah?"

"Yeah."

Was that burning in my cheeks the onset of blushing? Oh gosh. It was.

"I, well," I stammered. "I wouldn't even know what to wear."

"Something blue," Leo said. "To match your eyes."

He knew what color my eyes were?

I realized that I'd never, not even once, looked at his eyes. Not really. I did and got the strangest feeling in my tummy. It was exactly the same as when I was a kid and got up really high on the swings.

His eyes were brown. And they were kind.

I couldn't look at them too long without feeling just the tiniest bit light-headed.

What in the world was happening to me?

"What do ya say?" he asked. "Wanna go?"

"Why not?" I answered.

"Swell."

He winked at me.

For the first time I understood why other girls got the giggles around boys. I clenched my teeth hard so I wouldn't giggle in front of Leo. Nothing but nothing would be more humiliating than that.

He helped me balance the pie on top of my books and watched me walk to the back stoop, making sure I could get inside without dropping anything.

I couldn't decide which was better, sliding into home or seeing the way Leo smiled at me before he headed toward his house.

four

FLOSSIE

I was in no mood to talk to anybody. So, as soon as I got home, I stomped my way up the stairs—after slamming the front door and dropping my schoolbooks on the floor—and jumped into bed, pulling the covers all the way over my head.

No one followed me to check and see if I was okay.

Good!

I hadn't wanted them to anyhow.

It had been the lousiest kind of day and I wanted to be left alone. Completely. And I sure didn't want or need anyone's pity.

It got awfully boring, though, hiding under my blankets that way, waiting for somebody—Mam, Dad, Bertha—to barge in. So I got out of bed and borrowed the book off Bertha's bedside table.

The Catcher in the Rye.

"Oh, goodie." I rolled my eyes.

Another book about baseball.

But then I saw that it had a carousel horse on the cover and thought it couldn't hurt to give the book a try.

Sitting cross-legged on my bed, I read about a boy who was—surprisingly—not a baseball player. But he was more miserable than anybody else in all the world, including me.

Good grief, that Holden Caulfield was a whiny boy.

He certainly was no Gilbert Blythe.

Oh! Just the thought of Gilbert made me weak in the knees.

Dreamy Gilbert.

I feared that no boy would ever hold up to my expectations because of him.

It took all of my resolve to put aside thoughts of Gilbert Blythe and return to grumpy Holden Caulfield. I sighed. The book was boring me out of my skull. I couldn't figure out what made it so doggone popular.

So—I hated to admit it—I jumped ahead. Nothing much was happening anyway. That was when I saw a word that I knew was bad. It was probably the very worst word someone could say other than taking the Lord's name in vain.

I didn't know what made it bad, but Jimmy O'Shea had said it once on the playground, and when Miss Lange found out, she'd made him bite the bar of soap from the classroom sink. Then she'd sent him straight to Mr. Braun's office where—I had to guess—he'd gotten the paddle.

I pulled the covers over my head and pressed my face into the pillow and whispered the word just so I could know what it felt like to say something so wicked.

It was wrong and my Sunday school teacher would have been so ashamed of me for it. But my curiosity got the better of me yet again. I couldn't hardly help it.

I stopped whispering that very sinful word when I heard footsteps on the stairs that walked right up to my bedroom door.

"Flossie, dear?" It was Mam. "Are you in there, love?"

She pronounced that last word *loove* because she was from England and that meant that she said things differently than anyone else in the neighborhood.

Mam knocked on the door before coming in.

"Ah, there you are," she said, glancing at the book on my bed. "What in heaven's name are you reading?"

She crossed the room in three steps and put her hand out for me to give it over. Instead, I opened the book to the page where Holden Caulfield says that terrible, dirty word.

"What does this mean?" I asked, pointing at it.

She looked and gasped, grabbing the book away from me.

"It means you're too young to read it." She closed it and held it between her thumb and pointer finger. "Where did you get this?"

"From Bertha."

"Well . . ."

"What does that word mean?" I asked again.

"Nothing nice, that's what," she said, wrinkling her nose. "If I ever hear you say it, you'll be sorry."

"What if I say it and you don't hear me?"

She raised her eyebrow in the way that said, "Don't test me, young lady," and tossed the book on Bertha's bed.

Mam told me that it was time for me to have my tea. Most mothers gave their children milk and cookies after school, but not my mother. She always had tea and biscuits—which were cookies by another name, but they still tasted sweet.

After tea and before supper I snuck back upstairs to read more of *The Catcher in the Rye*. All right, all right. So, I complained about how awful Holden Caulfield was. And I still believed it. But something in the middle of my chest felt sorry for him too.

I didn't really understand everything that happened, and I skipped over some of the more boring parts—he really did go on and on. But I did know that he was sad even if he never said so.

His brother died before the book even began. If Chippy died, I'd be wretched for a long time too. Not only that, but nobody—*nobody*—liked Holden. Not even his mother.

I knew a little bit about how that was. Nobody—*nobody*—at school liked me. Not even my teacher.

But Mam liked me a whole lot. So did Dad and Chippy and Bertha.

The cat? Well, he was a cat, so his opinion didn't count for much.

Anyway, I knew the tiniest bit what it was like to be a kid like Holden Caulfield. It was the pits.

I turned all the way to the second to last chapter. Holden talked about watching a bunch of children playing a game too close to the edge of a cliff and how he wanted to catch them all before they fell.

I didn't know why he imagined that. Dad would have been able to explain it to me. He always understood stuff like that. But if I asked him, he'd know I'd been reading a book that I was too young for.

So I just leaned back against my headboard and imagined being in that field that Holden talked about and inching up to the edge to see what was down below.

five

BERTHA

Most of the world—well, the reading world, at least—knew my father as William S. Harding, author of books like *This Working-Day World* and *A Strange Eventful History*. His novels were reviewed in all the most popular papers and journals that called his writing "a revelation" and "stunning" and even declared him "the next John Steinbeck."

When Dad's editor sent him clippings of those great reviews, Mam would paste them into a scrapbook she kept on a shelf in the living room.

Of course, though, not everyone thought he was so very brilliant.

I only knew that because Mam also stuck those less-than-flattering reviews into the old scrapbook.

"Harding's characters fall flat, the plot is uninteresting, the pace slothful," one read. "If some other readers think him a Steinbeck, then I say Mr. Harding is unnecessary. We've already got a Steinbeck. We little need a dime-store imitation."

Another called my father "dangerous," claiming that his novels "smack of Stalinist sympathies." That one went on to say that "Wm. S. Harding's work will be lost to history and for that the world should be glad."

Ouch.

Someone—my guess was Mam—had written a big old "HA HA HA!" in red under each of the negative reviews.

However, I suspected that, if Mam ever had the opportunity to, she wouldn't have just laughed in those reviewers' faces but might have pinched them on the back of their arms where the skin was tender and given them a hefty dose of grievance on Dad's behalf.

As for Dad, he did his best to ignore all the reviews—good and bad.

"Nothing but distractions," he'd say. "'Sound and fury signifying nothing.'"

He'd go into his backyard shed-turned-office regardless of what the papers said and get to work on the next story.

Sometimes that next story kept him working late into the evenings and he couldn't be convinced to come in for supper. On nights like that, it was Flossie's or my job to take a tray out to him. That night it was up to me and I didn't bother with a coat even if it was still below freezing. It hardly seemed worth the hassle if I'd only be out there all of two minutes.

"Dinner delivery," I called, managing to get myself into the shed while balancing the tray on one arm.

What I lacked in homemaking skills I sure made up for in coordination.

He paused in his typing to put up one finger, letting me know to wait just a second longer. Then he went back to clickety-clacking.

Still holding the tray, I looked at the collection of framed photos he'd hung on the wall long before. Him and Mam on their wedding day. All of us kids sitting on the porch with enormous slices of watermelon. Mam holding a newborn against her chest, eyes closed and sweet smile on her face. And that was just for starters.

Golly. Dad had a lot of pictures on his wall.

Newest in the collection—one I couldn't remember having seen before—looked to be the oldest. It was of my dad and his brother Matthew when they were boys. In the photo they had their arms around each other's shoulders. They both had baseball gloves on. Uncle Matthew's on his left and Dad's on his right.

"Matt and Southpaw" was written in ink on the white border of the photo.

"What's for supper?" Dad asked, getting up and taking the tray from me. "Chicken and dumplings, huh?"

"Mam's specialty," I answered. "Say, where did you get this picture?"

"Oh, that? Matthew sent it to me." He nodded at the food. "Where'd you get the pie?"

"I made that at school today," I said.

I'd saved the best-looking piece—the one that wasn't too terribly lopsided—for him.

"Oh, and I have coffee for you." I grabbed the thermos out from under my arm.

"Good girl."

"How's the writing going?" I asked, struggling to twist the top off the thermos.

He hated that question, and I could have just kicked myself for asking it right off the bat like that. But it had slipped out before I could catch it. He grimaced, and I told him I was sorry.

With a wave of the hand, he brushed off my apology and grabbed the thermos, straining but able to get the top off.

"Your mother is awfully strong," he said.

I nodded.

He took a swig of coffee directly from the thermos, sighing after the first swallow.

I'd heard of lots of writers who drank booze all day and all night while they were writing. Dad had been one of them for years—that's what I'd heard from Mam at least.

But once my brother Chip was born, he swore off it.

Mam's version of the story was that she told him he'd better or else she'd lock him out of the apartment.

Either way, Dad tried to stay away from the stuff.

"Some men can hold their liquor," he'd told me once. "They can stop at just one or two drinks. I wasn't that kind of man."

So, he'd replaced the whiskey and bourbon with coffee and Tootsie Rolls.

As far as I knew, he'd only returned to it once since.

I shook off that memory, not liking to think of it.

Dad took another long drink of the thermos before putting the top on—twisting it with less vigor than Mam had.

"Thanks, Bertha," he said. "That really hit the spot."

"You're welcome," I said. Then, nodding at the typewriter, "I guess I'll leave you to it."

"Can you stay to visit?" he asked, stepping over my words. "For a little bit?"

It was a rare invitation, and I was so surprised by it that I didn't answer right away.

"Unless you have something better to do." He set the thermos on his desk. "I wouldn't mind a little reprieve from that." He motioned toward the page hanging out from the top of his typewriter.

"Is that it?" I asked.

"If by *it* you mean the new novel, then yes. That's it," he said. "And to answer your question from earlier, it's going rough. Well, today it is."

"Tomorrow will be better." I dragged the rocking chair from the corner of the room to be closer to the propane heater. "Don't you think so?"

"I hope so." He pointed at the slice of pie. "You said that you made this?"

"In class." I drew in a deep breath, nervous that he might not like it.

"Well, it looks fine." He picked up his fork and dug in.

No one's opinion mattered quite so much to me as my dad's.

He lifted the bite to his mouth, and I did my very best not to lean forward and inch up to the edge of my seat. When he closed his eyes and leaned back in his chair, I worried for the flash of a second that I'd poisoned him after all. I had visions of the Brewster sisters and elderberry wine and having to hide bodies in the window box like they did in *Arsenic and Old Lace*.

We didn't even have a window box!

"Dad?" I asked.

His eyes popped open. Thank goodness!

"It's just right," he said. "I'm going to save the rest of it for after I've had my supper."

Dollars to donuts he was just trying to spare my feelings. The way he took another slug from the coffee thermos convinced me it was true.

"Say, I read something in the paper you might be interested in," he said, cutting a dumpling in two with the edge of his fork.

"You did?" I asked.

He took a bite of chicken, veg, and gravy before nodding and half standing to riffle through a pile of papers on a shelf by his desk.

"Now where did it get off to?" he muttered to himself. And, "I really need to organize this desk."

Every few months Mam would tire of the clutter in Dad's writing shed. She'd wait until he'd gone out for a pack of Lucky Strikes or come into the house to take a phone call. Then she'd rush out with a trash can and a feather duster and take a quick sweep of everything that wasn't nailed down.

Luckily for Dad—and the rest of us—she'd never tossed a single page of a manuscript he was writing. That was our family's bread and butter. At least she hadn't yet.

If my father feared anything in the world, it was that Mam would snatch away whole chapters in the name of order.

"Ah, here it is," Dad said, pulling a page of newspaper out from the bottom of a stack of books. "Right where I left it."

He turned so that I could look at the paper over his shoulder, pointing at a short article in the middle of the page. I read it once all the way through. Then again. Before I read it a third time, I grabbed the paper from him.

WORKINGTON STILL IN LEAGUE

by Al Rogers

After a full year of talks and negotiations, Justin "JuJu" Eames announced earlier today that the Workington Sweet Peas are officially in for the 1952 season of the All-American

Girls Professional Baseball League (AAGPBL). According to Eames, the team was nearly dissolved after last year's losing season. But our "Girls in Green" will get another go at it this summer!

Waning interest in the Sweeties was also a concern of team owner Edward Wilson, who said that this year, more than others, it's important that fans get to home games to show their support.

So, mark your calendar and get ready to cheer on our gals! See the game schedule on page 5.

"That's swell," I said. "We'll have to make a few of the home games."

"Maybe we could convince Flo to come along. Your mother too." He paused, eating a single square of carrot. "Heck, I'll try to get the whole neighborhood to go. Anything to keep the team chugging along until you graduate from high school."

When I was seven years old, I told my parents that what I wanted to do when I grew up was to play baseball for the Workington Sweet Peas. Dad—one prone to audacious dreams—had been thrilled. Mam had been less excited.

She hadn't discouraged me from playing ball with the boys, though, because she thought it would help me get the baseball out of my system.

So far, no luck.

It only made me love the game all the more every time I played.

"You hold on to that," he said, nodding at the clipping. "Pick out which games you want to go to. Looks like the first game is against Grand Rapids. Maybe we could make a day out of it."

"Uncle Matthew could meet us there," I said.

"I'll bet he would." He winked at me before turning to his typewriter.

That was my cue to head back to the house, that Dad was itching to get to work.

On my way out, I flipped the paper over in my hands and read the headline that scrawled across the top of the page.

RED MENACE IN MICHIGAN!
Communism's Spread Across the USA

"Hey, Dad?"

"Uh-huh?" He didn't look up from his typewriter.

"Is this true?" I held up the headline for him to see.

He tilted his head so he could see it through his reading glasses.

"Eh. That's nothing new." He turned back to his work. "They're holding a bunch of trials in Detroit. Nothing but fuss and bother, if you ask me. Scared people buy papers, so they want to keep stirring up the hysteria. That's all."

"But are they in Michigan?" I asked. "The Reds?"

"Of course they are."

"Do you know any?"

"I used to," he said. "Back in the '30s. They were good people with good intentions. The ones I knew wanted things to be better. They had some funny ideas of how to help out. But they weren't selling state secrets to the Soviets, I can tell you that."

"But . . ." I started. "You weren't one of them. Were you?"

He tilted his head and wrinkled his forehead.

"Bertha, you don't need to worry about that." Dad shook his head. "What you need to worry about is making good grades and helping your mother. All right?"

"All right."

"You're a kid. Worry about kid things." He scratched at the back of his neck before turning away from me again. "Good night, sweetheart."

"Night, Dad," I said. "Love you."

"Love you right back."

Bonaventure Times
March 10, 1952

RED MENACE IN MICHIGAN!
Communism's Spread Across the USA

Editorial

After another day of testimony in the House Un-American Activities Committee (HUAC) hearings, the public knows more than ever about the spread of the cancer which is Communism throughout the city of Detroit.

Outside the glow of Detroit's lights, we of Bonaventure Park could be lulled into a sense of counterfeit safety, thinking that the tentacles of The Red Menace can't reach us. This simply is not true. Communism is able to wheedle its way into any workplace, any school, any home if given even an inch of entry.

It is up to the citizens of our great State of Michigan to stop this Red Menace in its tracks. Be on the lookout for Red activities in your office, neighborhood, and social clubs. Report any tips to . . .

six

FLOSSIE

The Bonaventure Park Public Library didn't open until 3:30 on weekday afternoons. That meant that if I wanted to check out a book, I had thirty whole minutes to spend first. That day I walked as slowly as I could and lingered outside the five-and-dime to see the spring things already on display in the window.

Dad had told me that morning that he'd seen five robins the day before. And he'd said we'd have to watch for Mam's yellow flowers to start blooming soon.

"It'll be here before we know it," he'd said. "'Daffodils, that come before the swallow dares, and take the winds of March with beauty.'"

That was Shakespeare.

Dad was always quoting something from Shakespeare, then getting a faraway look in his eye. I couldn't usually make heads or tails of any of it.

I got to the library at 3:25 and took the hard marble steps toward the stone lion that guarded the books inside.

"Afternoon, Archie," I whispered.

For real and for true, that lion was named Archie.

Well, Archibald if we're talking about his Christian name.

He'd been named for Archibald Phineas Bonaventure—what a mouthful!—the man who founded our little town.

When Dad had wanted to teach me the meaning of irony, he'd

told me about how Archibald Bonaventure—the man, not the cat—had actually been deadly afraid of lions after seeing one at a circus when he was a little boy. It had been a long-held Bonaventure family secret, though, until after he died and one of his kids snitched about it. The townspeople thought they'd done a good thing by collecting money to have Archibald—the lion, not the man—built in his honor.

Dad had always gotten a kick out of that story. I did too.

If it hadn't been so cold that afternoon, I would have sat on the slab of marble next to Archie to wait for the librarian to let me in. Instead, I stood beside him, dug in my school bag for the book I needed to return, and scowled at it.

I didn't get very much time to give that book dirty looks, though, because with the chiming of the clock on City Hall, Mrs. Maxwell came to unlock the door of the library.

"Good afternoon, Flossie," she said, holding the door open for me.

"Hello, Mrs. Maxwell. Thank you," I said.

Then I followed her as she walked toward the rows of shelves full of every kind of book imaginable. She stopped right before stepping into the aisle of biographies and looked at me over her shoulder.

"What did you think of *The Little Prince*?" she asked, whispering, of course.

"I didn't like it," I said.

"Oh dear." She squinted at me. "Why not?"

"It was weird." I wrinkled my nose.

"Well, the author *is* French."

I closed my left eye—something I did when I was thinking—and tried to figure out why that would make a difference.

"Didn't you like his friend the Fox?" Mrs. Maxwell asked.

"It was sad," I said.

She nodded and her eyes were soft, like she might start to cry.

"What happened to the prince? Did he die?" I asked.

"Do you think he did?" she asked.

One thing I liked about Mrs. Maxwell was that when she asked me a question, it was because she really wanted to know my answer. And if my answer was different from hers, she never said that either of us was wrong.

Then again, she only asked me questions about stories.

I knew it was okay to have different ideas about stories.

If she'd asked about math, that would have been an entirely different matter.

"I hope he didn't die," I said.

Mrs. Maxwell bent at the waist so that she was nearer to my eye level, and she smiled when she grabbed my hand.

"Flossie Harding, you are a brilliant girl," she said. "Don't let anybody change you. Okay?"

I nodded even if I wasn't entirely sure what she meant.

Then, she got a little sparkle in her eye.

"We got a brand-new book on Monday that I think you might like instead. It's about a prince, but it's very different. Would you like to see it?"

"What is it?" I asked, moving just a little closer to her.

"This way."

She kept hold of my hand, and we walked together to a shelf on the other side of the library. She grabbed a book with a blue cover and held it to her chest, looking down at me with a wide smile.

"I read it last night," she said. "It is wonderful."

"What is it?" I asked, folding my hands under my chin.

"A new Narnia book." She held it out to me. "*Prince Caspian*."

"Narnia?" I whispered. "A prince in Narnia?"

She nodded.

I wondered what he was like. Was he noble like Aslan? Or wicked like the White Witch? Oh, I had so many questions. I didn't ask Mrs. Maxwell any of them, though, because I wanted to find out for myself.

"Would you like to check it out?" Mrs. Maxwell asked.

"Yes, please."

On the way to the desk where I'd be the first to sign the card, I saw the display that was dedicated to my dad's books. On the shelf was a framed picture of him—the one that the publisher put on the dust jacket.

I'd never cared for that picture all that much. Dad looked too serious in it, his tie tight around his neck and his hair slicked back. That was the William S. Harding the rest of the world knew. But the one I knew was quick to smile and only ever wore a tie if he had to meet his editor in New York City or Mam insisted on him wearing a proper suit to church.

My version of Dad—the one who went by Will—always let his hair grow wild until Mam came at him with her trimming scissors.

Mrs. Maxwell stamped the inside of *Prince Caspian* and told me it was due in three weeks.

On my way out, I patted Archie again.

I would have whispered for him to have a good evening, but there were too many people around and they would have thought I was strange.

All the way home I held the Narnia book close to my heart.

seven

BERTHA

When I was eight and Chip was eleven, we found a crate of kittens outside the grocery store. The little dears were all ginger colored except for one, the runt. He was charcoal gray and huddled in the corner of the box, out of the way of his rambunctious littermates.

"They're free," Chip said, pointing at the sign on the side of the crate. "We ought to take one home."

I had one of the orange ones in mind, the one that was at the moment busy climbing up the side of the box, stepping on another kitty's head for a boost. Chip, though, had another idea.

"Not that one," I said when he picked up the runt. "He's too small."

"But he needs rescued," Chip said. "The others, they'll be fine. This guy, though . . ."

He brought the kitten up to his cheek and nuzzled it.

"Oh, all right."

We'd brought the little guy home with the name Sultan of Swat—Chip had let me pick the name. Sully for short. Mam had protested at first, saying that she little needed another creature living in the house.

"But, Mam," Chip had said. "He can't go back. The other kittens were mean to him."

Well, that got our mother's heart.

She had always been one to take the side of the downtrodden.

And so Sully became a Harding. And that little gray runt had grown into an oversized, very well-fed ball of fuzz.

The person that ball of fuzz loved most, of course, was none other than Chip.

When Chip and Peggy got married in December of last year, we all expected Sully to move to the apartment across town along with them. As far as I knew, my brother had that in mind too.

Peggy hadn't agreed.

She'd claimed that their landlord didn't allow pets. I didn't buy it, though.

So, Sully had stayed behind, skulking in the room he'd shared with Chip, yowling in the middle of the night, and scowling whenever one of us tried to console him.

The only time the poor dear was happy was when Chip came home to visit. Peggy he didn't care about.

Wednesday nights were for family suppers, which meant that the newlywed lovebirds joined us for dinner.

Mam cleaned and cooked all day long in anticipation. Dad came out of his writing shed and put a comb through his hair—but only because Mam insisted—and changed clothes if he smelled too musty. I would tidy the living room and set the table in the dining room.

Usually Flossie bounced around the house, too excited to sit still.

That night, though, she sat on the sofa, wrapped in an afghan and reading some book she'd gotten at the library.

She was so engrossed in it that she didn't seem to notice when Peggy came through the front door with Chip following behind, arms loaded down with dresses.

"What are those for?" I asked.

"For you to try on," Peggy said. "A little bird told me you got asked to the dance."

"It's not a big deal," I said, grimacing. "It's just a sock hop. I don't think I need anything that fancy."

"Maybe not. But, anyway, it's always fun to play dress-up." Peg's eyes lit up. "Don't you think so?"

As a matter of fact, I didn't think so. Playing dress-up sounded more like torture to me than anything. Especially when, I was sure, just one of the dresses cost more than my entire wardrobe combined.

The last thing I needed was to spill something on a dress I could never replace on my meager allowance.

"Where should I put these?" Chip asked. "They're sort of heavy, you know."

"Upstairs," Peggy said.

"Need help?" I asked.

"Nah. I got it." Chip hoisted the load. "By the way, hiya, Flopsy."

"Hiya, Chippy," Flossie said, turning the page of her book.

And up the stairs he went.

"Leo Schmidt, huh?" Peggy said, crossing the room and grabbing both of my hands. "Charles didn't believe me when I told him. He said the two of you'd been friends too long for something like that. I reminded him that romance can bud out of any branch."

"Right," I said, trying to make sense of that business about buds and branches and coming up blank.

She dropped my hands and took one step backwards, looking me up and down.

"You're lucky Leo's tall," she said. "He's, what, six foot?"

"Something like that."

"Then you can wear heels."

"I don't have any," I said.

"That's all right. You can borrow some of mine." She narrowed her eyes. "I'm afraid my brassieres would be a tad too big for you. We'll have to go shopping for something to give you a little more shape."

She pointed at my chest—as if I didn't know what she was talking about—and I crossed my arms over myself, wishing I could curl up and roll under the coffee table.

"As for that hair . . ."

"Lookie who I found," Chip said, interrupting at just the right time. "It's my furry friend."

If Flossie or I had ever dared to carry Sully like a babe in arms, he would have scratched our faces off. But Chip did it and the beast purred so loud I could hear him clear to the other side of the room.

"Oh, Charles," Peg said—or rather scolded. "You're getting absolutely covered in fur."

"That's all right, honey," Chip said. "Old Sully's a good boy. Aren't ya, buddy?"

Peggy rolled her eyes and said she was going to see if Mam needed any help in the kitchen.

"Don't you girls ever give this guy any attention?" Chip asked, going to the couch and sitting next to Flossie. "Poor neglected kitty."

"He stinks," Flossie said.

"Nah." Chip kissed Sully on the forehead. "He smells like roses. Don't ya, boy?"

Old Sultan mewed at Chip as if he was agreeing.

What a cat.

After supper—Mam made a roast—Peggy dragged me upstairs to try on every dress she'd brought, going to great pains to tell me the entire story of each occasion upon which she wore the specific outfit.

"Oh, this was what I was wearing when Charles kissed me for the first time," and "I was crowned Miss Junior Bonaventure Park in this one," and "I wore this on my honeymoon."

She paraded me in front of the full-length mirror in the corner of the room so I could see myself in the pink chiffon or the teal brocade and on and on and on. I hardly recognized myself in any of them.

"Last, but not least," she said, struggling to zip me into something a little more my speed, even if it was a bit too tight. "Suck it in a little, would you?"

I wasn't sure what I was supposed to suck in, but I did my best. Once the zipper was all the way up, Peggy clapped her hands, declaring me an "absolute vision."

She handed me a crinoline to put on under to make the skirt flare just right before she spun me around to see myself in the mirror. Her hands on my shoulders, she stood behind me.

"What do you think?" she asked.

"It's beautiful," I said, feeling the soft fabric. It was just the right shade of blue to match my eyes. "Maybe a little too fancy for a sock hop."

"Don't slouch." She put the heel of her hand into the small of my back and pushed, making me stand up straighter. "You could always wear this one to prom."

"Prom?" My eyes got wide. "Who'd want to ask *me* to prom?"

"You never know," she said. "Play your cards right at this sock hop and Leo just might want you on his arm in May."

"Gosh, I don't know."

"He's a nice boy. Don't you think so?"

"Sure." I touched my collar bones, trying to think of a way to change the subject. "Shouldn't it have sleeves or something?"

"No, silly. It's a strapless." She tilted her head. "We'd need to get you a new brassiere."

"One without straps?"

"Of course!"

"But how does it stay up if there aren't any straps?" I asked.

"It doesn't matter how, just so long as it does the job."

"It matters to me," I muttered.

"I never wore that dress anywhere," she said, ignoring my last sentence. "My mother talked me into it. It's fine. Just not the right cut for my figure. If you haven't noticed, my shoulders slump."

"I never have noticed," I said.

"But you have nice, broad shoulders." She looked me up and down. "You should keep that dress."

"I couldn't."

"It's a gift," she said, pulling the hair back from my face and twisting it into a bun, holding it at the nape of my neck. "You know, I guess I never realized how pretty you are before this very moment."

"Thank you?"

"You should have no problem nabbing yourself a husband right after high school."

"Why would I want that?" I asked, scrunching up my face.

"Well, what else would you do?"

"Oh, I've been thinking I might try out for the Sweet Peas." I turned so she could unzip me.

"The whosits?"

"It's a baseball team."

"Ah." She unzipped me and held the dress while I stepped out of it, making sure I didn't trip over the skirt. "Charles said you liked to play. You wouldn't be on a team with men, though, would you?"

"No." I laughed, throwing on my plain Jane button-up blouse. "The Sweet Peas is a girls' team."

"I guess that's a little better, then." She had her back to me, hanging up the dresses. "I'll be honest, I don't know anything about baseball."

"Neither does Chip."

"That's probably true," she said. "But, if you make the team, we'll come to every game we can. And we'll be the ones cheering loudest."

"Louder than Flossie?"

"Maybe not."

eight

FLOSSIE

Every morning we'd read silently while Miss Lange sat at her desk, correcting papers. We could read whatever we wanted provided the book didn't have any cuss words—or other questionable content— and we didn't make any noise louder than the turning of a page.

I'd finished *Prince Caspian* three times, so I grabbed a book off the living room shelf on my way out the door that morning.

Ever since Mam had caught me with *The Catcher in the Rye*, I was supposed to ask permission before reading a grown-up book. But I figured *Of Mice and Men* couldn't really be for grown-ups. It wasn't long enough for adults. Besides, it was about mice.

At least that was what I thought when I'd grabbed it.

It was not, as it turned out, about mice. And it had a lot of bad words in it.

I kept reading it, though, because I wanted to know what would happen to Lenny. I wanted to know if he'd finally get to go to the place where he could pet the rabbits.

When silent reading was over, I just hid it behind my arithmetic book, looking up every once in a while and squinting at the blackboard so it seemed like I was paying attention to the lesson.

When it was time to go home for lunch, I grabbed the book and read while I walked down the sidewalk. I was in the alley that went behind our row of houses when I read a part in the book that made me stop in my tracks and yell, "What?"

I slammed the book and stomped my feet the rest of the way home.

I hated, hated, hated John Steinbeck.

And I would hate, hate, hate him forever.

Instead of going inside the house, I barged into Dad's shed and dropped into the chair beside his desk, waiting for him to look over at me from his typewriter. When he didn't, I cleared my throat just in case he'd missed the ruckus of an entrance I'd made.

"Hello, dear," he said, still typing. "You seem to be in a capital mood."

"Why did George do that to Lenny?" I asked.

"Ah, you've been reading Steinbeck." He dropped his hands from the keys and let them rest in his lap as he swiveled in his chair to face me. "I didn't think he was fifth grade reading."

"I'm in sixth grade."

"Huh." He lowered his eyebrows. "Must have lost a year somewhere."

I frowned at him, but he didn't seem to notice.

"Why did he do it?" I asked. "He was supposed to be Lenny's friend. He was supposed to take care of him."

"What might you have done?"

"I would have kept running away," I said. "I would have found the place with all the rabbits."

"Hm." Dad lowered his eyebrows. "You think that place was real?"

"Of course I do. Why else would George talk about it so much?"

"Well, I'm not sure that I know."

He knew. He had to. My dad knew everything. But he also liked keeping secrets, and it sometimes made me so angry.

"How about I bring a couple sandwiches out here?" he said. "Give sweet Mam a quiet lunch. What do you think about that?"

He didn't wait for me to answer before he left. I watched the clock while he was gone. Five whole minutes! But when he came back, he not only had our usual sandwiches, he also had a cup of cocoa for me.

"I think," Dad said, handing me my plate of food, "that George thought what he did was the very best thing he could do for Lenny."

"The best thing?" I balanced the plate on my knees. "That doesn't make any sense. Not even a little bit. I think it was the worst, worst, worst thing he could do. He killed him, Daddy!"

There. I'd said it. George had killed his friend just when Lenny had needed him the most.

"I know it," Dad said.

He got a bandanna out of his slacks pocket and handed it to me. Doggone it. I was crying. Stupid John Steinbeck.

"He didn't have to do that," I said, sniveling. "Mr. Steinbeck shouldn't have made him do that."

Dad leaned forward in his chair so that we were almost nose to nose.

"You still have hope in your heart, don't you?" he asked, whispering.

"Don't you?"

"Well, honey, some days more than others."

"I'm sorry," I said. "I don't think I understand what you mean."

"It's all right." He put his hands on either side of my face and ever so gently pulled me toward him so he could kiss the top of my head. "Someday you will."

I left that book with Dad even though I hadn't read the last page and a half. I didn't think I ever would.

On the way back to school, I reached my right hand into my coat, right under the lapel, and held it on my chest the way I always did when I said the Pledge of Allegiance at school.

I tried to feel the hope that Dad said was there, but all I felt was the thumping of my heart.

nine

BERTHA

I saw my first baseball game when I was seven years old. Dad had bought me my very own box of Cracker Jacks, and I only allowed myself to eat ten pieces per inning in the hopes of making it last until the very end of the game.

It was the first year of the All-American Girls League and toward the end of the season, so the seats had filled up fast for the game between the Workington Sweet Peas and the Kenosha Comets.

"Who are you cheering for?" Dad had asked me.

I hadn't known what the right answer was and told him that.

"There is no right answer." He'd smiled at me. "You could even say you were cheering for both and that would be all right by me."

That had seemed swell to me, so I ate a few Cracker Jacks and watched the game.

At the top of the third inning, the announcer said the Sweet Peas were sending in a substitute pitcher.

"Let's hear it for Dottie Fitzgerald, folks," he called over the speakers. "What a gal!"

She skipped out to the pitcher's mound and waved at the crowd. I waved back, thinking for sure that she could see me. Then she'd blown kisses, but only to those of us sitting in the Workington fan section.

She'd won me over. In that instant I became a Sweet Peas fan.

By the time the game was over, I still had half a box of Cracker

Jacks because I'd forgotten all about it. I'd been so distracted, falling in love with baseball.

"I'm going to be like her," I told my father that day.

I'd pointed at Dottie Fitzgerald, who was at that moment shaking hands with the pitcher from the Comets.

Any other dad might have patted his little girl on the head, thinking it was a cute thing for her to say. Or he might have told her that it wasn't realistic to dream such a thing when she'd just grow up to be a housewife anyway.

Any other dad might have ignored his daughter.

But my dad wasn't like any other.

"Yes, I believe you will be," he'd said. "How about we go meet that Ms. Fitzgerald?"

The line had been long and moved slowly. Dad stood with me, holding my hand so that he wouldn't lose me in the crowd. I'd held his hand because I was nervous, and knowing he was near had given me courage.

When we finally got to the front of the line, Dad asked each of the players to sign the program.

"A keepsake for my daughter," he'd said.

Then we reached Dottie. She had her back against the chain-link fence and was chewing gum like it was her job. She looked down at me and winked.

"Hi there, babydoll," she said. "You look like a ball player to me."

I nodded even though I'd never played a day in my life.

"What's your name?" she asked, taking my program.

"Bertha Rebecca Harding," I'd answered.

"Bertha, huh? You ever go by Bert?" She snapped her gum. "I grew up with a kid named Bert. He was a good fella. Liked animals. Seem to remember he had a pigeon he trained or something."

"A pigeon?" I asked, wrinkling my nose.

"Yeah. How do you like that?" she asked. "Most boys train dogs. My pal Bert had a bird."

"Bert the bird boy?"

"Oh, I never thought of calling him that." She smacked her

forehead with the palm of her hand. "Talk about a missed opportunity! I'll try and remember that one for next time I see him. You got yourself a good brain, Bertha. This your dad?"

"Yes."

"Mister, you got yourself a good girl," she told Dad. "If she ever wants to be a Sweet Pea, you let her. Okay?"

"You have my word," Dad said.

"Tell you what, I'm gonna write my address here under my picture." She started scribbling, and I worried that it would be so messy I'd never be able to read it. "You write me anytime. Got it? I'm going to be looking for a letter from you."

I wrote her a letter the very next day on stationery Mam had tucked away in the junk drawer. It had pink roses in the corner, so pretty that it made my poor penmanship look that much messier.

Every day for a week I checked the mailbox to see if she'd written back. Finally, exactly one week after my letter went out, I'd gotten one from her.

"Listen here, Bert," she'd written. "If those silly little boys won't let you play ball with them, you let me know and I'll come up there and give them what-for."

I'd written back to tell her about the baseball I'd gotten with my own money at the five-and-dime.

She sent me a postcard from Rockford, Illinois, where she'd played against the Peaches.

I sent her a picture Dad had taken of me holding a bat, pretending that I was on my very own baseball card.

She wrote to tell me about seeing Lake Michigan from the other side when they drove through Chicago to get to South Bend to play the Blue Sox.

"I'm telling ya, Bert," she'd written, "there's something about the lake that makes me understand how strong God is. You believe in God, don't you?"

I'd written back to tell her that I believed in God. Of course I did. But I'd never been to Lake Michigan.

We exchanged letters, Dottie and I, for a good six months. We'd even gotten each other Christmas cards. And on my birthday, she'd sent me a tiny glass jar of dirt.

"A little bit of Judd Field just for you," she'd written.

Then, all of a sudden, her letters stopped coming. No matter how many I sent her way, she didn't write me back.

The next season, Dottie's name wasn't on the Sweet Peas's lineup. I didn't hear her name again.

Every once in a while, I'd dig out the stack of letters from her and read them all over again. I'd find the little jar of dirt and let myself dream.

Nobody knew that I still sent her letters once or twice a year. Sometimes more, but only if I had something to say. Dottie Fitzgerald became, to me, like a diary where I could trust that my secrets would be safe.

I couldn't know if she got them for the lack of response.

But the letters never came back "return to sender" either.

She'd fallen off the face of the earth. At least that was how it had seemed.

So, when I saw her name in the sports section of the paper, I very nearly choked on my grapefruit.

Dottie Fitzgerald was making a comeback.

What a gal.

Bonaventure Times
March 13, 1952

ALL-AMERICAN GIRL RETURNS TO WORKINGTON

Fitzgerald's Long Road Back Home

by Al Rogers

WORKINGTON, MI: Delores "Dottie" Fitzgerald was once a household name in Workington. In her first (and only) season as a Sweet Pea, she outplayed her teammates but was so nice about it none of them resented her success, happily giving her the title of MVP. There was talk around the All-American Girls Professional Baseball League (the AAGPBL) that she'd be recruited to a winning team like the Rockford Peaches.

There were even rumors that Steve O'Neill (manager of the 1943 Detroit Tigers) was considering having her play a game or two with the boys.

But early in 1944 Workington's sweetest Sweet Pea seemingly disappeared without a trace.

In the next season, Sweet Pea fans chanted "Oh where, oh where has our Dottie gone?" at every game.

Never finding an answer, they gave up the chant smack-dab in the middle of the summer.

I was on the horn that year, announcing games on the radio. I well remember those days, pining over the best of us. Our own little girl lost.

Imagine my surprise when Workington issued a press release stating that Sweet Peas manager JuJu Eames had hired none other than Dottie Fitzgerald as chaperone for his 1952 season.

When asked where Fitzgerald has been all these years, Eames demurred, simply stating, "She's been where she was. If you don't already know where that is, maybe it isn't your business. She's here now and she's ready to do the job. End of comment."

Mr. Eames is holding tryouts for the Workington Sweet Peas on April 12 . . .

ten

FLOSSIE

Miss Lange had told me that I couldn't read *Johnny Tremain* at school because it was a boy's book. When I pointed out that the author was a woman—her name was Esther, after all—she'd told me it didn't matter.

It was a book about war, and books about war were for boys. She wouldn't change her mind.

Then she handed me a copy of *Caddie Woodlawn* and told me to go back to my desk and read.

But I'd read *Caddie Woodlawn* a hundred times!

At the end of the day, I went to the public library and, in an act of utter rebellion against Miss Lange, I told Mrs. Maxwell that I wanted to check out a copy of *Johnny Tremain*. She didn't flinch and she didn't argue that it wasn't a book for me.

Mrs. Maxwell was a good egg.

If everything went according to my plan, I would get home just in time for a cup of tea—with extra lumps of sugar because it was Friday. I'd ask Mam if I could sit in the living room next to the fire to have my tea and whatever kind of goodie she'd made to go along with it. Then I would read my library book all the way until suppertime.

When I got home, though, I found Mam on the telephone instead of in the kitchen making tea. She hadn't gotten around to

59

making scones or cookies or cake. And when I looked in the cupboard to see if there was a sugar cube that I could suck on to hold me over, all I found was an empty box.

Besides, there wasn't a single log for the fireplace.

"I'm sorry, love," Mam said after hanging up the phone. "Tell you what, I'll put the kettle on if you'll run over to Mrs. Sanders's house and ask to borrow a cup of sugar."

"Mrs. Sanders?" I asked. "Why not Mrs. Schmidt?"

"Because I borrowed an egg from her yesterday."

"Okay. I could ask Mrs. Abrams."

Mam pinched her lips together and shook her head. "Flo, I asked you to go to Mrs. Sanders's house."

"But, Mam, I don't like going there," I said. "She's not very nice."

"Oh, dear, she's plenty nice." Mam turned on the faucet, filling up her old kettle. "She's shy, that's all. Best hurry."

Mrs. Sanders lived across the street and a few doors down from us in a house that was far too big for just one person. Mam had told me that Mrs. Sanders lived alone because she was a widow and her children were all grown up and moved away. But the kids in the neighborhood all said that it was because she was a wicked witch who turned into a tarantula when no one was looking.

I stood on the sidewalk looking up at Mrs. Sanders's house, trying to work up my nerve to knock on the front door and trying to convince myself that the woman wasn't a witch. She was just a grumpy old lady. That was all.

"Hello, Mrs. Sanders, how do you do?" I whispered, practicing what Mam had told me to say. "My mother wondered if we might borrow a cup of sugar, please?"

I tapped the bottom of the measuring cup against the palm of my hand and willed myself to get a move on.

There was no answer when I knocked, so I tried again. I might have looked in through the window next to the door, but Mrs. Sanders always—but *always*—kept her curtains drawn.

"Florence?"

I turned when I heard my name. Mrs. Schmidt—Leo's mother—was on the sidewalk, paper bag on her hip.

"Mrs. Sanders isn't home, honey," she said. "Did you need something?"

She glanced at the measuring cup in my hand.

"My mother needs a cup of sugar," I said, still standing on Mrs. Sanders's porch. "She sent me here because she hasn't asked Mrs. Sanders for anything in a long time."

"Oh, well, I have plenty of sugar. You go on home and I'll bring it by in a few minutes."

True to her word, Mrs. Schmidt knocked on our door just a couple of minutes later with a whole bag of sugar. But the way she walked in and took off her coat, I could tell she intended to stay for a little while.

That could only mean one thing with Mrs. Schmidt. She had gossip.

Mam poured me a cup of tea and spooned a little extra sugar in. She put a butter cookie on my saucer and told me I could sit in the living room—what I'd wanted all along.

Suddenly, though, I wasn't as interested in Johnny Tremain and the Revolutionary War. I could read about that any old day. What I was interested in was whatever juicy rumor Mrs. Schmidt was dying to tell Mam.

If I stood in just the right spot in the hallway, I could hear everything someone said in the kitchen—even if they whispered—without being seen.

The two of them went through the grown-up lady routine where they pretended that the visit was just for drinking tea and swapping small talk. I waited, nearly giving up listening while they talked about Leo and Bertha going to the dance together.

But just before I went to my seat and cracked open my book, I heard the start of the gossip Mrs. Schmidt had come to share.

"You know Mrs. Sanders is in trouble, don't you?" she started.

"Trouble?" Mam asked. "Why, whatever could you mean?"

"Oh, Louisa, it's horrible."

She drew out that last word so she sounded like somebody'd slowed down a record player.

"She was named during the hearings," Mrs. Schmidt went on. "You know the ones I'm talking about. The Un-American ones."

"The Communist trials?" Mam asked.

"Well, I don't think that's what they're calling them, but sure. Those."

"No. I can't hardly believe it." Mam's voice went up in pitch. "Marjory Sanders. A Communist?"

"Didn't you see the paper?"

"Oh, I don't bother . . ."

"You should read the paper," Mrs. Schmidt said.

"What will happen to her?" Mam asked.

"I couldn't say. Now, I need to ask because Leo will forget. What color is Bertha's dress for the dance? I want to make sure the corsage matches . . ."

I knew it. I just knew it!

Well, I hadn't known that Mrs. Sanders was a Communist. But I had known that she wasn't a very nice lady.

But, as far as I was concerned, it was close to the same thing.

She was a traitor to her country!

In the comfiest chair in the living room, wrapped up in the thickest afghan, I cracked open *Johnny Tremain*.

Bonaventure Times
March 14, 1952

HOUSEWIFE AMONG THOSE
PROVED RED

DETROIT, MI: The widowed housewife wore a woolen dress, more suited for a secretary than a grandmother, when she testified in Washington DC last week. She wore her hair in finger curls and had pinned a cameo brooch on her lapel, looking more like she'd come from the 1930s than these modern days.

Her name is Mrs. Marjory L. Sanders of Bonaventure Park, Michigan, where she has lived for nearly a decade. She revealed in her testimony that her neighbors and friends little knew of her involvement with the Communist Party.

Mrs. Sanders garnered a gasp from those in attendance when she disclosed that she'd spent nine years among Michigan Reds. In that time she worked as record keeper for "The Party," taking attendance and collecting dues at meetings.

We are still learning about this unlikely informant and the consequences she will pay for her involvement with the Red Menace. One thing we do know is that she is scheduled to appear before the House Un-American Activities Committee (HUAC) next week to give more testimony and, potentially, reveal the names of those who are now and those who have in the past been involved in "The Party."

eleven

BERTHA

It poured all day long. And all day long the temperature fell so that the raindrops turned to shards of ice. The roads and sidewalks were slippery and treacherous. But once the rain let up and the clouds parted, the sun made the iced blades of grass and branches sparkle. It was as if everything turned to crystal in a matter of hours.

"It's so pretty," I said, walking down the school steps.

That was just before the heel of my saddle shoe slid on a particularly icy patch and I tumbled my way down the rest of the stairs.

"Whoa there, slick," Leo said, grabbing my elbow.

He'd single-handedly saved me from landing hard on my keister, and for that I was glad. However, my stupid pride prevented me from declaring him my hero and swooning into his strong arms.

Instead, I swatted at his hand and told him I was fine.

"Uh-huh." He squinted at me. "Sure you were."

I pursed my lips and glowered at him.

"You don't have to be such a tough guy all the time," he said. "There's no sin in letting somebody help you every once in a while. You know that, right?"

"Yeah, yeah." I rolled my eyes. "I guess no baseball today, huh?"

"Nope." He frowned. Then his face brightened and he lifted one finger, pointing straight up. "Eureka!"

"What?" I asked, trying—unsuccessfully—to hold in a laugh.

Leo really could be the most ridiculous person in the world.

"Brilliant idea," he said. "How's about you and me go get a malt? Or a hot fudge sundae? Or a banana split?"

"*That's* your brilliant idea?"

"Sure is."

"Well, I guess it's a pretty okay plan."

He offered me his arm, and I glared at it.

"Just, you know, to keep you steady on your feet," he said.

"Oh, all right," I groaned before linking my arm with his.

At home I had a stack of all the newspaper clippings that Dottie Fitzgerald was ever mentioned in. I'd read and reread every single one of them at least a hundred times over the years.

In one of them—an interview with sportswriter Al Rogers—she said that, unlike other girls on the team, she wasn't interested in going on dates during the baseball season.

"There's enough other stuff that'll take my mind off the games," she'd said. "The last thing I need is for those distractions to come in tall, dark, or handsome."

Leo was tall and he had dark eyes and hair.

I wasn't exactly sure about the handsome part. It wasn't until recent days that I'd even thought of him as someone who could be handsome, so I was still trying to decide what I thought about his looks.

When I glanced up at him and he grinned down at me, though, it made my heart beat funny and my head dizzy.

Maybe that meant he really was handsome.

I could see how he could become a distraction. And how!

The diner on the corner was full like it always was after school on Fridays. Guys and gals ordering milkshakes with two straws—Leo best not think I was interested in sharing—and making eyes at each other over the swirl of whipped cream.

Rosemary Clooney was playing on the jukebox, singing "Come On-a My House," and Leo snapped his fingers to the rhythm while leading me to a couple of empty stools at the counter. Once we were both up on our seats, he signaled to the soda jerk.

"What'll you kids have?" the guy behind the counter asked.

"I'll have a root beer float," Leo said. "How about you, Bert?"

"Oh," I said, glancing up at the chalkboard menu on the wall. "A strawberry shake."

"Sure thing," the soda jerk said, spinning away from us to fill our order.

I grabbed the change purse out of my skirt pocket and pulled it open, counting out my nickels and dimes.

"What are you doing?" Leo asked.

"I have to pay for my milkshake, don't I?"

"That's what I'm here for."

"But I have money," I said.

"That's not the point." He turned on his stool to face me, his knees spreading to either side of me. "I asked you on a date. That means I've gotta pay. Make sense?"

"I guess so." I returned the purse to my pocket.

Rosemary's song finished, and the next song that played—picked by some goofball—was Spike Jones's version of "You Always Hurt the One You Love," zany sound effects and all. Leo shifted so he was facing the counter again and glanced at me when I tittered at the song.

The soda jerk delivered Leo's float and my milkshake, and neither of us said much of anything for the next two or three songs.

All that time I didn't think about baseball once.

The only thing I could seem to think about was how close his hand was to mine and wondering what it might be like to grab on to it.

I supposed Dottie had been right. It was easy to forget about everything else when it came to boys.

But, oh, how fun to be distracted.

twelve

FLOSSIE

On Saturday mornings Chippy came to give me piano lessons. Usually he spent half the time cringing at my creative interpretations of the music—what he rudely called "errors"—and the other half of the time getting after me for not practicing. Then he'd walk me to the candy store to buy me a treat because he felt badly for making me cry.

Piano lessons with Chippy were full of frustration, hurt feelings, and boring old scales. But I wouldn't have traded them for all the gold in Fort Knox. It was a whole hour of my brother's full attention and the best sixty minutes of my week.

That morning, though, Chippy called to say he'd be late and that I should start on my Edna Mae Burnam exercises while I waited.

I did them. Not with vim and vigor. But I did all dozen I was supposed to do.

When he still wasn't there, I played through "Skip to My Lou" as slow and moody as I could, only stopping halfway through because the telephone rang.

It was Chippy, begging off the lesson because Peggy was sick.

Even though I wasn't supposed to, I slammed the lid over the keys and pouted.

"Now, love," Mam said, pulling on her green gloves that matched the lining of her spring coat. "I won't have you sulking. Poor Peggy's unwell."

"I don't care." I crossed my arms.

"You should." She grabbed my arm. "Come along. You'll be coming to the deli with me."

I dragged my feet for three blocks, and Mam didn't notice. So I walked normal the rest of the way because I didn't need to ruin my shoes.

Mam asked for a pound of Swiss—"Sliced thick, if you will"—and all different kinds of cold cuts. When she saw me eyeballing the barrel of pickles, she said I could have one if I promised to help her put together the sandwiches for her bridge club.

Mr. Abrams fished two out. One for right then, one for after I helped my mother.

"Thank you," I said in my very sweetest voice.

We left the deli, Mam carrying the grocery bag in one arm and me holding the for-right-then pickle in my hand. I liked the pickles at Mr. Abrams's deli better than the garlicky ones at Kowalski's on the other side of town.

"Are you up for stopping at the bakery?" Mam asked.

"Sure," I said, following her.

I was a little disappointed when, instead of going two blocks away to get to the Dutch bakery, we crossed the street to the new one. It was called Lazy Morning, and it didn't have the cream puffs I liked from the other place.

"It's closer," Mam said, taking my hand before we stepped off the curb to walk across the street.

"I don't need you to hold my hand," I said. "I cross the street all the time by myself."

"I know, sweet." She gave my hand a little squeeze. "I miss you being little, is all."

Never had I hoped so hard that I wouldn't see anybody from school. The last thing I needed was to give them an idea for another verse to their stupid Baby Bumpkin song.

When we got to the other side, Mam dropped my hand and headed for the bakery. As soon as she opened the door, we heard the yelling.

I went right in before Mam could stop me. I wanted to know what in the Sam Hill was going on in there.

Mrs. Sanders—the Communist!—was at the counter, waving dollar bills in the face of the woman behind the counter.

"I have money," Mrs. Sanders yelled. "Why won't you take my money?"

"Like I said, we don't serve the likes of you," the woman yelled back.

"I want a loaf of bread. That's all I want." Mrs. Sanders slammed her fist down on the counter. "One lousy loaf of bread."

"See here," Mam said, stepping up to Mrs. Sanders's side. "Why won't you let her buy bread?"

"Because she's a Pinko," the lady behind the counter said. "We don't sell to Commies. I told her that already."

"Well, surely you can make an exception, can't you?" Mam kept her voice calm. "Just this once. She still needs to eat, doesn't she?"

"But I'm a good American and Christian," the woman behind the counter said.

"What's more American and Christian than making sure everyone has what they need?"

The bakery lady crossed her arms. She wasn't going to let Mrs. Sanders have that loaf of bread no matter what Mam said.

Mrs. Sanders kept her head high while she stormed out.

The woman behind the counter smirked like she'd just won a fight. Maybe she had.

Mam went to the window and watched Mrs. Sanders stomp down the street.

"Can I help you?" the lady asked.

"Yes," Mam answered, turning. "One loaf of bread, please. No. Two."

"Anything else?"

"That's all."

I tugged on Mam's sleeve and mouthed the words "black and whites" to her. But she shook her head.

"None of those today, love," she whispered.

We walked home together, Mam and me. She held my hand, and I didn't argue.

When we neared Mrs. Sanders's house, Mam told me to wait on the sidewalk.

She took a loaf of bread to the porch.

She didn't knock. She just left it on the doorstep.

Bonaventure Times
March 15, 1952

150 MICHIGAN REDS NAMED

Granny Spy Single-Handedly
Takes Down Party

DETROIT, MI: In testimony as informative as it was long, Mrs. Marjory Sanders revealed the inner workings of the Communist Party in Detroit. The widowed housewife detailed, year by year and name by name, the activities of the Red cause.

Along with telling about Party procedure, Mrs. Sanders revealed names—150—of those associated with the Reds. Many of these, she said, also belong to the local UAW. A few others are professors at the University of Michigan and Michigan State. Still others are in places of influence over the hearts and minds of our Nation.

Mrs. Sanders also produced a list of what she called the "Century Club" of those who contributed $100 or more to the Party each year. As her testimony continued, the list of names grew. Doctors and teachers, office workers and housewives . . .

It seems as though no workplace is safe from the cancer that is Communism.

Once finished with her testimony, members of the House Un-American Activities Committee each in turn commended her service. Committee Chairman Wood (D., Ga.) along with Reps. Potter (R., Mi.) and Jackson (R., Calif.) showed the utmost appreciation, telling Mrs. Sanders that her testimony was heroic and had the potential to dismantle the Party altogether.

Other witnesses will be called to give testimony. We can only hope they are as forthcoming as she.

CONT on page 3

thirteen

BERTHA

On Sunday mornings every household in Bonaventure Park hustled and bustled about to get ready for church. Leo and his mother went to the Lutheran church a quarter of a mile away, and Mrs. Higginbottom's family were Baptists. Violet Lancaster's dad was a Methodist minister, and Bobbo's folks had them drive the next town over for Mass. Stinky Simon and his family were Jewish, so they went to synagogue.

We Hardings went to the church where Reverend Lancaster preached because Mam liked how he told a lot of stories in his sermons.

The only person I knew in Bonaventure Park who tended to dillydally on Sunday mornings was my dear old dad.

He'd stay in his robe, reading the paper instead of rushing to get dressed. He'd lollygag over his breakfast until it was far too late for him to make it on time for Sunday school. Mam, Flossie, and I didn't wait for him. We'd climb into the car and leave him behind.

That's not to say that Dad skipped out on church. Not entirely, at least. He had it timed out perfectly so that he'd miss Sunday school and the chatting time before the service. He'd slip into the pew beside Flossie just as the congregation sang "amen" on the last hymn.

He always brought an envelope of money for the offering plate and he sometimes took notes during the sermon.

72

Then he'd slip out during the closing prayer and walk home so he could make sure Mam's Sunday roast didn't burn in the oven.

Dad believed in God, read his Bible, and said his prayers. He just didn't go in for all of the socializing and singing.

His Sunday morning routine irked Flossie to no end. She could not abide tardiness in any form. So, every week she tried a different method of convincing him to get to church on time.

That morning, she sat on the arm of the chair Dad occupied—cat curled up on his lap—holding him tight about the neck. With her lips mere centimeters from the side of his head, she proceeded to sing "Come Thou Fount of Every Blessing" directly into his ear.

For his part, he hardly looked up from his paper.

Flossie met my eye and winked at me as if I was in on her scheme to trick Dad into going to church with us.

I shook my head and rolled my eyes so she'd know I wanted no part of it.

"Florence Mable," Mam said, coming into the living room, cup of coffee in hand. She set it on the end table beside Dad's chair. "You stop that this moment. You're going to make him deaf, singing into his ear like that."

"Oh, Mam," Flossie said. "I was just getting to the good part."

"Flo." Mam's tone was one of warning.

"All right."

Flossie slackened her hold on Dad's neck but didn't leave her little perch. She pushed one side of her white-blond bobbed hair behind an ear. Her too-short bangs stuck up in all different directions.

"Come, love," Mam said, waving her over. "Let's see to that hair before we go. Come."

Flossie obeyed, but not before turning and giving Dad a peck on the temple.

At that he looked up from the paper, surprise on his face as if he hadn't known she was even there until that very moment.

Mam and Flossie bustled up the stairs, no time to waste or else we'd all be late for church.

"Did you bring this to me?" Dad asked, nodding at the cup of coffee.

"It was Mam," I answered.

"Ah. She's kind." He pointed at the ottoman next to him. "Take a load off."

I folded my coat—the red one I'd gotten at Christmas—over my arm and took a seat.

"Goddess of chaos," he said, squinting at the morning crossword puzzle. "Four letters."

"Loki?" I asked.

"Hm. Starts with an e. And Loki's male." He tapped the eraser on the paper.

Sully didn't like that and made a groaning protest and tucked his nose under his tail.

"Oh well, doesn't matter." He tossed the paper and the pencil onto the coffee table. "You said something weeks ago about your ball glove not fitting anymore. Is that right?"

"Yeah." I rubbed my palms together. "It's all right, though. It doesn't bother me all that much."

"Well, I got you something." He pushed his hands under the cat like he was a forklift and picked him up, thrusting the critter at me. "Here, take him."

"You didn't have to get me anything," I said, struggling to get a hold of Sully that wouldn't end in my church dress and coat being covered in fur.

"Don't worry. It's small."

"A nicer cat?"

Sully wriggled his way out of my hands and slinked across the room.

"Nope," Dad said, opening the seat of the piano bench.

Clever place for him to hide something he didn't want me to find. He knew I'd never have looked there.

Sully glared up at me, licking his paw as if wanting to rid himself of the stink of me.

"Close your eyes," Dad said.

I did and jumped a little at the slamming of the piano bench

74

but kept my eyes shut. I didn't particularly like surprises—that was more of Flossie's thing. They made me nervous.

"Is it alive?" I asked. "You have to warn me if it is."

"Used to be, I suppose." His voice was closer. "Put out your hands."

I smelled it before he even put it in my hands. Brand-new leather. That smell always got my heart racing. I lifted my palms higher and tried to hold a giggle in. I wasn't successful.

My eyes opened as soon as I felt the ball glove touch my skin.

It was the most beautiful thing I'd ever seen.

"You didn't have to get me a new glove," I whispered.

"No, I didn't," Dad said, hands on his hips and warm smile on his face. "I wanted to. You ought to try it on."

I worked my fingers into it. The leather would need to get broken in, but I knew where Mam kept the lanolin oil and thick rubber bands. It would be perfect in no time.

"Does it fit?" Dad asked.

"It sure does."

I punched my right fist into the pocket of the glove and then clamped my left fingers and thumb together like pinchers. It would do. It would do just fine.

"Look here," Dad said, turning my hand so I'd look at the backside of the glove.

There, under the webbing, in the space where thumb met hand, was a tiny daisy burned into the leather.

"Dad . . ." I jumped up from the footstool and threw my arms around his neck.

It was the first in a very long time that I'd hugged him like that. He laughed and hugged me back.

I'd only read one of his books—Flossie was the reader among the three of us kids. But a year ago I'd been home sick a whole week and needed something to occupy my time. So I grabbed a copy of *This Strange and Eventful History* from the shelf.

It was good. Better than most of the things I had to read at school.

No book—not even *Little Women*—had ever made me cry. Not

like I did when I finished reading my dad's book. The thing was, I wasn't sad. If someone had asked me why I'd gotten emotional reading it, I couldn't have explained it.

I'd gone straight out to Dad's shed, book in hand and still in my flannel nighty and robe even though it was in the middle of the day. And I told him that it was the best thing I'd ever read.

"What was your favorite part?" he'd asked.

"This," I said, turning to the very last page and reading to him, "And no matter how many times they mowed those daisies down, they always came back, star-shine in a sky of green."

"Well, isn't that interesting?" Dad had said. "You know, when I wrote that sentence, I was thinking of you."

Mam hustled Flossie back down the steps with no small ruckus, and I let go of Dad. Flo's hair was smoothed and tidy, so I guessed Mam had won that struggle. But my sister's face was bright red and her lips pursed, so I guessed she wasn't done fighting the war.

"Coats," Mam said, grabbing her own off the rack.

I pulled the glove off my hand and held it to my chest, the daisy just over my heart.

fourteen

FLOSSIE

Mam was next door, having tea with a couple of neighbor ladies, and Dad was in his writing shed. Bertha was—well, I had no idea where she was. She could have been sitting in a tree with Leo, k-i-s-s-i-n-g for all I knew.

I had the entire house to myself.

Unfortunately, Mam had told me to have the living room dusted by the time she got home. Fiddlesticks! She never let me have any fun.

I put Bertha's Mary Ford record on and turned the sound up all the way. Then, feather duster in hand, I tried to make my way from one end of the room to the other by the end of the song.

"There's mu-u-u-sic," I sang, waggling my tail end and tapping my feet, flicking the feathers over the picture frames hanging on the wall. "How high the moon."

I might not have known every word in the song. So when it got to a part I didn't know, I just belted out a loud "ah" and flung my arms out to my sides, turning in circles, duster passing over the knickknacks on the shelves and mantel.

My dusting was just about done—not necessarily to Mam's standards, but close enough—but I didn't make it to the end of the song because someone chose that moment to knock, with enthusiasm, on the front door.

I wasn't supposed to answer the door if my mother wasn't

home. But Dad was just in the backyard, so I thought it was probably okay. Just to be safe, though, I grabbed Sully from where he was napping on the sofa. He wasn't happy about it. Well, phooey on him. He was answering the door with me anyway. He could wriggle and yowl all he wanted. I wasn't going to let him go.

When I opened the door, the man glanced down at me and smiled. I didn't smile back. His face was smarmy—that was a word I'd had to look up after Dad called a reviewer that once. The man on the doorstep squatted low so that our faces were level.

"Hello, little girl," he said.

It made my skin crawl.

"I am not a little girl," I said.

"Okay. Hello, young lady." He winked. "That better, honey?"

I ought to have tossed Sully in his face right then. The only reason I didn't was that curiosity had gotten the better of me—once again—and I wanted to know why the man was at my house.

"Is your father home?" he asked, taking his fancy hat off his head, revealing hair so tightly slicked that I imagined it hadn't moved since last Easter.

"He is."

I shifted, struggling to hold Sully. He was a very fat cat. He made a screaming noise that made him sound like a mountain lion, and the man on the front porch straightened up.

"Could you go get him?" the man said.

Well, he didn't say please, so I decided I didn't have to be polite either.

Mam would have choked, but I closed the door, leaving the man on the porch. It wasn't cold. He'd be fine out there.

I didn't want him wandering the house while I ran out to get Dad.

For his part, Sully was glad when I dropped him to the floor. I would have to remember to reward his courage with a pinch of cheese.

Dad was typing furiously when I barged into his shed. He was so deep into his work that he didn't hear me until I'd called for him four times. And he only snapped back to reality because I was right next to him, stamping my foot on the slatted floor.

"Huh?" he said. "Not now, Flossie. I have a lot of work to do."

"There's a man here," I said, tugging on his arm. "He's smarmy."

Dad blinked his eyes a bunch of times fast before pushing back in his chair and getting up.

"Smarmy, huh?" he asked.

"Yes."

"Well, I wouldn't want to leave my daughter to deal with a man like *that*."

He grabbed his cardigan—the one he'd had since before he met Mam—and shoved his arms into it.

"Where's your mother?" he asked.

"Next door." I stopped on the back stoop. "I didn't let the man in. I left him on the front porch."

He held the door for me like a gentleman. "We'll have a conversation about hospitality later."

I shrugged and went inside.

Even though Dad told me not to snoop, I stood in the hallway and tried to listen when he invited the man inside. Then, when I heard them swapping loud greetings, I stopped hiding and went into the living room to see the two shaking hands so hard I was surprised they didn't get hurt.

"How the heck are ya, Will?" the man asked, slapping Dad on the back.

"Fine, I'm fine," Dad answered. "What are you doing in town?"

"Oh, I was in Detroit," the man said, pulling a gold cigarette case from his jacket pocket and offering it to Dad. "You want one?"

Dad shook his head.

The man shrugged.

"Had a meeting with some young hotshot. He's a hel—" He spied me out of the corner of his eye. "Heck of a guy."

He might as well have said the actual word, I already knew what it was.

I had, after all, read *Catcher in the Rye*.

"Say, Roger, you've never met my youngest, have you?" Dad asked, waving me over. "Roger, meet Florence. Florence, meet Mr. McClinton. He's my agent."

"Pleasure to meet you, Flo," the man said. "You as talented as your old man?"

"Yes," I said.

"Well, good for you. Anyway, I was in Detroit, scouting out this young writer. Heck of a poet." He sat in the wingback chair. "Name of Landrum. You ever hear of him?"

"Can't say I have." Dad dropped onto the sofa. "You want something to drink? My little waitress over there works for tips. Don't you, honey?"

I nodded.

"You mix drinks, little lady?" the man asked. "Maybe you know how to make an old fashioned?"

"I know how to pop the top off a bottle of Coke," I said.

"I don't suppose you have anything to put into that Coke." He looked at Dad.

"Not in the house, Roger," Dad said. "You know that."

"Then let's you and me go out," Mr. McClinton said. "We ought to go to Jacoby's in the city. They've got a corned beef that's so tender it'll make you cry. Don't ever tell my mother, but it's better by far than hers."

"Your secret's safe." Dad pretended to zip his lips.

"So, you coming or what?" Mr. McClinton leaned forward to tap the ash off his cigarette into the dish on the coffee table. "Will it convince you if I say we've got celebrating to do?"

"I'm listening."

"I got a call from a guy I know out in LA." There it was, the smarmy grin. "Hollywood's calling your name, Will. They want *This Working-Day World*."

Dad fell back and put his hand on the top of his wild, uncombed hair.

"You're kidding," he said.

"Never would." Mr. McClinton clapped his hands together. "I told you I'd make a star out of you. Didn't I?"

"You did." Dad laughed. Then he turned toward me. "Flossie, honey, you can't tell anybody. All right?"

"Oh geez," Mr. McClinton said. "I forgot you were here, girlie.

Tell you what. I'll give you a little hush money. You know what that is?"

"Roger, no . . ." Dad started.

"It's a little something to make sure you remember our secret." He pulled the wallet out of the inside pocket of his jacket and grabbed a bill. "Don't spend it all in one place, kid."

He handed me a ten-dollar bill. A whole ten dollars! I could buy a lot of lipstick for that.

"Now you," the man said, looking at Dad. "Go get cleaned up. We've got lots to talk about."

Dad kissed me on the forehead on his way out.

fifteen

BERTHA

Dad came home late, long after Mam served a quiet dinner for the three of us and Flossie and I cleaned up afterward. After we listened to *The Halls of Ivy* on the radio. He came home hours after us girls cleaned our teeth and got into our nighties and Mam had us say our prayers, kneeling beside our beds.

After Flossie finished her recitation of "Now I Lay Me," Mam had added, "Bring him home safe," and I knew she meant Dad.

By the time Dad got home, Flossie was in my bed—she'd insisted that she was lonely in her own—and I was sitting on the window seat because my sister kicked in her sleep.

From my bedroom window I could see the glow of the Detroit lights that stayed on all night, every night.

It was well past one o'clock in the morning when a car pulled up in front of the house, the engine still running as Dad stepped out. He leaned back into the car, and I heard a loud laugh—it had to be loud for me to hear it through my closed window—before he closed the door and headed for the house.

I left my room with the intention of meeting him at the front door. But halfway down the steps I saw Mam standing there, holding it open and waiting for him.

"Louisa," he said when he stepped inside. "What a beauty you are."

She dodged his kiss, something I'd never seen her do before.

Granted, it was rare that they showed any sort of affection toward each other in front of us kids—they usually saved that for anniversaries or Christmases. Still, when Dad did go in for a kiss, Mam nearly always welcomed it.

"Where were you?" she asked, keeping her voice quiet. "Your daughter said she wasn't allowed to tell anyone."

Dad cringed. "I think she misunderstood."

"She told me Roger gave her hush money." Mam crossed her arms.

"Yes, well." Dad laughed. "Roger is a character."

He walked past her, and she followed. I lowered down a step or two so I could see them but backed into a shadow so they wouldn't see me.

"So, where were you?" Mam asked again.

"Some place in Detroit." Dad dropped his coat on the back of a chair. "Jockeys . . . Jackies . . . something like that. Either way, they've got great corned beef."

"And booze, from the smell of it."

Dad's shoulders slumped, and he turned toward her.

"I only had one drink."

"William."

"To celebrate," he said. "A producer wants to make a movie out of my book."

"You promised not to touch the stuff."

"It was one drink, Lou," he said.

"We both know it can never be only one with you, Will."

She grabbed his coat and walked it back to the hook on the wall. If she'd looked up the stairs, she would have seen me. I held my breath and kept perfectly still, and she didn't notice me.

"One becomes two becomes drinking every night," she said. "Then to starting the day with a bit in your coffee and so on. I won't have that life again."

"And I won't make you," Dad said. "I promise."

He came to her and put a hand on her cheek. She closed her eyes and leaned into his palm.

"I promise, Lou," he said. "And I'm sorry."

"Don't make a liar out of yourself, love."

"I won't."

Then he leaned close to kiss her, and she didn't move away.

"Tell me about the movie," she said, nodding toward the sofa.

They moved out of sight, but I stayed and listened for a few minutes.

"Well, Roger's going to push for Nunnally Johnson to write the screenplay," he said.

"I don't know who that is," Mam said.

"He did the script for *The Grapes of Wrath* film."

"Oh. That was a good one, wasn't it?"

"It was," Dad said. "Real good."

"Not particularly cheery, though," she said.

"No." He laughed.

I slept in Flossie's bed that night, lumpy as it was.

sixteen

FLOSSIE

Both Mam and Dad had taken me aside before school to remind
me not to tell anybody about what they called "the movie business." Mam said that it could get Dad into heaps—*heaps*—of
trouble if the news leaked before all the paperwork was signed.
Dad reminded me of Mr. McClinton's hush money.

He didn't say anything about Roger being part of the mob,
but I wouldn't have put it past him having a squad of goons at
his beck and call.

"If you can keep the secret," Dad had said at breakfast, "we'll
all take a trip out to California to see the movie set."

"Can I be in the movie, Daddy?" I'd asked.

"I'm not sure about that."

"Everybody says I look just like Doris Day." I blinked at him
slowly. "Is Doris Day going to be in your movie?"

"I don't think there's a part for her."

"Well, if she is and she needs someone to play her daughter, I'll
do it," I said. "You won't even have to pay me."

Dad said he would keep that in mind and then scooted me off
to school.

I made it most of the morning without saying anything. But
doggone it. The worst part about good news was not being able
to brag about it.

When Miss Lange left the classroom during quiet reading time,

Iris Markowitz started bragging about her father's job—a thing she did regularly—and I couldn't hardly resist spilling the beans. To my credit, I rolled my lips between my teeth and clamped down so I'd remember to hold it in.

Oh, but it was bubbling and gurgling and threatening to burst out of me one way or the other.

"My father got another promotion," Iris said. "We'll have to go to Florida at least twice a year for his work."

"Oh, Iris," Ethel said. "I wish I could go to Florida."

"We might have to move there." Iris puckered up her lips. "My mother said that if we do, I can get a bikini."

All of the girls—including me—gasped at that part of the news. None of our mothers would have agreed to that. As a matter of fact, Mam had told me I might as well just sit around in my underwear because it covered more than a bikini would.

The very thought of Iris being allowed to wear one made me feel so jealous that I was sure my skin was turning green.

"You can't move to Florida," Janey whined. "It's so far away."

"I know," Iris said. "I'd probably never see you ever again. But my father's job is so important, you know. We all have to make sacrifices for the good of everyone."

"We might have to move for my father's work too," I said.

The girls all looked at me.

"Oh, really?" Iris said, looking down at her book.

"Yes. We might have to go to California."

That got Ethel to raise her eyebrows.

"Hollywood, to be exact," I said.

Iris narrowed her eyes at me.

"They're making a movie from one of his books," I said. "And Doris Day is going to be in it. And Cary Grant too."

"You aren't joshing, are you?" Ethel asked.

"No. Honest to goodness," I said. "And they might let me be in it too. Doris Day saw a picture of me and said I was a dead ringer for her."

"Oh, Flossie," Ethel said. "That's wonderful. Do you think you could get Cary Grant's autograph for my mother?"

"I'll ask."

The classroom door opened, and we hushed up real quick and went back to reading. Well, the other girls did. I, on the other hand, could hardly focus on my book. I'd gone and done it. Told the secret I was absolutely, positively not allowed to tell.

And for what? To outdo Iris Markowitz.

I thought I was going to be sick.

What if Mr. McClinton found out that I'd told? He'd want his ten dollars back, that was sure. But I couldn't know if he'd be so angry he'd take it out on Dad.

"You'll never write another book again!" I could almost hear him yelling.

Then I imagined Dad crumpling on the couch, hands over his face, despairing. And all because of me.

I dragged my feet when the lunch bell rang, dreading going home. Mam would know that I'd told. Somehow the woman could always tell when I was guilty of something.

I was in for it, I just knew it.

"Hey, Flo," Iris said, standing with the rest of the girls by the schoolyard gate. "Tell Doris Day hello for us, would you?"

They all snickered behind their hands.

"Little Baby Bumpkin," Iris sang. "Gee, she ain't nothin'. Her pants're on fire 'cause she's a dumb ole liar."

"Oh, Iris," Ethel said. "Aren't you clever?"

Clever? My foot. Iris wouldn't have known what clever was if it came up and kicked her in the behind.

I didn't say anything to Iris or any of the other girls. I just shoved past them out the gate. They followed behind me chanting "Liar, liar, pants on fire" all the way to the end of my street.

By far, it wasn't the first time I'd been called a liar. But it was the first time I hadn't been mad about it. As a matter of fact, I was relieved. Iris couldn't have known the favor she'd done for me.

I hummed as I walked down the street, trying to get the new version of Iris's Baby Bumpkin song out of my head.

But I stopped when I went past Mrs. Sanders's house.

The curtains were closed, as usual. But what wasn't normal was the letters in red paint on the wooden siding.

"RED GET OUT!" it said, a thick swipe of paint underlining it.

I rushed home.

When I went back for the second half of the school day, I took a different way so I wouldn't have to pass Mrs. Sanders's house.

seventeen

BERTHA

Mam wasn't exactly pleased when I grabbed a couple of slices of toast and a sausage link on my way out the door. She liked us to sit down and eat breakfast together on Saturday mornings.

"At least eat an egg," she called after me.

But I was already out the door.

"Sorry," I said, walking backwards toward the gate, where Leo was waiting for me. "I've got to get to the sandlot."

"Don't be gone all morning." She stood in the doorway, arms crossed. "We've got a busy day, you know."

"I'll come home as soon as the game's over. Promise."

"And don't get hurt." Then, louder, "Take good care of her, Leo."

"I will," he answered, giving her a Boy Scout salute.

"Race ya," I said, running past Leo and not slowing down until we got almost all the way to the park.

I, of course, beat him handily.

"I let you win," he huffed.

"Yeah, right." I socked him on the arm.

"Hey," somebody yelled at us from the sandlot. "Quit making eyes at each other and come play ball!"

Usually something like that would have embarrassed me to tears. That day, though, I couldn't have cared if I'd tried. The two of us dashed across the bridge—Leo teasing that he was going to knock me off into the creek—to meet up with our team.

Every year on the third Saturday of March, we held the first ball game of the season. The Bonaventure Park Grizzlies—that was my team, of course—took on the Monument Park Bobcats. If it snowed, we brought shovels to clear paths between the bases. If it rained, we slid around in the mud. If the sun was out, it was all the same to us.

We'd play that third Saturday no matter what. We were all just antsy to get out on the diamond for a ball game.

The Monument boys lined up in front of their bench, trying to look tough by slamming their fists into their mitts or chomping on big old wads of gum. One of the kids even turned his head and spit a stream of brown mess.

It made me glad that my boys had a strict rule against playing with chaw in their lips.

"Looks like they got some new blood," Leo said, glancing over at them.

"Yeah. A family with a whole bunch of boys moved into the old Wright place. Guess they're farm boys." Bobbo scowled. "Big guys, every single one of 'em."

"Big don't mean good," Stinky said, puffing out his chest.

Leo turned and took off his jacket, tossing it on the ground by our bench.

One of the new Monument kids stared over at me, squinting his eyes and smirking. I didn't like the look of that one. Not one bit.

"Hey. Nobody told me you boys had a cheerleader," he yelled. "Who's the broad?"

"Just ignore him," I said, turning away from him. "Neanderthal."

I knew as well as anybody else that heckling was part of the game. It was used to distract, to get somebody off their stride, to crumble the confidence a little bit. Honestly, I usually thought it was funny the ways we poked fun at each other.

Then there were the kids who took it too far, picking fights and being downright nasty. I suspected that was the deal with Sir Neanderthal.

I was going to have to prove myself to him.

It always seemed to be that way when a boy first saw me on the diamond.

The only girl anywhere always had to be just a little bit better than the boys around her. And she didn't have much wiggle room to make mistakes.

She had to be good from the get-go or else the boy would always question her abilities.

What a stinker of a situation that could be.

Because we were the home team, we let the Monument boys bat first. Leo was catcher to Simon's pitching. They'd put me at shortstop and Bobbo at first.

They only got one run in the whole inning before we got them out—one, two, three. I tried not to let it get to my head that I'd caught everything that came my way.

Bottom of the first, the Bonaventure boys got in two runs—Bobbo and a kid named Ricky—before Leo struck out and a couple other boys hit fly balls that seemed to fall directly into the mitts of the outfielders.

Second inning same as the first. At least for the Monument team.

When it was our turn at bat, Vic Lancaster hit a double, and Stinky Simon eked his way to first just before the baseman caught the ball.

Then it was my turn.

The ground was still too hard for me to make a divot with my toe, and I was aware of the patches of ice here and there that I'd need to be careful of when I took off for first base.

Sir Neanderthal stood on the pitcher's mound, that same smirk still on his face. When I stepped up to bat, he laughed. He actually laughed.

"Isn't this rich," he said, holding his stomach as if he was about to bust a gut. "Are you sure you want to do this, honey?"

"Yup," I answered, deciding that I was not going to give him the satisfaction of getting to me.

"Tell you what," he said. "You go sit your pretty little behind back on the bench and let the men play."

I didn't answer him. Instead I lifted my arms over my head, warming up my shoulders.

"Hey, Zeke," he said to the kid manning first base. "You ever notice it's the plain ones that always wanna play with the boys or work with the men? Why is that?"

"Come on," the kid named Zeke said. "That ain't all right."

"You think maybe that's 'cause they don't like being girls?" the pitcher asked. "They wanna try their hand at being men?"

"That's enough," Leo yelled from the sidelines. "Cut it out or I'll—"

"You'll do nothing," I said, lifting the bat, cocking it to the right of my head. "He's just yammering. Doesn't mean a thing to me."

"You ready, babycakes?" Neanderthal asked.

"I don't know," I said. "Are you? Maybe let someone else pitch? You seem real scared of little old me."

That was when he shot me a look as if to say I'd better watch out.

He grinned at me, the smug little monster, and tossed the ball to me. Underhand.

I didn't so much as flinch, and I most certainly did not swing. I just let that lame pitch go by as if it never existed.

"That's strike one," he yelled, putting up his glove and waiting for the catcher to throw the ball back to him.

"Is not," I said, keeping my bat in place. "We play overhand. That one didn't count."

"You got a problem?" Leo yelled from the bench.

"Leave it, Leo," I said. "I can handle it."

The second pitch went wild. Ball one. The third I let go because it didn't feel quite right. Strike one. Or two if you asked that Monument kid.

I held my breath, determined not to get struck out. Not that day. When he threw the fourth pitch, I knew it was mine.

The swing felt exactly as it should have. Or at least it did until the bat connected with the ball.

Instead of a crack, the hit made a thunk. Then I was on my backside, the bat still in my left hand, my right holding my eye.

The stupid ball had bounced off the bat directly at my face!

"You did that on purpose!" That was Leo.

"Did not," the Monument Park boy said. "Told ya girls shouldn't play."

Then there was the sound of boy feet thudding on hard ground.

"Well, I oughta . . ." I thought that was Leo, although I couldn't be sure.

It seemed like all of the boys were yelling and hooting, ready for a fight.

"Oh, knock it off, won't you," I yelled, getting to my feet.

By myself.

The boys were all so busy preparing for battle that they'd forgotten all about me in the process.

Figured.

Boys and their posturing for position. It was exhausting just to watch.

"Hey," I yelled, trying to make myself heard over the rabble. "Are we gonna play or not?"

"Oh, gee," Leo said, running back to me. "You okay, Bert?"

"Think so."

"You're gonna have one heck of a shiner." He touched the skin around my eye.

"Ouch," I said, swatting at his hand. "That smarts."

"Bet it does." He squinted at me. "Want me to get you home?"

"Nope. I've got to get on base." Then I lowered my voice so only he could hear me. "I can't let him think I'm weak."

"You're such a tough cookie." He winked at me, and I could tell he was impressed. Then he turned toward the rest of the boys. "Play ball!"

We went all nine innings, the score going back and forth the whole time. It was anybody's game, we were so evenly matched. The year before we'd trounced them. But those new kids were good. The most annoying thing in the world was a cocky boy. The second most annoying was when he was cocky *and* good.

The game ended, and we were down just one run. One lousy point.

"We'll get 'em next year," Stinky Simon said.

Tired from playing hard and losing anyway, we Grizzlies walked home in a big pack, none of us talking. We were a hangdog crew if ever there was one.

One by one the boys splintered away from the group, taking the porch steps to their front door or heading down an alley that led to their family's home. Eventually it was just Leo and me, shuffling our feet down the sidewalk on Aurelius Avenue.

I didn't expect him to grab my hand, but when he did, I didn't pull away.

"I'll come get you at 6:45," he said once we stopped in front of my house. "Okay?"

The dance. It was that night. In all the excitement over the game, I'd completely forgotten.

"Yeah, okay," I said. "How bad is my shiner?"

He pulled his mouth into a cringe and wrinkled his nose.

"Hideous," he said.

"Oh, get out of town." I swatted at him with my free hand.

"It's not that bad," he said. "You'll look nice no matter what."

"You saying I don't look nice now?"

"I'm too smart to answer a question like that."

Leo looked down at our hands and smiled before letting go and heading to his house.

"See you at 6:45," I called after him. "Don't be late."

"Wouldn't miss it for the world," he yelled back.

I skipped to the porch and hopped up the steps.

eighteen

FLOSSIE

I didn't hurry to the butcher shop. For one, Mam hadn't told me to be quick about it. For two, I was sore that I'd been uprooted from my warm spot next to the fire to be sent out in the cold and gloom of the afternoon. And for three, I really hated going to the butcher's.

All that raw meat and skinned animals hanging from hooks for the whole world to see gave me the screaming meemies.

Deep down I hoped that I would take so long getting there that it would already be closed for the day.

Well, the laugh was on me. I got to the butcher's with five whole minutes to spare.

Drat!

"One steak, please," I said once I got to the counter. "My mother would like a very small one, if that's all right."

"Yup. That's fine," Mr. Gomez said, grinning at me. "Bertha get a black eye again?"

"Yes, sir," I answered. "She was playing baseball."

"I have just the thing." Mr. Gomez turned around and grabbed a chunk of meat before slapping it onto the scale.

I went up on my tiptoes to make sure he wasn't putting his thumb on it so he could charge more.

"My Roberto thinks a lot of her, you know?" he said, putting his hands up so I could see he was being honest.

"Oh really?" I asked, lowering back down. "Is he in love with her?"

"I don't know about that." He laughed as if I'd meant it as a joke.

What he didn't know was that I never joked about things as serious as romance.

"I would imagine a lot of those boys carry a torch for her." He looked at the scale over the tops of his glasses. "That'll be forty-nine cents. Unless you needed something else?"

I gave him the two quarters Mam had sent me with and waited for him to wrap up the little bit of meat.

Mrs. Gomez stepped in from the back of the butcher shop, newspaper in hand.

"Did you see this?" she asked her husband.

He glanced at the paper and then they both looked at me like I was a sad, lost puppy.

"Oh, hi there, Florence," Mrs. Gomez said. "How's your mother?"

She didn't smile at me like she usually would.

"She's fine," I answered. "Is something the matter?"

Mrs. Gomez shook her head, and her husband said something to her in Spanish that I didn't understand.

He finished with the steak and handed it to me over the counter.

"No charge," he said, pushing the quarters back at me. "We have to close now. Tell your mother we can't take her money here anymore."

Then he followed me to the door, locking it behind me.

Two shiny quarters! Just for me. Mam wouldn't know that Mr. Gomez had been nice enough to give me the steak for free.

I ducked into the five-and-dime for a couple of Charleston Chews and a tube of pale pink lipstick that I'd been eyeing for weeks. I even had a nickel left over to buy a pack of Doublemint gum.

With all the fuss over getting Bertha ready for the dance, I should have no trouble sneaking it all by Mam.

Huzzah! What a lucky girl was I!

I skipped all the way home. When I passed someone on the street, I waved and told them to have a nice day. It was the neighborly thing to do.

nineteen

BERTHA

Way back in February, when most of the girls in my home economics class were all paired up for the Valentine's Day Sweetheart Dance, Mrs. Higginbottom devoted an entire week to teaching us how a lady should conduct herself at such a soiree.

I hadn't been asked to the dance—which had been no skin off my nose—so I doodled on my paper instead of taking notes. After all, I'd assumed I'd never get asked to any dance by any boy I'd ever actually want to go with.

Boy, oh boy. How shortsighted I'd been.

Oopsy daisy.

So, when Peggy gave me pointers, I tried my very best to listen even as she tugged on my hair while brushing out the snarls and kept scolding me to put the steak back on my eye.

"Rule number one should have been not to run off and play baseball on the day of the dance," she said, shaking her head. "Only you, Bertha. Only you."

"It's not that bad," I said, lowering the steak and looking at my reflection. "At least my eye didn't swell shut."

"Well, we can thank goodness for small mercies, I guess." She stopped working on my hair and sighed. "I would give anything to go to a dance. Hold this."

She handed me the brush and reached around me for a couple of rollers.

"Well, Chip takes you out dancing, doesn't he?" I asked.

"Yes." She sighed again. "It's just not the same, is all."

Peggy was the sort of girl who had spent all four years of high school wanting to hurry up and get married already. But then, once she was married, she longed for the good ole days when she didn't have to worry about how much a pound of chicken cost or how often she should wash her sheets.

She rolled my hair, powdered my face, dolled me up in an outfit we'd both agreed on—a black and white polka dot skirt, white blouse, and blue cardigan.

"Just wait until Leo gets an eyeful of you," she said, staining my lips a glossy cherry red. "Bertha, he'll go absolutely bonkers."

I laughed and Peggy scolded me, saying that I'd smudge my lipstick.

The thing was, boys went bonkers over girls named Catherine or Victoria or Elizabeth. Gosh, they'd even go gaga over a girl named Betty or Sally. But boys did not get moonstruck over girls named Bertha.

It was the difference between having the name of a queen and the name of a German milkmaid.

"Leo will be here any minute," she said. "Are you ready?"

"I think I'm going to be sick," I said.

"Oh no, you'd better not." She grabbed my shoulders and turned me. "I don't have time to clean that up."

Then she bustled me out of the room and down the stairs.

My entire family—even Chip—sat in the living room, waiting to see me all gussied up. I had never been so embarrassed in my entire life.

Dad got up from his favorite easy chair and clapped, which made me snort and laugh like a big old oaf. Peggy cleared her throat, and I knew that the sound had displeased her high-brow sensibilities. But I just couldn't help it.

Ridiculous situations warranted ridiculous-sounding laughs.

"Did you stuff your bra?" Flossie blurted.

Mam put her hand over my sister's mouth, and no matter how Flossie tried to pull it away, she held firm.

"You look lovely, Bertha," Mam said.

"Hold on," Chip said. "*That's* Bertha? My kid sister? Can't be. I don't believe it."

"Knock it off," I said, raising my fist at him.

Peggy cleared her throat again, and I dropped it.

I stood by the door, waiting for Leo to come. My heart beat so hard and so fast, it was almost like I'd just run around the block three times.

Leo didn't come at 6:45 when he said he would. And he wasn't there at 6:55. Or five, ten, fifteen minutes later. By then I was antsy, wondering how long I was meant to wait and worrying that I'd understood him wrong. Maybe I was supposed to meet him at the dance. But Mam told me that wasn't done.

"A gentleman comes to pick up the young lady," Mrs. Higginbottom had said in one of her Sweetheart Dance lessons.

I'd remembered that, at least.

But what happened if the gentleman forgot or didn't have the nerve or got lost on the way? What then? Was the girl just supposed to wait forever?

When the grandfather clock struck half past seven, I'd had enough of waiting for Leo. Without a word, I grabbed my red coat and swung it around my shoulders, shoving my hands through the arms as I let myself out the front door, stepping over the evening paper that was rolled up on the porch.

Peggy called after me, but I didn't stop. Not even when Mam said my name.

twenty

FLOSSIE

Mam wouldn't let me spy out the window because she said that Bertha deserved some privacy. When I asked her if it was the same kind of privacy that newlyweds like Chippy and Peggy needed all the time, she'd laughed. Peggy turned bright red and went to the kitchen.

Chippy gave me a look that I didn't like before he ran off after her.

I had no idea what I'd done wrong.

Peggy was so sensitive.

I dropped onto the couch and grabbed *Little Women* from the coffee table. After just a minute or two, Peggy came back in the room and sat down next to me.

"I'm sorry," I said, not looking up from the page, still not entirely sure what I was apologizing for.

It just seemed like the thing she expected me to do.

"It's all right," she said. "You didn't mean it."

I licked the tip of my pointer finger and turned the page.

"What are you reading?" she asked.

"Have you ever read it?" I showed her the cover of the book.

"Of course. Bunches of times."

"This is my first time," I said. "I'm only partway through."

"Which March sister are you?"

"What?" I lifted my head. "I don't understand."

"Every girl is just like one of the little women." She leaned closer to me. "I'm like Meg."

"You *are* fancy," I said.

"Thank you." She smiled. "Bertha's like Jo, don't you think?"

I widened my eyes as big as they would go and nodded. She was right! There wasn't anyone else in the world so like Jo March than my sister.

"I like Beth most of all," I said. "She plays piano and is nice to everyone and never throws fits."

"She's the best of them, isn't she?"

Just then my big brother came back into the room and sat down at the piano in the corner. He didn't need sheet music. He had all the best songs saved up in his noggin. When he played by heart, he sounded better than anybody I'd ever heard on the radio.

He was the best of us. A dear and nothing else.

"Maybe Chip is like Beth," I whispered.

Peggy laughed. I pouted because, doggone it, that meant there was just one March sister left.

"But I don't like Amy." I shook my head. "Not even a little. She's horrible."

"Oh, come on," Peggy said. "It's not all bad. She does end up with Laurie."

"She what!" I cried, horrified. "That's not right. Laurie loves Jo. Why would he do a thing like that?"

"Oh," she said, cringing. "You just said this was your first time reading it, didn't you. I'm sorry. Forget I said anything."

How could I ever forget a thing like that? And just when I'd considered letting myself like Peggy, she had to ruin it.

I thought about making myself cry so she'd feel bad about it, but when the telephone rang, I forgot all about my hurt feelings and yelled, "I'll get it!"

I jumped up from my seat and dashed across the room before anyone else could answer the phone. It could have been news about Bertha and Leo, and I wanted to be the first to hear it.

"Harding residence," I said once I got the receiver to my ear. "This is Florence M. Harding speaking."

"Let me talk to your father," the deep voice on the other end barked.

No kidding. He sounded just like a junkyard dog that was frothing at the mouth, wishing he could bite somebody for walking past his fence.

"Well, that's no way to talk to a lady," I said. "Call back when you remember your manners."

Then I hung up.

"Flo," Mam said.

She'd turned around and looked at me like I'd been the rude one. If she'd heard the way that man had talked to me, she might have thought different.

Then the telephone rang again, and I reached for it.

"Don't you dare," Mam said, crossing the room, her pointer finger stabbing in my direction. "What has gotten into you, young lady?"

"The dickens," I said.

If looks could turn a girl into ice, I would have been a popsicle.

"Harding residence," Mam said once she'd picked up. "I beg your pardon?"

Whoever was on the other line talked so loud I could hear him when Mam pulled the receiver from her ear.

It was the very same guy. Woof, woof, woof.

"Well, I never." Mam touched the middle of her chest. "How dare you?"

Then she hung up, and I'd never been so proud to be her daughter.

"Who was that?" Dad asked.

"I don't know," Mam said, looking at the telephone like it had burned her. "But he was angry. Nasty."

"What did he want?" Chippy asked, sitting sideways on the piano bench.

"He wanted to talk to your father," Mam said. "Something about needing to talk sense into him."

"Maybe somebody didn't like one of your books?" Chippy asked, shaking his head.

Dad shrugged.

The phone rang a third time.

"Just let it go," Dad said. Then he looked me in the eye. "I mean it, Flossie. It does nobody any good to listen to a blunderbuss."

When I asked him what that word meant, he told me to consult the dictionary.

I hated it when he said that.

twenty-one

BERTHA

When Leo's dad left, I was the only one he told. We were in the eighth grade at the time and played catch every day after school in the alley behind our houses, even in the winter. When he'd told me, I pretended that I didn't notice him crying.

It hadn't taken long for the rumor mill to start cranking out the gossip about why Mr. Schmidt had gone away and where he'd ended up. For months, if a couple of women were talking behind their hands at the grocery store, there was a good chance they were telling stories about Mrs. Schmidt.

Now, Mam liked to indulge every once in a while in the tidbits of other people's lives. She wasn't a busybody exactly, but she would have said she liked to stay on top of things. But when it came to another woman's grief, she just couldn't bring herself to dish about it.

So, when one of the neighbor ladies tried to talk to her about Mrs. Schmidt, Mam would just say, "If you're so concerned about her, why don't you invite her over for supper? Or maybe offer to pay her water bill?"

Then, so as to not be a hypocrite, she'd invited Mrs. Schmidt to have dinner with us any Sunday after church she wanted to.

She'd never, not once, taken Mam up on it. But at Christmas

we always got a card from her and Leo. I sometimes wondered if we were the only ones in the neighborhood she sent one to.

I couldn't help but think of all that when I got to the bottom of the front steps to the Schmidt house. There wasn't another friend I'd ever made who was half as important to me as Leo. There wasn't anyone on the planet who I told secrets to. Only a couple people—aside from Mam and Chip—ever saw me cry. Leo was one of them.

If he had decided he didn't want to take me to the dance after all, it would hurt my feelings so much more than I would ever admit to anyone.

I shouldn't have let him convince me to go with him in the first place. I should have just laughed it off and acted like I thought it was a joke. At least then we could have gone on being friends like we'd always been.

Mrs. Higginbottom had never given us tips on how to navigate such a thing with grace.

I wondered why they didn't teach things like that in school.

Biting the inside of my cheek, I took the steps, touching the wood pillar once I got to the porch and trying to get my heart to stop thudding so hard before I knocked on the door.

No one came after half a minute—I knew it because I'd counted to thirty—so I knocked again before pressing on the doorbell.

"It's her," I heard Mrs. Schmidt say from inside. "Don't you dare answer it . . ."

This wasn't the way it was done, Mrs. Higginbottom had even said so. The girl wasn't supposed to pick up the boy. My entire home economics class would have been scandalized if they'd known I was at the Schmidts' front door, ready to insist that my date get his act together and escort me to the dance. It was backwards. But I didn't care. I needed to get to the bottom of whatever was going on.

"Ma," Leo said.

Then he opened the door.

I looked at Leo and saw the sad face he'd had just a few years before when he'd told me about his dad. My annoyance that had turned into anger melted to worry.

Something was wrong.

He hadn't even put on his tie.

"What's up?" I asked. "Come on. We're already late."

"You look really pretty," he said. "How's the eye?"

"Ugly. But it doesn't hurt too badly," I answered. "We'd better go or we'll miss the whole thing."

"I can't."

"What do you mean, you can't?" I asked, crossing my arms in the hopes of warming up.

I wished he would just let me step inside already. But he was blocking the way.

"My mother said I can't go to the dance." He swallowed hard, his Adam's apple bobbing up and down. "Well, I can't go with you, that is."

I opened my mouth to say something but couldn't think of any words. So, I shut my trapper and blinked. Hard. I thought I might start to cry.

"Why not?" I managed, my voice cracking.

"Tell her to go back home," Mrs. Schmidt called from behind him. "She needs to get off our porch. I don't want the neighbors to see her over here. And in a red coat. That's bold."

Leo lowered his eyebrows, and he wouldn't look at me.

"I'm sorry," he said.

"Don't apologize to her!" his mother yelled.

"I'm sorry." He whispered it that time.

"Tell her she isn't to bother us anymore," Mrs. Schmidt said, her voice deep and gravelly. "She isn't to talk to you at school or on the street or . . . or . . . anywhere. She's to leave you alone. Her and her whole family. Leave us alone."

"I don't understand," I said. "What did I do? Whatever it was, I'll make it right. I promise. Just, please, tell me what I did."

I hated to beg. And I hated the way my voice sounded weak and pathetic. But more than that, I hated the hollowed-out feeling I had right in the center of my chest.

"I'm so sorry," Leo said one last time.

That was when Mrs. Schmidt pushed past Leo, her eyes wide and mouth pulled into a tight line. She threw a newspaper at me. It hit my chest—right where the empty feeling was—and fell on the porch at my feet.

There on the front page was a picture of my dad.

Bonaventure Times
March 22, 1952

AUTHOR NAMED IN RED PROBE

DETROIT, MI: More than half a dozen names of those accused of affiliation with the Communist Party of Detroit have been released. These men were named in last week's hearing of the House Un-American Activities Committee.

Most notable among them is William S. Harding of 364 Aurelius Avenue, Bonaventure Park, MI. Harding is the author of critically acclaimed novels such as *This Working-Day World*.

Before naming Mr. Harding, Mrs. Marjory Sanders hesitated. When asked the reason for her pause, she said that of all those on her list, Harding was the most difficult revelation as he has been her neighbor for several years.

"I watched the Harding children grow, baked them cookies, played bridge with Mrs. Harding for years," she is recorded to have said. "It pains me to speak of his betrayal to our nation."

Because of her close ties to the Harding family, it was all the more courageous of her to take the stand in defense of democracy.

As of this printing, there is still no word on whether or not Harding will be summoned to testify before the HUAC members.

Neither Harding nor a representative of his publisher were available for immediate comment.

Others named by Mrs. Sanders were C. E. Carter, Jack Donan, T. Robert Main, Jacob Adams . . .

CONT on page 4

Part Two

Many of the great stories have some fool who's too blind to see the betrayal coming. I never thought my story was great or that I was a blind fool until betrayal hit me square on the chin.

From *This Working-Day World*
by William S. Harding

twenty-two

FLOSSIE

Bertha rushed in the front door, strangling a newspaper in her clenched fist.

"Did you know?" she asked, handing the paper to Dad.

"Know what?" He unrolled it. Then, looking up, "Louisa."

Mam stood at his elbow, reading. Then Chip looked over Dad's shoulder with Peggy close by. They all had very serious looks on their faces.

Doggone it. I was too short to see what they were looking at.

Last time everybody in my family paid so much attention to the newspaper was when the king of England died. Mam had cried so hard I would have thought he'd been her very own long-lost brother.

I thought that really would have been something, being related to royalty. It still wouldn't have made her the queen and me a princess. But I would eventually become a duchess, which was even better. All the money and family jewels without any of the boring meetings with dull old politicians.

Mam had read and reread every story she could about King What's-His-Name and the brand-new Queen Elizabeth for weeks after.

From the way Mam's jaw clenched that night, I thought the news was just as big and important. Maybe even more important, judging from how many times she said, "Oh goodness, oh gracious," as she read.

I tried to keep my questions of "what does it say" and "what's going on" to myself so they wouldn't send me out of the room. They were always sending me upstairs when there was something important and "grown-up" for them to talk about.

Little pitchers like me had big ears, after all.

So I tried to keep my lips buttoned.

But when Mam opened the paper and I saw what was on the front page at the very top—a picture of my dear old, beloved dad—I couldn't hardly stay quiet.

"It's you, Dad," I said, with all the glee I could. "This is the berries! With cream and sugar! Is it about the movie?"

Mam looked at me over the top of the paper, and I couldn't figure why she wasn't smiling. In fact, her eyes were red and watery.

As a matter of fact, everybody in the room had gloomy expressions on. Nobody talked or cheered or clapped Dad on the back in congratulations.

I didn't know what in the world was going on.

But then I remembered the way Mr. and Mrs. Gomez had looked at me at the butcher shop. They'd had the paper too.

It was bad news. I could tell.

I grabbed the paper away from Mam and read the headline. Then I went on to read the article.

By golly. My dad was a Red?

And Mrs. Sanders had been the one to tattle on him?

I dropped that paper like it was covered with biting ants.

"How could you?" I asked, looking directly at Dad.

"Say, Flopsy," Chippy said, picking the paper up. "It's not true. Right, Dad?"

"Not in the slightest." Dad knelt on the floor in front of me. "Listen, kiddo, folks are scared. Mrs. Sanders is scared too, believe it or not. She did something wrong, right? And she got caught, didn't she?"

"I guess so." I sniffled.

"Do you know what these people who say they're rooting out un-American activities do?"

I shook my head.

"They tell people like Mrs. Sanders that if they tattle on other people—people who were Communists like they are—then they won't get in as much trouble." Dad put a hand on my shoulder. "Do you understand what I'm saying?"

"I think so."

"So, she probably got scared and rattled off a bunch of names," Chippy said. "Maybe she didn't know that they'd get in trouble too."

"Oh, she knew," Bertha said. "I'm sure of it. She was just trying to save her own bacon."

Mam sat on the bench, facing away from the piano, and chewed her thumbnail.

I thought about how Mr. Gomez had said he wouldn't take our money anymore. He'd told me that after looking at the newspaper, and I'd thought he was being nice. But he wasn't.

I understood.

We were no better than Mrs. Sanders. Not anymore.

twenty-three

BERTHA

We Hardings kept our saddest mementos stowed away in a trunk under the basement stairs. Once tucked in, those relics of our sorrows were supposed to be out of sight, out of mind. At least we didn't bring them up in conversation.

"You can't well see where you're going if you're looking back," Mam often said.

Stiff upper lip and all that.

After Chip and Peggy went home and everyone else had gone to bed, I grabbed the newspaper and rushed down the basement stairs. The bare bulb hanging from the ceiling gave off just enough light for me to see if there was anything on the floor I might trip over.

I'd need a flashlight in order to inter the bad news where it belonged.

The trunk was the same one Mam had packed her things into when she left England on a ship headed for America. She'd been seventeen—just one year older than I was—and had somehow convinced her mother to let her go.

I grabbed the flashlight that Dad kept on an old metal shelf and had to give it a couple of good whacks before it flickered on.

The trunk was dusty, a sure sign that things had been good for quite some time. Nobody'd had a need to hide bad news, I supposed. I knelt on the floor beside it, glad that I'd changed out of

Peggy's skirt and into a pair of pajama pants. As it was, the floor was cold as stone through the flannel. With one hand I held the flashlight, with the other I flipped open the latches of the trunk one at a time.

The hinges made a crackling, creaking sound when I lifted the lid.

What I should have done was just toss the newspaper in, drop the lid, latch it closed, and make my way to bed. I wasn't usually much of a crier, but that evening I'd done more of it than I liked to. It was exhausting. I sure didn't need to spend a moment longer kneeling before my family's troubles.

But what I did was point the flashlight into the trunk. That was a whopper of a mistake on my part.

There on the very top of the pile was a picture I hadn't seen in years. I dropped the newspaper on the floor so I could reach in and pick up the old photograph.

If anyone else had been around I wouldn't have, but I was alone, so I held the picture to my chest like I could absorb it into myself.

Completely ridiculous.

I was not so sentimental. Not on a normal day, at least.

When it came to my baby brother, though, I couldn't help it.

Amos had come along when Flossie was barely a year old. I'd been six and Chip was nine. As was the case with Flossie, he'd been a surprise.

Unplanned. But completely wanted.

He was born with a full head of soft hair that stood up on end no matter how Mam tried to smooth it after his baths. His little cheeks were covered with the tiny bumps that babies sometimes get, and he had a little pink spot on his forehead that Mam had said was the mark where an angel had kissed him before sending him to us.

I used to kiss him in that exact spot.

Between all of us—Mam and Dad, Chip, and me—Amos hardly ever got put down. It put Flossie's nose out of joint, seeing him get all the attention she'd grown accustomed to.

Maybe that was why she'd turned out to be such a drama queen. She'd had to work hard to get us all to look at her in those days.

I pulled the picture away from the front of my pajama shirt and held it in the beam from the flashlight. It was the only picture we had of us as a family of six. Dad and Mam stood on the front porch, Mam holding Amos and Dad with his arms around both of them. Chip had Flossie on his hip. She, of course, had refused to smile. I stood next to Dad, my head resting against his elbow.

We were so happy.

One morning I woke up and Dad told me that Amos had died in the night. He'd been sleeping and stopped breathing.

"It happens sometimes," he'd said. "I don't know why."

Mam busied herself with taking care of the house and the three of us kids. Dad busied himself with emptying as many bottles of bourbon as he could get his hands on.

He earned himself a lot of nights locked out of the house. So many that he went out and bought himself an old army cot for his shed.

I never knew what happened to make him straighten up. Kids aren't always privy to the ways of adults. All I did know was that Uncle Matthew came for a few days, and after he left Dad bought himself a box of Tootsie Rolls and got back to his writing.

My father wasn't a perfect man. He had his faults and flaws just like anyone else.

But one thing I knew, he was no Red.

I dropped the newspaper into the trunk and very carefully lowered the picture of my family, laying it on top.

Before I went upstairs, I grabbed the American flag that we sometimes hung off the front of the house on the Fourth of July or Armistice Day.

If ever the neighborhood needed to observe an act of patriotism from us, it was then.

Bonaventure Times
March 24, 1952

"I AM INNOCENT"
A Letter to the Editor
by William S. Harding

If you were to come to my house for a cup of tea or a coffee (which many of you have enjoyed over the years), you would witness my eldest daughter rushing off to play baseball with the neighborhood boys. My younger daughter might regale you with theatrics that could rival the likes of Bette Davis. My son and his new wife could pop in for a visit or for a bit of advice.

My wife, British-born immigrant that she is, would show you the photograph of the day she became a citizen of the old U.S. of A., her standing beside the Stars and Stripes along with a half dozen other newly minted Americans.

That day remains one of her proudest. Mine too.

You might find me tucked away in my office, mashing the keys of my typewriter as I take a stab at writing the "great American novel." I'd likely be happy to take a break for a chat with you about the weather, sports, the family. If we had the time, I'd gladly take you for a ride in the Ford I recently bought at the local dealership.

It's a Custom Deluxe and the best car I've ever owned. The engine purrs like the family cat, Sultan of Swat, and has plenty of get-up-and-go (unlike old Sully). It rides like a dream, that car. And I'm proud to know it was built by the hands of my countrymen, my fellow Michiganders.

If you were to stop by the Harding home, you would be treated to a glimpse at the All-American family.

I suspect that if ever I was honored to be invited into your home, I would find the same.

This week I was accused of being in league with the Communist Party of Michigan. I am, apparently, under investigation by the House Un-American Activities Committee. It leads me to ask, what is this un-American activity in which I've supposedly engaged?

Is it an accusation of being a free thinker? Then I am guilty.

Of wondering about ideologies and systems of government and methods of improving the lives of my neighbors? Guilty am I.

Is it because I desire safety and fair pay for workers and equality for the men and women in my community? Well, I can't defend myself there.

However, if the accusation is based wholly on the supposition that I am now or have in the past been a member of the Communist Party, I can declare with perfect honesty that I am innocent.

Next time you find yourself on Aurelius Street, I hope you'll stop by for a cup of tea. If it's coffee you prefer, we can have that too. I'll sit with you on the front porch and we can talk about the Tigers or the struggles you're having at work. Maybe we'll even share the dreams we have for our children.

Come on over. We'd love to have you.

Bonaventure Times
March 26, 1952

WM. S. HARDING: "I'M NOT A RED!"

Though William Harding of Bonaventure Park has yet to be called to testify before the House Un-American Activities Committee (HUAC), he is still the focus of much public scrutiny.

"I always knew there was something funny about him," said a neighbor of Harding who wished to remain anonymous. "He's always out in that shed of his doing goodness knows what."

Virgil Whitmore of 328 Tulip Street, owner of The Book Store in downtown Bonaventure Park, has pulled all copies of Harding's books from the shelf.

"I never liked his writing," Mr. Whitmore said. "I do my best to never sell anything quite as subversive as that in my shop."

Whitmore has suggested a book burning of Harding's work, proposing the fire be started in front of Town Hall. Mayor Ebbert has said that, while he encourages civil engagement, the burning of books could pose a hazard.

So far no plans for such an event have been set.

William Harding, however, maintained his innocence when reached for a comment.

"As I said earlier, I am not now nor have I in the past been a participant in any Communist Party activities," he said.

When asked if he knew of anyone who belonged to the Communist Party in Michigan, Mr. Harding simply stated that he could not be compelled to accuse another of such.

It should be noted that Mrs. Marjory Sanders claims that Mr. Harding attended no less than three meetings of the Communist Party in Detroit dating back to 1933. As of yet, she has not produced any evidence to back up that accusation.

Meanwhile, the *Times* has recently learned that Mrs. Marjory Sanders has been cleared of all charges of Communist activities after her cooperation with HUAC in rooting out more members of the Communist Party.

She is scheduled to appear before the committee in New York City in the next few weeks to offer testimony against the Party there.

twenty-four

FLOSSIE

Honest Abe, I had been sick every single day that next week. On Monday it was a tummy ache. Tuesday my throat was scratchy and I'd lost my voice. Wednesday I woke up with a sick headache, and Thursday it was a combination of all of the above.

Still, Mam made me go to school each day, miserable as I was.

She hadn't bothered to take my temperature even though I was absolutely sure I was burning up. Boy, would she ever be sorry if I fell into a coma or ended up having tuberculosis or scarlet fever just like Beth March in *Little Women*.

Had I ever bawled my eyes out when she died.

Why did writers always kill off the best characters in their books? Was it just because they liked to make people cry? That had to have been it.

I thought about how if I ever got to be a character in a book, I would want to be the kind who wasn't so good that the author would want to murder me or so bad that the reader would want to see me dead.

"I could be dying," I'd told Mam every morning at breakfast.

"You aren't dying, love," Mam had said. "Eat your oatmeal."

"But you don't know that." I slumped in my seat. "The Marches didn't know Beth was dying until it was too late."

Mam pushed crumbs off the edge of the table into the palm of her hand and carried them to the garbage.

"We won't hide away, Flo," she had said. "No matter how much we'd like to."

And so, I'd gone to school, even though I got chased around the schoolyard during recess every day so the boys could play "Catch the Commie."

It didn't take much of a genius to figure out who the Commie was.

"Catch, catch, catch the Commie," they'd sing. "Hang her from the tree. That is how we get our daily glee."

I never thought I would miss the Baby Bumpkin song so much.

During Thursday's recess, while running from the boys, I tripped on a root and skinned up both of my knees, the blood soaking all the way through my white tights. The bullies gathered around me, singing the song and laughing like a bunch of buffoons. I'd been so scared that I wet myself. Not enough for them to notice. Just enough that I worried all day that someone would find out and add that to the list of reasons for them to tease me.

I hadn't told any of the teachers or Principal Braun because I figured they wouldn't do anything about it. I was cursed because my father was against America and an enemy to Uncle Sam himself.

It wouldn't have surprised me if they'd all thought that Dad shot bald eagles for sport and used strips of Old Glory instead of toilet paper.

I'd had a terrible week.

So, on Friday morning I decided that it didn't matter what Mam said. I wasn't going to school. Not that day. Not any other. I was done.

That time I meant it.

So once Bertha went down for breakfast, I hid in the closet behind the long dresses. I pulled a quilt over my head for good measure.

If Mam couldn't find me, she couldn't force me to go anywhere.

I sat there for so long that I thought they'd forgotten all about me. Just when I started to feel sorry for myself that I could be so easily put out of mind, I heard footsteps on the stairs.

Someone was coming for me after all. My brain told the rest of my body to keep still, but my body just wasn't having it. I got the nervous hiccups that only ever seemed to plague me when I was trying to be extra quiet like in the library or at a funeral or when I was trying to hide from my parents in the closet.

I tried thinking of all the ways to get rid of hiccups—standing on my head, drinking water upside down, getting the ever-loving life scared out of me—but I couldn't do any of those without making far too much noise.

So I did the only thing I could. I held my breath as long as I could stand it, which didn't turn out to be very long at all.

"Flossie?" Dad said, letting himself into my room.

The only answer he got was a creaky-sounding meow from Sully, who happened to spend every morning snuggled up in Bertha's bed.

"Oh, Sultan," Dad said. "Can you tell me, please, where Flossie went?"

I knew what he was doing. I hadn't been born yesterday! He was trying to make me laugh so I'd give away my position. I was not going to fall for it.

"Under the bed, you say?" Dad went on.

I heard the rustling of blankets.

"No. I'm afraid she isn't there," Dad said. "In the dresser? Oh, silly kitty, she would never fit in there."

Sully meowed.

"You're right," Dad said. "It can't hurt to check anyway."

I knew he'd pulled out the middle drawer because that was the one that stuck and needed a firm jostle to get it to open.

"Huh." Dad cleared his throat. "Do you suppose she let herself down the laundry chute?"

Sully responded with a deep mew.

I thought Dad must have been pinching that stinky old cat to get him to answer right on time the way he was.

"No? Yeah, I don't think so either. We would have heard the thud at the bottom."

He, I was sure, thought this game was cute and charming and playful. But I found it nothing short of aggravating.

"I suppose I'll sit here and wait for her to come back." He paused for a second. "Oh well. I was going to ask her about that book she wanted me to read. Do you know the one I mean, Sultan? Perhaps you've read it. Then again, I suppose not. We haven't taught you to read yet, have we? We really must remedy that. Well, the book I'm thinking of has a lion, a witch, and a wardrobe in it. And some strange fellow with hairy feet by the name of Bilbo Baggins stumbles into that world . . . is it The Shire?"

"It's Narnia!" I yelled from the closet, unable to contain myself any longer.

I pushed the quilt off of me, feeling the static pull my hair up on end. Against my better judgment I crab-walked my way out of the closet, a dress falling off its hanger and onto the floor behind me. I didn't pick it up.

"Aslan lives in Narnia!" I yelled, getting myself up and stomping my foot on the floor. "And he never, ever, ever meets Bilbo Baggins and he doesn't go to Bag End. That's a completely different story. It's a completely different author."

"Ah. There you are," Dad said, standing up and looking at the cat. "Why didn't you tell me she was in the closet?"

Sully just tucked his little face under his fluffy tail.

No-good, lousy fur ball.

"Flossie," Dad said. "You need to get ready for school."

"No, thank you," I said. "I respectfully decline."

I tilted my head to the side and waited for Dad to say how impressed he was with my manners. Instead he raised one of his eyebrows.

"You decline?" he asked.

"Respectfully."

"Hm." He crossed his arms. "Well, I kindly reject your refusal."

Well. I didn't know what to say to that. Then I remembered one time Mam telling me that if I was at a loss for words that I could do one of two things. First, I could say nothing at all. Second, I could say the truth.

I knew myself enough to realize that I wasn't going to keep my mouth shut. So I decided to try saying something that was true.

"I don't want to go to school anymore because the kids are mean to me," I said. "They say awful things to me and chase me around. Just look what they did."

I pulled the hem of my nighty up so he could see my scabbed-over knees.

Dad's shoulders slumped like he'd gotten the very worst news, and he sank down onto the end of my bed. He patted the spot next to him, but I climbed up on his lap instead. I nestled my head into the space where his neck became shoulder. He'd shaved so his skin was smooth, and he smelled like Lifebuoy soap and Aqua Velva. Just the way every dad should smell, as far as I was concerned.

"Are they mean to you because of me?" he asked. "Because of what was in the paper?"

"Yes," I said.

I didn't tell him that most kids were mean to me before. But all the hubbub about him had made it a hundred thousand times worse.

"I suppose it wouldn't help to tell them that it's not true," he said.

"Already tried it," I said. "They told me that was exactly what a Communist would say."

"Hm. They probably thought that was pretty smart of them, huh?"

I shrugged.

"I'm smarter than they are," I said.

"Smart enough not to brag about it," he whispered. "Right?"

"Of course."

"That's my girl."

He kissed the top of my head.

"It isn't true, is it?" I asked, sitting up so I looked him in the face. "Because if it is, if you really are a Communist, you should tell me. I promise I won't tell anybody. Not even Mam if you don't want me to."

The space between his eyebrows creased.

We had the same color eyes, my dad and me. "Blue as a stormy sea," Mam called them. Not as icy blue as Bertha's—hers were more like Mam's. Not green like Chip's. No, Dad and me, we had brooding eyes.

But that morning his eyes were sad too.

"I'll still love you even if you're a Red," I said.

"I should hope so," he said. "Flossie, I'm not perfect."

"I know you aren't."

"It's good that you agree with me on that." He smiled. "Anyway, I've made mistakes and I've been wrong. But something I've never, ever been is a Communist."

I put both of my hands on the sides of his face and gazed as deeply as I could into his stormy-sea eyes.

He was telling the truth.

"Mrs. Sanders told a bald-faced lie, didn't she?" I said.

He sighed and let his shoulders droop again. Then he helped me off his lap so he could get up.

"You're going to be late for school," he said, going to the door.

"But why would she say that if it wasn't true?" I asked. "Why would she fib?"

He stood in the doorway, his back toward me. When he turned to face me, he kept his eyes on the floor.

"Why would she pick on you?" I whispered.

"I don't know." He stepped out of the room and grabbed the knob, pulling the door closed behind him. "Please get ready for school."

I didn't want to. I thought about climbing back into bed and pulling the covers over my head. Instead I got myself dressed and brushed my hair.

There was a pair of old tennis shoes that Bertha had outgrown a few years before, and I thought about wearing those in the hopes that they might make me run away faster from the bullies.

But I decided on my patent leathers instead.

I was sick of running.

twenty-five

BERTHA

If I hadn't known any better, I might have thought there was a four-foot force field—try saying that ten times fast—around me as I walked down the hall. I might have thought that my body odor had become so repulsive that nobody could stand sitting next to me in class. I might have believed that I was a leper in need of a bell to alert passersby that I was unclean and that they ought to stay out of my way if they didn't want what I had.

But I did know better.

I was in the middle of being shunned by everyone in my high school.

Violet Lancaster shunned me in home economics.

Emily Perez shunned me in the hallways.

Bobbo and Stinky Simon shunned me in the cafeteria.

But worst of all was that Leo Schmidt shunned me everywhere.

I wanted to believe it was because he was obeying his mother, him not talking to me. With each day that he averted his eyes, though, it got harder and harder not to think he had come to hate me.

By Friday I had resigned myself to being as good as Hester Prynne. All I needed was a bright red C to sew onto my dress and a weird little girl following me all over the place.

Well, I did have Flossie.

Anyway, it had been almost an entire week of shunning, so it surprised me when Leo walked past my desk during Latin and dropped a crumpled-up slip of paper on top of my textbook.

I covered it with my hand so that the teacher wouldn't see it and slipped it down to my lap before pulling it open. It took a couple of good, fortifying breaths to give me the courage to see what the note said.

Honestly, I worried that it would tell me to eat dirt and die or something to that effect.

But that wasn't what it said. Not at all.

"Meet me at the park after school," he wrote. "The gazebo. You know the place."

I did know the place.

As far as town legend went, Archibald Bonaventure had hired builders to put a gazebo on land that he had set apart for a park. The way he'd planned it, the gazebo would overlook a small pond where he would keep koi fish, lily pads, lots of shade trees. The works. It was in that gazebo where he wanted to ask for the hand of the prettiest girl in town.

Her name was lost to history because it turned out that he never had the chance to ask her.

It wasn't as tragic as it sounded, though. She didn't die on the way to the proposal in a fiery accident or come down with dropsy or anything like that.

He never got the chance to ask because another guy got to her first.

His name was also unknown in town lore.

It was how Archibald would have wanted it.

The gazebo was built, but hardly anyone ever visited it anymore. That too, it seemed, was a casualty to time.

When the last bell of the day rang, I didn't waste any time getting out of the school and on my way to the park and the trail that would lead me through the woods to the gazebo.

It wasn't until I was there, waiting for Leo on the bench, that I realized I was a sitting duck out there. That it would be the perfect place for an ambush. For nearly an entire minute I worried that it was a trick, a setup.

But then, crashing through the woods, well off the trail, came Leo. The big galoot.

"What are you doing?" I called.

"Didn't want anybody seeing both of us take the trail," he said, stepping over a tree that had fallen years before. "Just being safe."

Then, in a move that didn't look all that safe to me, Leo climbed up the outside of the gazebo—not, apparently, taking into account that it had been around since before his grandparents were born—before hefting himself over the side of an especially crumbly railing.

He gave an old goofy grin once he was standing in front of me.

I could have cried for how nice it was for somebody to smile at me.

"Your eye looks better," he said.

"Yeah. Thanks." I touched it. "I'm a fast healer."

He shoved his hands into his pants pockets and leaned back into the beam of the gazebo where dozens of kids afflicted with puppy love had etched their initials and carved imperfect hearts.

I reached out and traced a couple of the letters with my fingertip. I didn't realize how close I was standing to Leo until he turned, shoulder to the beam, facing me. Inches. His face was inches from mine.

I'd never been that close to him. I thought he realized it too because he swallowed hard. Neither of us moved away, though.

"You doing okay?" he whispered.

"Do you want the true answer or the polite one?" I said.

"The true one."

"I'm doing rotten. It's awful, Leo. Just horrible."

My voice cracked a little bit, and my eyes burned in the inside corners. It felt like I'd swallowed a rock and my throat was clamping on it to keep it from slipping further down.

"Are you . . . are you going to cry?" Leo asked.

"Yes."

And I did.

Now, I was not a dramatic crier. I didn't heave and shake and sob. That was Flossie. I, on the other hand, was the kind to cover my face while my shoulders bobbed up and down just the slightest bit. The only sound I made was from the huffs of breath going in and out real fast.

It had been years since I'd cried in front of someone else. Usually I could make it somewhere private when I felt the boo-hoos coming on.

Poor Leo. He would be the first person to see me cry since we were ten and I rolled my ankle while making a run for second base. As bad as that had hurt, I thought it was broken. Leo had carried me home that day, piggyback. And he'd told me jokes the whole way to take my mind off the pain.

It ended up being a sprain. Still, Leo came to visit me every day to make sure I kept my foot elevated and to give me a play-by-play of the day's game on the sandlot.

He hadn't been embarrassed to be my friend then. It hurt all the worse to think that now he'd only talk to me if he thought nobody was looking.

Part of me wanted to tell him to go away, that he was no kind of pal. But the other part, the weaker part, was just glad to have him beside me.

He patted my back and waited for me to finish crying. I wished he'd tell me a joke. I really could have used a good laugh. But he didn't.

I supposed that having a father who was accused of being a Communist was a bit more serious than a sprained ankle.

"I'm sorry," he said instead of a joke.

"It's all right," I managed to get out, the worst of the crying over. "It's not your fault."

"No, I'm sorry. I shouldn't ignore you at school. I should be the one standing up for you. And I'm sorry I went out of my way to get here so nobody'd see us together. It's not right. I shouldn't have done that." He grabbed my wrists. "Would you look at me?"

I wouldn't let him pull my hands away from my face.

Some girls—like Violet—were gorgeous when they cried. There was something about the tears that made their eyes a more vibrant color, and they kept their faces relaxed even when they frowned.

I, on the other hand, turned bright red and my eyes got bloodshot. My face pinched up and I looked wrinkly as a raisin. Add to that a runny nose and I looked like a creepy Halloween mask that had gotten too close to the radiator and melted a little bit.

It didn't make sense, me worrying about how I looked in front of Leo. He'd seen me covered in mud and with my hair tangled in a rat's nest, not to mention sweaty and bloody and dressed in my brother's old clothes.

But there was something scary about having him see me in the state I was in under the cobweb-laden roof of the gazebo. There was something vulnerable about it, the slow loss of hope.

"Bert, it's me," Leo said. "Look at me, please."

I let him pull my hands down.

"Don't laugh," I said.

"Why would I?"

"Because I look horrible." I heaved a sigh. "My eyes are puffy, aren't they?"

"Yup." He grabbed a hanky from his pocket. "Here."

I took it and wiped under my eyes. "This is clean, right?"

"Sort of." He cracked a smile.

"Oh you." I shoved him. "Get out of town."

There was an open spot in the railing, and I imagined it was where old Archibald dreamed of sitting with his fiancée to watch the fish. It was just high enough that they could have swung their legs over the water without getting their feet wet.

Leo stretched his arms behind him, palms on the wooden floorboards, and leaned back. I pulled my feet up, bending at the knee, and wrapped my arms around my shins. We sat and listened for a few minutes. Somewhere in the trees a bird trilled, and I tried to remember what kind it was. My dad would have known.

Leo put his arm around me, and I let him pull me to him. I rested my head on his shoulder.

"I'll understand if you don't talk to me at school," I said.

But I didn't say that it would hurt. It would. Like all get-out.

133

"I'm done with that, Bert." He tilted his head so it was resting on top of mine.

He walked me all the way home that afternoon, and even though I didn't look, I could feel the housewives goggling us the whole way.

If I could have only one friend in all of the world, I was glad it was Leo Schmidt.

twenty-six

FLOSSIE

It turned out that wearing my patent leather shoes to school was a bad idea. I'd stayed inside at recess to clap the chalkboard erasers. Not because I was in trouble. I wasn't. I'd volunteered. So, I didn't get chased then.

And I'd hung around after school to scrape wads of gum off the bottom of Dean Coyer's desk. It was a nasty job, but it bought me time.

Once I finally went outside, I thought the schoolyard would be clear of kids. Silly me. I'd underestimated the bullies' patience. There, blocking the only way out of the yard, were three of the meanest, ugliest, biggest boys at school.

I had two choices. I could wait until those boys got sick of standing there and went home. Or I could push past them and run.

Of the two, I decided to wait. But then the boys started moving toward me, singing the "Catch the Commie" song.

They were, of course, out of tune. But I didn't think that was the time to let them know.

I backed up against the school doors and tried to open them. They wouldn't budge. I was locked out. And when I slammed on the glass, nobody came.

I was down to one choice.

I ran.

My greatest advantage was that I was small—half the size of

those boys—and that made me quicker. The shoes were slippery on the pavement, but somehow I didn't fall down when I zigged and zagged, dodging them and slipping out of the schoolyard.

Their heavy footfalls thudded behind me. I didn't have to look back to know that they were coming.

The only thought in my head was a memory of the time Mrs. Maxwell had told me that if I ever needed help, I should come to the library.

Boy, did I ever need help!

I wasn't in a pickle. I was in a whole barrel of them.

I wasn't sure if the boys were going to hang me like they were singing in the song. After all, they didn't have a rope. But they sure weren't chasing me so they could shake my hand.

When I saw Archie the lion, I picked up speed, knowing I was nearly there.

The summer before, the movie theater in town had played a bunch of old films on a Saturday. Mam had given me a handful of nickels—enough for a ticket and a bag of popcorn—and told me I could stay as long as I liked, provided I was home for supper.

That was the day I saw *The Hunchback of Notre Dame*.

To be honest, at first I was a little bit afraid of Quasimodo and I almost left for home at the beginning of the movie. But I decided to stick around because the next movie on the schedule was *The Wizard of Oz*. And in Technicolor, even!

All I could think of as I got closer and closer to the library, the three boys hot on my heels, was Quasimodo lugging Desdemona to the church and yelling "Sanctuary! Sanctuary!"

So, when I finally got to the doors of the library, I yelled it too.

"Sanctuary!" I yelled, flinging the doors open.

"Sanctuary!" when I ran past a scowling old woman.

"Sanctuary!" up the stairs where I found Mrs. Maxwell pushing a cart of books to be put back on the shelves. "Sanctuary!"

I yelled it one more time for good measure even if everybody in the place was shushing me.

"Flossie," Mrs. Maxwell said, rushing to me. "What in the world?"

She ushered me to the back of the library by the dusty old reference books that nobody ever used.

"They're after me," I said, out of breath from all the running and hollering. "You've got to hide me."

"Who's after you?"

I told her the names of the boys and about the song they were singing. As I talked, her eyes got more and more narrow, and I worried for a second that she was angry with me. But then she grabbed my hand and squeezed it.

"Come on, sweetie," she said. "I'm going to talk to them."

Her kitten heels clicked on the floor, much louder than was allowed in a library. But nobody told her to be quiet.

She pushed through the doors and found the boys sitting on Archie's back. They all slid off when they saw Mrs. Maxwell.

"Are these the boys who were chasing you?" she asked me.

"Yes," I said. "Al Thomson, Patrick Gardner, and Matty Mc-Dermott."

"And they were threatening to hurt you?"

"Yes."

"Boys, I'm disappointed in you." She pointed her finger at them with great purpose. "I'll be calling your mothers."

That was, of course, the very worst she could do to them. I resisted the smug smile that tugged at the corners of my lips.

"Furthermore," she went on, "if I hear that you've bothered her in any way, I will personally revoke your library cards and tell your mothers about the fines you've each accrued."

The look of terror in their eyes made me think they had enormous fines. Maybe even over five dollars!

"Go on, then," Mrs. Maxwell said. "Go home."

Those boys scrammed, Al looking back once and then scurrying down a side street.

Mrs. Maxwell told me that she'd escort me home herself as soon as she closed the library for the day. She even called Mam on the telephone to let her know that I was all right. Then she got me a book to read—*Emily of New Moon*—and told me I could sit at her desk if I wanted while she finished her work.

I settled into her chair, fully intending to shush anyone who I thought was making too much noise. But no one made a ruckus, so I started reading my book. Only a chapter in and I thought the book was fine. Emily was no Anne Shirley. Then again, no one ever could be quite that wonderful.

I'd been reading for a while before I looked up. And then, it was only because I heard a loud voice coming from among the bookshelves. Well, it was about time I had someone to hush.

Standing as tall and straight as I could, I marched around the desk and toward the hubbub with the authority of a junior librarian.

Of course, Mrs. Maxwell had never told me that was what I was, but I knew she wouldn't have minded.

Lo and behold, the loud voice came from Mrs. Lyons—a lady we went to church with! I never would have thought she had it in her, as mousy and meek as she always was at the potlucks. And the person she was speaking so noisily to?

None other than Mrs. Maxwell.

I slapped a hand over my mouth to catch my gasp.

"I'm disappointed in you, Jenny," Mrs. Lyons said. "It's a dangerous book, don't you know. A child could come in off the street and read it."

"Oh, I doubt any child would be interested in Mr. Harding's novels." Mrs. Maxwell smiled, her hands held together in front of her. "Besides, I would strongly discourage them from checking them out. They're far above most children's reading ability."

"That's not what I mean and you know it." Mrs. Lyons held her hands in fists at her sides. "I want those books gone, and I want to watch you get rid of them."

"No." Mrs. Maxwell didn't drop her smile. "Now, if there's nothing else . . ."

"They're dangerous, Jennifer," Mrs. Lyons said.

"Please, tell me, what's so dangerous about them?"

"Why, they're chock full of Communist ideas, don't you agree."

"I don't," Mrs. Maxwell said.

"Well, they have profanity in them," Mrs. Lyons said.

"Many books do."

Mrs. Lyons huffed and put both hands on her hips.

"Sylvia, have you read any of Mr. Harding's books?" Mrs. Maxwell asked.

"Well, I . . ."

"I recommend them if you haven't. They're actually quite beautifully written."

Mrs. Lyons puffed and dropped her hands back to her sides.

That was when Mrs. Maxwell glanced at me and winked.

Maybe there weren't many in the world who were quite so loyal and strong as Anne Shirley. But Mrs. Maxwell was among them.

I decided that I was glad that I could live in a world where there were librarians.

Bonaventure Times
March 30, 1952

LOCAL LIBRARIAN SAYS, "NO!"
Won't Ban Subversive Books

Mrs. Jennifer Maxwell, librarian at the Bonaventure Park Library, is standing firm against those who would have her take William S. Harding's books off shelves due to subversive content.

Harding, recently accused of being a Communist, is the author of eight books, one of which is to be adapted for the "silver screen" late next year.

Maxwell has received many letters and telephone calls from concerned citizens, worried about the books indoctrinating young readers with Communist ideology.

"The fact is," Mrs. Maxwell said in a statement, "that Mr. Harding's books are not meant for children. Furthermore, they are no more a threat to our society than *The Grapes of Wrath* or *In Dubious Battle* by John Steinbeck. I would even contend that the books by both authors are a gift to our nation. Like Steinbeck, Harding seeks to hold up a mirror to Americans. Whether or not they like what they see in their reflection is not Harding's concern."

When asked if they were dangerous, Maxwell said, "Absolutely. Then again, aren't all the best books?"

In short, Maxwell is standing firm. All books authored by William Harding will remain available for loan at the public library indefinitely.

Harding continues to insist that the claims against him are false.

twenty-seven

BERTHA

At Christmas Peggy had tried to do a nice thing by giving Mam a new teakettle to replace the old, dinged-up copper one that was in constant use in our kitchen. When Mam opened the box, she'd made much of the gift, whisking it away to the kitchen to "give it a go."

The new kettle was shiny and clean and electric. It must have put Peggy and Chip back a little bit to buy, especially on their newlywed budget. It was a very good gift. So thoughtful.

But, as soon as Chip and Peg left at the end of Christmas Day, Mam had tucked that new contraption away in the cupboard and kept using the copper one.

That old kettle had been around a hundred years or more— "Two hundred, if you'd have asked your nan," Mam would say— and was one of the few things she had packed in her trunk when she left Cumberland. Regardless of how many hundreds of years it had been around, it had boiled more English water than American. Mam said that no other kettle in the State of Michigan made tea that tasted right.

"It tastes like home," she'd say.

Then she'd get a far-off look in her eye.

She'd never gone back to England. My mother had missed the births of her nieces and nephews, the death of her mother. She'd

141

even been away from that side of the family for an entire war, watching from the sidelines and fretting all the while.

Dad had offered to buy Mam an airplane ticket so she could visit. She wouldn't accept it, calling such a thing an extravagance that was "too dear," meaning we couldn't afford it.

Three thousand miles was a long way from home.

Chip and Peggy were expected at dinner after church, so Mam had pulled the electric kettle out and plugged it into the wall. And when Peggy came into the kitchen and asked Mam how the kettle was working, Mam had smiled and said, "Like a charm, love."

Then she'd winked at me.

"I'm so glad," Peggy said.

"Bertha, be a lamb and get the flour, please," Mam said, turning to whisk the gravy on the stovetop.

"How are you holding up?" Peggy sidled up to Mam and lowered her voice. "This must be so hard for you."

"It's all right," Mam said. "We carry on, and it will all be behind us soon enough."

"I couldn't believe it when Charles told me they wouldn't serve you at the butcher shop."

"Well . . ." Mam started.

"What?" I interrupted. "What do you mean they wouldn't serve her?"

Peggy looked at me and pulled her lips into a cringe. "Oh, I'm sorry. I thought you'd heard."

"I was turned away," Mam said, taking the flour container from me. "Not just from the butcher. It seems I must needs do my shopping in Monument for a while."

"But why?" I asked.

Mam measured the flour and dumped it into the gravy, not answering me.

Peg caught my eye and mouthed the word *communism*.

"Your sister got chased all over town by a pack of wild boys on Friday," Mam said. "Thank the Lord Mrs. Maxwell was there to protect her. Who knows what they would have done if they'd caught her."

Flo had told me about that late at night when we were both sup-posed to be sleeping. She'd been sure that they meant to string her up if they got hold of her. I'd tried to convince her that they were just idiotic boys blowing off steam. I wasn't so sure that was true.

They might not have hanged her. But that wasn't the only way to hurt a kid.

"You should teach her how to fight," Peggy said, looking at me. "Charles said you punch as hard as any boy."

"I'd rather she not have to fight in the first place," Mam said.

She poured the gravy into its boat—one that matched the dishes—and handed it to Peggy to deliver to the dining room.

Then, when it was just the two of us still in the kitchen, she rubbed her fingertips into her temples.

"Mam?" I asked. "Are you all right?"

"Yes, dear." She rolled her lips between her teeth and dropped her hands. "This has been a good home for us, hasn't it?"

"Of course it has."

"Your father and I have been talking about spending the sum-mer away." She tilted her head. "Maybe take you girls to a nice cottage on a lake up north somewhere. Wouldn't that be nice?"

"Yeah. It would be swell," I said. I swallowed.

"Yes, well." She patted my shoulder before walking around me. "We ought to get dinner served before the roast gets cold."

She left me standing there in the middle of the kitchen. From the dining room I heard Dad tease her about serving last year's canned succotash instead of a fresh vegetable from the market.

He didn't know.

He didn't know that she'd had to drive two towns over for the roast. And she would never tell him.

twenty-eight

FLOSSIE

It was night and the house was quiet. Well, except for Bertha's log sawing from across the room. Her snoring was so loud that night that I couldn't get to sleep no matter how many sheep I counted or how many times I tossed and turned.

Whenever I couldn't sleep, I had Mam warm a cup of milk for me.

But she wasn't up, I could tell when I peeked my head into her room. Bertha had inherited the snoring from our dear, delicate mother.

I was eleven years old—very nearly twelve. I could warm up some milk on my own. And I could grab a couple of the cookies Mam had baked earlier in the day. Why not? It couldn't hurt.

I snuck down the hall and down the steps. I stopped at the very bottom of the stairs, trying to work up my nerve to dash across the living room. It didn't scare me in the daytime, walking from one side of the room to the other. And it wasn't bad at night provided that the lights were all on. There was just something about a room in the dark—the way the shadows made monsters on the wall and how different the settling of the house sounded when it was the only noise in the whole neighborhood—I got the willies from it no matter how brave I talked myself into being.

"Don't be a baby," I whispered, scolding myself. "Nothing's going to jump out at you."

It was just a dozen steps or so to the hallway leading to the kitchen. I could make it that far. All I had to do was move one foot in front of the other and not think about monsters.

Or witches.

Or boogeymen.

Or mummies, zombies, ghosts.

Or Gollum from *The Hobbit*. Especially not him.

"Just go," I told myself. "Then you can have a cookie."

Clenching my fists, I took the first step, reminding myself that nothing was going to eat me in my own house.

I made it halfway before the sound of breaking glass—a high, shattering, ear-splitting noise—made me scream. Falling to the floor on the other side of Dad's leather chair, I curled up into a little ball, making sure my head was tucked in between my knees like they taught us at school.

Then another smash. And another. And one more. Each one made me scream all over again.

"Get out, Commie!" somebody yelled.

Then more words that I knew weren't all right to say in mixed company. Even the one word that had nearly made Holden Caulfield lose his mind. I screamed louder.

"Leave me alone," I screamed. "Go away!"

At first, when I felt someone grabbing on to me, I tried pushing them off. I flailed my arms and legs and yelled. I would have hit and bit, but then I heard Mam's voice.

"Flossie, love, it's me," she said.

It was the voice that had sung me to sleep when I was tiny and upset that I had to go to bed so long before Bertha. And it was the voice that comforted me when I was sad or scolded me when I needed it. Mam's was the voice of all the characters in the books she read to me and the voice I listened for to call me down for supper.

And it was the voice that told me that I was going to be okay. That the bad men were gone. That the police were going to come and make sure we were all safe.

It was the voice that I'd never heard shake so much as it did that night.

145

"You're all right, dear," she said. "The worst is over."

"I'm so cold," I said.

It surprised me how much I trembled. And I wasn't even doing it so I would get more attention.

Mam pulled an afghan off the couch and wrapped it around me. It helped a little.

Bertha helped get me to the couch and stayed with me while Mam and Dad waited for the police to come.

"They're sure taking their time getting here," my sister muttered under her breath.

And it was Bertha who went to the kitchen for my cup of milk while Mam started sweeping up the glass. She brought out a cookie for me even though I hadn't asked for it. Just the thought of eating it made my stomach ache a little, and she said I didn't have to if I didn't want to.

"We'll save it for tomorrow," she said.

When I shivered again, she gave me the blanket she'd been using and started a fire—"just a small one"—to keep us warm while Dad nailed boards over the broken windows.

She let me rest my head on her lap when I got tired, and when she started snoring, I didn't complain.

When I woke up sometime in the night, Bertha wasn't with me anymore. I wasn't even on the couch. Someone had gotten me to my bed. Probably Dad.

Sully was curled up under my blanket and made a humming sound when I touched his head.

The door was open, and I could see that the light was on in my parents' room. They were talking just loudly enough for me to hear them.

"Louisa, it will blow over," Dad said. "I keep telling you that."

"I know you do," Mam said. "But tonight . . ."

"Won't happen again."

"How can you be so sure?" Her voice went up higher. "I worry for the girls every day they go to school. Worry that someone will say something cruel to them. Afraid the bullies will catch Flossie and do goodness knows what to hurt her. We aren't safe here."

"So we let a couple of goons chase us off?" Dad asked. "If we leave, they win."

"Let them." She paused. "This is not some sort of competition, Will."

"I don't want to go," he said. "This is our home."

"And we can make a home somewhere else," Mam said. "Wherever we're together is home."

"Chip won't come with us."

"I know."

Neither of them spoke for a few minutes, so I got out of bed and tiptoed my way to the hall so I could peep into their room.

They were both sitting on the bed, their backs to me. Mam's shoulders were rolled forward and Dad's face was turned toward her.

"I'm sorry," he said, reaching for her hand. "Please don't cry, Lou."

"I don't want this family to fall apart." Her voice shook and she sniffled. "But I will take the girls and go somewhere safe. You're welcome to stay here if you'd like. I won't have them sacrificed so you can save face."

Dad got up from the bed, and I didn't have time to get back to my room before he found me pressed against the doorjamb. He stopped and smiled at me before heading downstairs.

I followed him. Why wouldn't I? I was up, after all. I might as well. But I stopped halfway down the steps and spied on him between the slats of the railing.

He picked up the telephone receiver and turned the dial.

"Hello, sorry to call at such an ungodly hour," he said. Then he waited a second before saying, "Yeah, it's Will. Listen, Matt, we've got a problem over here."

Dad paused and scratched the top of his head.

"No, everybody's okay. We just need to get out of town."

Another pause.

"Indefinitely," he said. "Do you mind if we stay at your place for a little while? Just until we find something permanent?"

I leaned back against the wall.

Uncle Matthew lived in a tiny, nowhere town all the way up north. The place was called Bear Run, for goodness' sake. We'd never been to his house, but I wouldn't have been surprised if it was smack-dab in the middle of the woods with nowhere for a girl to do her business but an old, dirty outhouse.

"Thanks," Dad said into the phone. "We'll be there tomorrow, if that's all right."

I slinked my way back to bed.

Sully had moved to my pillow and I didn't dare move him. So, I went to Bertha's bed and climbed in beside her.

"What on earth . . ." she muttered. "Flo, go back to your own bed."

"Wake up," I said, elbowing her. "I have something important to tell you."

"What?"

Boy, did she sound annoyed.

"We're being exiled," I whispered.

"We're what?"

"Exiled."

"Sounds good to me," she murmured.

Then she fell right back to sleep. Honest to Pete. Whoever could sleep under such circumstances?

The light went off in my parents' room.

Part Three

We walked toward our own exile, our knees knocking
all the way. But, oh, how steady it made us in the end.

From *O! Wonder! And Other Short Stories*
by William S. Harding

twenty-nine

BERTHA

By ten o'clock in the morning Flossie had run out of patience for being trapped in the car. She jittered and fidgeted and asked 137 times if we were there yet. She begged for yet another pit stop less than half an hour after the last one. The kid would have climbed her way from the back seat to the front to visit Mam if I hadn't grabbed her and pulled her down.

For crying out loud. The girl was liable to make Dad steer the car off the side of the road if she didn't settle down.

It would have been better if she could have read a book. But she couldn't while the car was moving without getting sick. None of us wanted to deal with that.

I thought maybe we should have put her in a basket for the trip instead of poor Sully. He, at least, was hunkered down, content to sleep through the whole ordeal.

At least it would have kept Flossie contained.

She was nervous. And when Flossie got nervous, she became restless. And her restlessness made all of us suffer.

Even Mam was nearing the end of her patience when Dad offered to tell Flossie a story if she promised to sit still.

One of the best things about having an author for a father was that he came up with really great stories.

"This is the story of how the town of Bear Run got its name," Dad started.

I let Flo snuggle up next to me, her head resting on my arm.

"A hundred years ago it wasn't uncommon to find a crew of loggers working in the deep woods, felling trees that had been around since before Christopher Columbus sailed the ocean blue," Dad said. "A good many of them worked for a lumber baron named Johannes Huebert."

Flossie opened her mouth wide in a yawn.

Dad would need to pick up the pace of the story or he was going to lose her. She'd be bouncing on the seat before we knew it.

"There was this one particular logger by the name of Booger . . ."

"That was his name?" Flossie sat up and then slapped her thighs. "What a name!"

He'd gotten her back.

"Well, he was the last kid in his family," Dad said. "His poor mother'd had a dozen boys before him, and by the time he was born, she'd run out of suitable names."

"What was his last name?" she asked.

"Snot."

"William," Mam scolded.

He shot her a sly smile.

"Booger Snot," Flossie yelled, laughing so hard I was afraid she might wet herself.

"Well, our pal Booger was brand-new to the job. It was his first time in the woods, even," Dad said. "He learned how to chop a tree down and when it was best to yell 'TIMBER!' He got good at burning the Huebert brand onto the felled logs. He did pretty well for a guy named Booger Snot."

That got a fresh snort out of Flossie.

It only earned a groan out of Mam. She was less impressed by what she called "loo humor" than my little sister was.

"About halfway through the workday, Booger needed to . . ." He stopped himself and turned to Mam. "Apologies, my love. Booger needed to relieve himself."

I was behind Mam, so I couldn't see the expression on her face, but I could imagine it was one of utter disgust.

"What's a man to do when there's no toilet within a hundred

miles? He goes off into the woods where nobody can see him," Dad said. "I won't go into the nitty-gritty of it, but once he'd finished with his business, Booger realized he wasn't quite as alone as he'd thought."

Flossie's eyes got big as platters and she sat stock-still. Quiet as she could, she whispered, "Who was it?"

"Old Booger turned around and saw something that took his very breath away," Dad said. "There, sitting on an old stump, watching his every move, was a little baby bear."

"Aw." Flossie clapped her hands. "Did he pick it up?"

"He did." Dad turned and cringed at us. "Which made that baby bear start to cry. Have you ever heard a baby bear cry? It sounds surprisingly similar to a baby human."

"Poor baby," Flossie said.

"The trouble with a crying baby bear is that it gets the attention of the mama bear."

"Uh-oh."

"Mama Bear wanted her baby back. Any mother would, right, Lou?" Dad asked.

"Maybe not if my baby was named Booger Snot," Mam said.

I might have expected Flossie to giggle at that, but instead, she sat on the edge of the seat, waiting for Dad to continue with the story.

"Now, Booger was like us," Dad said. "He was from the city. So he'd never encountered a bear before. I'm sure you suspected as much when he picked up the baby. That was his first mistake. The second was that he ran."

"Why shouldn't you run from a bear?" Flossie asked.

"Because they're faster than you are," I said.

"Oh boy." She shook her head slowly. "Booger's in for it."

"The third mistake was that he held on to that baby for dear life while he ran," Dad said. "He ran all the way back to the camp. Once he got there he yelled, 'BEAR! RUN!' And that, my dear, is how the town got its name."

"Is that story true?" Flossie asked me. "Or is he pulling my leg?"

"I think he's pulling both of them," I said.

"Daddy!"

"Fiction is my bread and butter, honey," Dad said. "I can't help it."

Dad turned on the radio, paying more attention to finding a station than driving. When Mam got after him for it, he argued that it was fine. The road was straight from where we were all the way to Uncle Matthew's house.

"Mind the road anyway," Mam said. "I'm certain these woods are full of deer."

Dad gave the dial one more little twist and found Frank Sinatra singing "I'll Never Smile Again," a song that always made me a little melancholy.

Especially that day.

Every mile that got us closer to Bear Run took us farther from a life I'd loved.

thirty

FLOSSIE

Uncle Matthew liked to keep to himself. That was what Mam told me when I asked why he didn't come to visit us very often. And it was why when he was in Detroit to see a Tigers game, he stayed in a hotel room instead of sleeping on our couch.

I'd asked Mam if that was why he'd never gotten married, and she'd said that was none of my business. Then she'd told me I'd best not ask him a question like that.

How was I supposed to get to know the man if I couldn't ask any of my questions?

When I'd told Dad that I was sure Uncle Matthew didn't like me, Dad said it was more that he didn't know what to make of me. I couldn't be sure, but it sounded like I was as big a mystery to Uncle Matthew as he was to me.

I guess I didn't mind that too much.

The last time I'd seen him was when he came for Great-Aunt Lena's funeral a whole year before. He hadn't talked the whole time. He just sat in the very back of the sanctuary even though we'd saved a seat for him in the family pew. Then, at the luncheon afterward, he ate nothing but drank cup after cup of coffee. Before anybody'd even gotten to dessert, he was gone.

He hadn't even bothered to say goodbye to anyone.

It was my opinion that Uncle Matthew was the oddest of ducks.

After sitting in the car for what felt like a hundred years, I was

155

relieved when Dad pulled into a driveway and said, "This is it."
What a relief! I didn't think I could have survived another minute
of traveling.

But when I got a look at the house, I was sure we'd gotten lost.
There was no way on the green earth God made that somebody
like Uncle Matthew lived in a place like that. It wasn't the fanciest
place I'd ever seen. But it was huge. Bigger than any of the houses
on our block in Bonaventure Park.

Just when I was about to tell Dad that he must have taken a
wrong turn, Uncle Matthew stepped out onto the front porch. He
didn't smile and he didn't lift a hand to greet us. He just stood
there watching us drive up to the house.

"Uncle Matthew really lives here?" I asked.

"You've been here before, Flo," Dad said.

I furrowed my brow so he'd know that I had no recollection
of it.

"She was small," Mam said.

I turned to Bertha. "Do you remember?"

"Yes," she said.

"Why didn't you tell me that Uncle Matthew lives in a mansion?"

"It's not a mansion," Mam said.

"It sure looks like one."

Dad stopped the car, but before I could get out, Mam said my
name and reached over the seat to grab my arm.

"Now, remember," Mam said, her icy blue eyes burrowing deep
into me. "Don't overwhelm him. He scares easily."

"Okay," I answered.

Then Mam winked at me twice with her left eye. That was the
signal to me that I should remember to be "seen and not heard."
I touched the end of my nose to let her know that I got it.

I didn't like it, being forced to act like a wallflower. But Mam
had made it very clear that it wasn't up for debate. I would do as
she said. That was that.

"There's a good girl," she said.

I dropped my finger from my nose. Then I slid off the seat and
hopped out of the car.

"He's just shy," Bertha whispered to me. "It takes him a little bit to warm up."

"Like a car?" I asked.

"I guess you could say that." She grabbed the basket Sully was in. "Don't worry. He won't bite."

"Are you sure?"

"Mostly."

Well, *that* didn't make me feel any better.

"Hi there," Dad called to Uncle Matthew.

Uncle Matthew nodded.

That was it. A nod! Not a how-was-the-trip or did-you-find-it-okay. Just a nod.

And he didn't budge to help us get our things out of the trunk.

If he wasn't coming to say hello to us, I'd go to him. I marched myself and my suitcase right up to the front porch and said, "Hi, Uncle Matthew. Boy, is this house ever big. Do I get my own room? Is your house haunted? I only ask because it looks old. Golly, this suitcase is heavy. Could you carry it for me, please?"

He looked down at me with his mouth pulled down into the sort of frown that adults sometimes got when they were considering something.

"Florence," Mam called after me.

If I'd turned around to look at her, I was sure I would have seen her left eye winking over and over again.

"Hello," Uncle Matthew said, taking my suitcase. "You can go inside if you want."

I got the door for my own self—apparently Uncle Matthew wasn't in the mood to play gentleman—and stepped into the house. He didn't follow behind me, so I didn't feel too bad about gawking.

Our house back in Bonaventure Park was full. Every wall had at least half a dozen framed pictures and not one piece of furniture matched another.

Uncle Matthew's house, on the other hand, was a lot neater. More orderly. Much more tidy. All of the furniture in the living room matched. Blue sofa, blue easy chairs, blue area rug. And there were just two pictures on the mantel in frames.

The strangest thing was that there were bookcases on either side of the fireplace. There wasn't a single book on the shelves. Not even one.

Dad came in behind me, a couple of suitcases in hand.

"Where are all the books?" I asked, motioning to the empty shelves.

Dad squinted at me and shrugged one shoulder.

"Matthew's not much of a reader," he said, taking the luggage up the stairs.

Not much of a reader? How was that even possible? Maybe he and Dad weren't really brothers after all.

It was a good thing I'd thought to pack a bag of books to hold me over until the movers brought all the rest of them.

I zipped past Uncle Matthew, who was still on the front porch, and between Mam and Bertha, who were making their way up the sidewalk—Mam with one suitcase and Bertha with Sully—and ran around to the backside of the car. Somebody had closed the trunk, so I had to fiddle with the latch until it opened.

Oddly, the bag of books wasn't there.

I checked the back seat and the front.

No bag.

Someone must have gotten it and I'd been too hurried to notice.

"Mam," I yelled, slamming the passenger-side door. "Do you have my school bag?"

"No," she answered, stepping up to the porch. "Did you ask your father?"

When I asked my father, he told me he didn't remember having seen it.

"Did you ask your sister?" he asked, lighting a cigarette.

I found Bertha in the bedroom across the hall from mine—we got to have our own rooms!—trying to coax Sully out from under the bed.

"You dumb cat," she said, lying on the floor and reaching for him.

"Did you bring in my school bag?" I asked.

"Which one?" She sat up.

I didn't tell her that she had a cobweb in her hair.

"The one with my books," I said. "It was next to my bed."

"I put it on the porch for Dad to load into the trunk." She got up and went to the doorway. "Dad?"

"Yes?" he said, popping his head out of the door of the room he was sharing with Mam.

"Did you get the bag I put on the porch? Back at home?"

"No." He scratched a spot behind his ear. "I only packed the suitcases."

Bertha hesitated before turning to me. When she did, her face was white as a sheet, and she lifted a hand to her mouth.

"Flo, I am so sorry," she said. "I was sure Dad would put it in the car."

I bit my bottom lip so hard that I was surprised it didn't start to bleed.

All of my most beautiful books were still on the porch at home. They may as well have been on the other side of the world. Shutting my eyes, I pictured them sitting in my bag under the broken windows that Dad had boarded up the night before.

"It's okay," I said through my clenched teeth. "I think I need to rest for a little bit."

I went to my room—the one that wasn't mine at all and never really would be—and shut the door.

—— From the Desk of Florence Mable Harding ——

Dear Chippy,

When are you coming to Bear Run to visit? Please say it is soon because Dad forgot to bring my books when we left home and I am bored to death without them. We've only been here since this afternoon. Still, I need them and soon.

Dad doesn't think the men with the moving truck can get them here before next weekend. Next weekend, Chippy! I'll never make it that long!

You, dear and sweet brother of mine, are my only hope against complete despair.

You can find them in my school bag on the front porch.

Will you bring them, please-pretty-please-with-chocolate -frosting-on-top? Come as soon as you can.

I suppose you can bring Peggy too if you have to.

Love and hugs,

Hopsy

P.S. Sully already caught a mouse and brought it to Bertha. She screamed and jumped on a chair when she realized the poor little rodent was still alive.

P.P.S. I screamed too.

P.P.P.S. So did Mam.

P.P.P.P.S. And Dad.

P.P.P.P.P.S. It was the first time I've ever seen Uncle Matthew laugh.

thirty-one

BERTHA

It didn't take Sherlock Holmes to see all the evidence of my uncle's lifelong bachelorhood. For instance, there was the kitchen with just one pot, one pan, and exactly three dinner plates to go around. Not to mention that all he had in the Frigidaire could fit on just one shelf with room to spare. "Store's closed for the day," he muttered, grabbing the package of Oscar Mayers from the fridge before dumping them in the pot and drowning them in water.

At least there would be a hot dog for each of us.

"It's all right, Matthew, dear," Mam said, taking the pot from him. "I'll stop in at the store first thing tomorrow."

When he wasn't looking, she poured out most of the water before sticking the pot on the stovetop.

"Uncle Matthew," Flossie asked, doing the best she could to set the table, "is there a public library nearby?"

The poor girl. I didn't know if she would ever recover from the shock of having nothing to read. Well, unless she wanted to read through the stack of *Old Farmer's Almanacs* I'd found on the shelf in my closet.

Uncle Matthew had scrounged up one half of an old camping mess kit and the lid of an old Charles Chips canister to use for the plates he lacked.

"There's a library in town," he answered, staring into his silverware drawer.

"Oh, thank goodness," Flossie said. "Can we go tomorrow?"

"It's not open on Tuesdays." He grabbed forks from the tray—it was close to a miracle that he had enough for all of us.

Stricken. That was exactly the expression on my little sister's face.

"That's okay," she said. "I can wait until Wednesday."

Good old Flossie. She was trying so hard to be a good sport. What a gal.

Uncle Matthew handed the forks to me and left out the kitchen door. The screen door clapped closed behind him.

"That's Matthew for you," Dad said from behind a newspaper. Mam just shook her head.

"Is he upset?" I asked, putting the forks beside the plates and noting that half of the napkins were washcloths.

Golly, I hoped they were clean.

"No way of knowing," Mam answered. "See if there's anything in that bread box, would you, lass."

It didn't surprise me that all he had in there was half a loaf of stale bread.

"Well, that won't do." Mam sighed and went about checking the cupboards for something, anything that we could eat with hot dogs. "Ah. I should've known."

She had to go up on her tiptoes to reach the top shelf, where Uncle Matthew had at least six cans of baked beans.

I wondered if he ever heated them up or just had them straight from the can while he stood over the kitchen sink.

We were busy rummaging through drawers for a can opener when Uncle Matthew came back carrying an old crate.

"Oh, thank heavens," Mam said. "Matty, where do you keep your can opener?"

He put the box on the floor and then grabbed a little piece of aluminum off the top of the fridge and handed it to her. Mam held it like she wasn't sure what in the world it was. Luckily, I'd seen Leo use his Boy Scout jackknife enough to know what to do with it. It took a couple of tries before I successfully stabbed through the top of the can.

162

I didn't mind the look of admiration Mam gave me.

Seemed I wasn't completely useless in the kitchen after all. Mrs. Higginbottom might have been a little proud of me if she'd seen me in action.

"The woman who lived here before left some books behind," Uncle Matthew said, pointing at the crate by the door.

Flossie rushed to look inside, picking a book up off the top of the pile, rummaging through the books until she found one that she wanted.

"Anne! You have Anne Shirley!" she yelled. "How did you know that I love her most of all?"

"I . . . I, uh, didn't," he said, clearly flustered.

"Thank you, thank you, thank you," she said, hugging the book to her like a long-lost friend.

"It's okay."

Then, much to everyone's surprise—and Uncle Matthew's consternation—she threw both arms around our uncle.

He didn't know what to do, so he patted her on the head.

thirty-two

FLOSSIE

Uncle Matthew dragged a folding chair outside so I could sit on the porch and read *Anne of Green Gables*. He made sure to put the chair in the sun. It was still early in the morning and not as warm as I would have liked.

It was awfully nice of him to bring out a blanket for me when he saw me shiver.

But I didn't thank him by giving him a hug. I'd learned my lesson the night before. Uncle Matthew would rather get a kick to the shin than a hug around the waist.

So, I just used my words to tell him that I appreciated it.

"Oh. Sure," he said back. "Do you like that book?"

"Yes. I've read it before, of course," I said.

"Did you forget what happened in it?"

"No, silly. I practically have it memorized."

"Then why would you read it again?" he asked, scrunching up his face at me.

"Because Anne Shirley's my friend."

The words were out before I could stop them. Shoot. Uncle Matthew was going to think I was a nut.

But he didn't say anything. He just relaxed his face and crossed his arms, saying that he needed to get to work.

"I'm late," he told me.

"Uncle Matthew?" I asked.

"Yeah?"

"Where do you work?"

"Uh. The grocery store," he said, feeling the outsides of his pants pockets until he figured out which one held his keys.

"What do you do there?" I asked.

"A little of everything." He cringed then made to leave. "Bye now."

"Will you get in trouble for being late?"

He shook his head.

"You must have a very nice boss."

"Well." His lips twitched, and for the first time I saw a little resemblance between him and Dad. "I am the boss."

"You're the boss of the grocery store?" I jumped up from the chair. "And you don't have any food in your house?"

"Yeah." He shrugged then stepped off the porch. "Bye."

"Bye," I called after him.

I watched my uncle while he walked down the street and thought it was quite the coincidence that he and Matthew Cuthbert shared a name. For one, they were both bachelors. For two, they were both shy. And Matthew Cuthbert loved Anne just as much as I knew Uncle Matthew loved me, even if he had no idea how to show it.

I wrapped myself in the blanket and settled back into the chair and—because I knew Mam wasn't looking—I rested my feet up on the porch railing, propping the book on my lap. And pretended to read.

Really, though, the reason I was out on the porch in the not-warm-enough-to-be-outside morning wasn't so I could read by the brand-new light of the sun. Truth be told, I would have preferred sitting on the blue couch in the living room with Sully snoozing on my feet.

I was out there because Uncle Matthew had said something to Mam at breakfast about the little girl who lived next door and how she was "just about" my age.

Now, I was certain that Uncle Matthew didn't know how old I was. On my last birthday he'd sent me a See-Em-Walk dog that was exactly like the one a toddler down the street dragged along behind him on a twine leash.

Then, at Christmas, he'd given me a bottle of lavender perfume from England.

It was almost as if he couldn't decide if I was fresh out of diapers or ready to start my own family.

Anyway, he'd told Mam that he would be glad to make introductions if I thought I might want to "play" with the girl next door.

I'd piped up and said that I wasn't sure if I did. That I needed to see her first.

At that, Uncle Matthew had screwed up his face like I'd said a dirty word.

Well, I didn't explain to him that the last thing I needed was to spend time around a girl as snot-faced as Iris and her group of meanies. If this girl next door was worth my time, I'd be able to tell at first glimpse.

So, I sat out on the porch in the hopes of seeing her before she went to school. That was, of course, if she was old enough for school. There still was the chance that she was a baby.

It took more than a little patience, but a few minutes before eight o'clock a woman stepped out of the house. She had on a pretty pink coat and black high heels. Not kitten heels like what Mam wore during the week. These were glamorous, for-special-occasion kind of shoes. And the woman was wearing them on a Tuesday!

Then, coming out behind her, was a girl in a matching pink coat and black patent leather Mary Janes. And, judging by the size of her, she was probably about my age or a year younger. Close enough. Not bad guessing for my otherwise oblivious uncle.

The two of them walked to the curb just in time for the bus to come roaring down the road, stopping just long enough for the girl to climb up and in.

The lady stayed in her spot on the sidewalk, blowing kisses and waving until the bus was gone again.

When she turned to walk back up the driveway, I held the book so she wouldn't know I'd been spying on her.

I flipped to the page where Anne Shirley and Diana Barry first became friends and decided that the only right thing to do was ask Mam if I could have a tea party and invite the girl from next door.

She seemed like a nice girl.

Well, I hadn't really seen her. Her scarf had been pulled up over most of her face and she'd been all the way across the yard from where I was sitting.

But I wanted to believe that she'd be kind to me.

At three that afternoon I sat in that chair again, watching the neighbor lady walk out to the curb to greet her girl. Then the next day I went out in the morning and afternoon again. That day the mother and daughter were both wearing teal coats and red shoes.

What kind of people matched every day like that? And how rich were they to have more than one winter coat?

It was baffling.

And a little intimidating, if I was to be honest.

"Why don't you go introduce yourself?" Bertha asked.

"Because," I said.

But that was all I said because I didn't have a good reason not to other than I was afraid that the girl would end up being mean to me.

"Okay. Have it your way." Bertha rolled her eyes. Then she pulled a letter out of her skirt pocket. "By the way, you got mail."

"I did?" I squealed.

When I saw that it was from Chippy, I forgot about the little girl for the rest of the day.

Chippy had sent me, and only me, a letter.

If that didn't make a girl feel special, I didn't know what would.

My Dearest Flopsy Cottontail,

The minute I read your letter I hopped in the car and raced over to the house for your bag of books. I got there just in time too. The mice of Bonaventure Park heard about Sultan of Swat's attack on their Bear Run cousin and were in the process of storming the house (tiny torches and pitchforks in hand). They were squeaking their little heads off in rage.

Fortunately, I was able to talk them out of burning the house down. Phew! It sure was a close call.

Oh, and I grabbed the books and put them in the trunk of my car where they'll stay until Peg and I can make our way to you (we're hoping by the end of the week, will that be soon enough?).

Give everyone a hug for me. Well, except for Uncle Matthew. For him, I send along a firm handshake.

Love you, kiddo.

Chippy

thirty-three

BERTHA

Our first few days in Bear Run were spent setting up housekeeping and turning Uncle Matthew's sparse rooms into something more suitable for habitation. After a couple shopping trips, some rearranging, and a whole lot of elbow grease, Mam was finally satisfied that we'd be comfortable living there, even if it was temporarily.

In the process of making the place more homey, I found a whole box of baseballs in the cellar. No kidding! There had to have been at least two dozen of them. Not a one of them used. Clean and white as the day they were sold. The red stitching on every single one of them was perfect.

More snooping down there paid off when I found a Louisville Slugger. Also brand-new.

I carried that whole box, the bat balanced on top, up to the dining room, where Dad had his typewriter and stack of pages. When I asked if he thought Uncle Matthew would mind if I used the balls, Dad just waved me off.

"Take your sister with you," Mam called after me. "She could use some fresh air."

"Flo, let's go," I yelled, using my backside to push through the screen door.

The yard behind Uncle Matthew's house went on for what seemed like forever and ended at Bald Creek. When I'd asked him why the creek was called that, he said he had no idea. Flossie was aghast at how completely uncurious Uncle Matthew was.

I lugged the box far enough away from the house that I didn't need to worry about breaking a window—Mam would have had my hide—but not far enough that I'd lose all the balls in the creek. Flossie plopped down on the ground in the early growth of grass and opened her book.

Just over a hundred yards from me was a weeping willow. I decided that was second base. I put my mitt at my feet for home plate. My goal would be to hit the ball past that tree on either side. Well, and I'd try my very best not to hit it.

I tossed the ball up just high enough so I had time to get a good swing to hit it. Over and over.

Toss, swing, hit.

And then again.

Toss, swing, hit.

Until the box was empty.

"Hey," I said to my sister. "Wanna help me find all of the balls?"

"No, thank you," she answered, turning the page of her book. "I'm busy."

"Come on. Please?"

"How much will you pay me?"

"I don't have any money." I pulled out the pockets of my jeans to prove it.

"Tough luck, I guess," she said.

So, I went it alone, picking up all twenty baseballs by myself. It turned out to be not so bad. I practiced my throwing aim, shooting them back into the box.

One of them went a little wild—I'd put a little more mustard on it than I probably needed to—and barreled straight toward Flossie.

She, of course, wasn't paying attention, so I yelled, "Heads up!"

Which, it turned out, was the wrong thing to yell at a kid who wasn't well acquainted with projectiles barreling toward her head.

Flossie popped her head up, right in the path of the ball. I was sure she was going to get beaned, but then she dropped flat on her face in the nick of time.

"Is the coast clear?" she asked, nose deep in the grass.

"Yeah," I said, jogging over to her. "You okay?"

She let me help her to her feet and then she proceeded to dust herself off.

"Why did you yell for me to put my head up?" she asked, clearly irked at me. "You should have said 'heads down.'"

"Well, heads up just means to watch out."

"That's dumb." She glared at me. "How would you like it if I threw a ball at your head?"

"I guess I'd think I deserved it," I said. "Matter of fact, go ahead. Grab that ball and chuck it at my head if it'll make you feel better."

"You can't duck," she said.

"Are you kidding me?" I asked.

"That's the deal."

I figured that was a fine deal on my part. With arms as skinny as hers, she couldn't throw the ball very hard.

"All right. I won't duck."

She didn't hesitate to grab that ball. Then she marched toward me, a look of fury on her face that scared the socks off of me. Once she was close—too close—she lobbed it at me.

Boy, was I wrong. That kid hurled that ball so hard it would have made Stinky Simon turn green with envy. Lucky for me, she didn't have any kind of aim to speak of, so it whizzed by my head. Still, I was impressed.

"Flossie," I said, throwing my arms out to either side. "That was amazing."

"It was?" Her eyes got wide.

"Yeah! You're a natural."

"I am?"

"Do it again." I grabbed a ball from the box and tossed it underhand to her.

She fumbled and dropped it. We'd work on that.

"Try for my hand," I said, pulling the glove on.

But she didn't wait for me to be ready; she lobbed another at me, and I hopped out of the way just in time.

"Again," I said, tossing another ball. "Try and control the throw a little."

"How do I do that?" she asked, looking at the ball in her hand.

"No clue. But you'll know it once you've got it figured out. Trust me."

"That doesn't make any sense."

I put my glove up. "Right here."

We played catch, my sister and I, until she said her arm was getting sore. We gathered all of the balls and put them back in the box. They weren't pristine anymore. The white leather had grass stains and dirt smudges.

I carried the box, and she got the slugger. She wanted to wear my mitt—the one with the daisy—and I let her, promising to give her my old one. I had, of course, packed it along with my clothes. You never could know when you'd need a spare glove.

We were most of the way back to the house when I noticed Uncle Matthew standing on the back porch, smoking.

Flossie took off running toward him, waving her gloved hand over her head.

"We played baseball," she yelled. "Uncle Matthew! We played baseball."

"Yup," he said.

When she passed him, he reached out and rustled her hair like she was a dog. I braced myself, thinking she'd snap at him for it. But, instead, she gave him her biggest toothy grin.

Wonders never ceased.

"I see you were in the cellar," he said, nodding at the box.

"I hope you don't mind." I rested them on the porch railing. "I used your bat too."

"It's okay." He took a drag off his cigarette. "I was watching you play. You're real good."

"I'm all right for a girl."

He squinted at me and raised one eyebrow. Such an intense glare he had.

"I really like baseball," I said, swallowing hard. "And I suppose I'm good at it."

"Hm." He relaxed his face. "You ever think about playing, you know, for the All-American Girls?"

"You mean like the Sweet Peas?"

"Something like that."

"Maybe," I said. "Someday."

"You know they hold tryouts every spring, don't you?"

I inhaled through my nose and nodded.

"Might be worth thinking about," he said before taking one more pull on his cigarette and stepping off the porch, headed toward the shed.

─────── Bear Run Crematorium and Taxidermy ───────

Dear Leo,

Ignore the heading. This was the only paper I could find in my uncle's desk. I thought about cutting off the crematorium/taxidermy part but decided against it. Then again, don't ignore it. Some things are just too funny not to share with a best friend.

I hope we're still best friends. We are, right?

It's hard to know if you're nodding or not because I'm not in Bonaventure Park to see it. Guess you'll just have to write me back to let me know your answer.

We left early Monday morning (in case you didn't notice) and drove all the way across Michigan to Bear Run where the woodland creatures outnumber the humans ten to one. No kidding. We're staying with my uncle, Matthew Harding, who lives in the second-biggest house in town. Again, not kidding.

It's nice out here, though. Quiet. At night it gets so dark that, if it weren't for the stars, I wouldn't be able to see my hand in front of my face. There's no Detroit lights keeping the place lit up at all hours.

Did I mention that it's quiet?

Anyway, how's it going back home? You boys play another game with the Monument fellas? I hope you beat the snot out of them for me. Tell me all the news. Every last bit of it.

Even if you have to make something up. I don't care. I just want to hear from you.

Your best girl (hopefully that's still true),

Bert

thirty-four

FLOSSIE

All during supper I watched Uncle Matthew. Of course, whenever he looked my way, I dropped my eyes. I wouldn't have wanted to make him feel uncomfortable.

He wasn't an ugly man. He wasn't exactly handsome, either. More like in between. He had more hair than Dad, but it was mostly gray. His eyes weren't blue like Dad's. To be completely honest, I wasn't sure what color they were because he seemed always to be squinting at me.

Uncle Matthew was the kind of man who ate everything he put on his plate and even saved his slice of Wonder Bread until the very end of his dinner so he could use it to wipe his plate clean.

He never read the paper at the table—he never read anything ever, as a matter of fact—and almost always minded his p's and q's.

I wondered what would make a nice man like him go his whole life without getting married.

So, I asked.

"Uncle Matthew," I said. "Why aren't you married?"

"Flossie," Mam gasped, clutching her pearls.

"It's a good question," Dad said. "I'd like to know myself, Matt."

"What's that?" Uncle Matthew said, perking up. "Did you ask me something?"

175

"I did." I put up my hand like I was in school. "Why didn't you ever get married?"

"Oh." Uncle Matthew sat up straighter in his chair. "I, uh, don't know."

"I'm sorry," Mam said. "You don't have to answer her."

"Couldn't hurt," Dad said.

"I just wondered," I said, "because you're not completely ugly. And you're only a little bit old."

Dad covered his mouth with his hand.

"My goodness, Flo," Bertha whispered. "Stop while you're ahead."

Well, I didn't know what she meant by that, so I plowed through to my next question.

"Haven't you ever been in love?" I asked. "And did she break your heart?"

Uncle Matthew's eyes got wide and his face red as a lobster. I worried for a second that he was about to have a heart attack.

"That's enough, Florence," Mam said.

"Oh boy," Bertha said.

She and I both knew that when Mam used my full first name it was meant to be a warning. Add the Mable to that and I was on my way to some sort of punishment. When she tacked on the last name for good measure, I might as well get myself right with God.

I pulled my lips in between my teeth so I'd remember not to say anything else for fear of getting my ear twisted.

Mam excused me from the table, telling me that I ought to spend a couple of minutes outside.

"Come on, Flo," Dad said, getting up out of his seat.

We sat on the porch steps because he said it was the best place to watch the sunset. I didn't want to watch the sunset because I knew that Mam had something special for dessert, so I picked at the peeling paint on the railing until Dad told me to knock it off.

"You know," he said, patting his shirt pocket where he usually kept his cigarettes, frowning because it was empty. "Your uncle had a lady friend some years ago. Would you like to hear about her?"

More than anything.

I turned to face him and crossed my legs like a German pretzel.

"What was her name?" I asked. "How did he meet her? Was it love at first sight?"

"Her name was Opal." Dad narrowed his eyes like he was squinting to see the memory clearer. "They met at a dance while he was still living in Detroit."

"Uncle Matthew can dance?" My jaw dropped open.

"Sure he can," Dad said. "He's no Fred Astaire, but as far as I know, he doesn't step on any toes."

Try as I might, I just could not picture it, Uncle Matthew gliding across a ballroom floor wearing a tuxedo with tails. The best I could get myself to imagine was him planted like a tall flower against the wall with a cup of punch, watching everybody else dancing.

"Anyway," Dad went on, "he lindy hopped well enough for Opal that she agreed to go dancing with him the next night. And the one after that. Soon enough he went to meet her folks and she came to meet us."

"Was I there?" I asked.

"You, my dear, hadn't arrived yet."

"Shucks."

"Opal, thinking that your uncle had started making plans for the future, started letting herself hope for a life with him." Dad put a finger up in the space between us. "Now, when you look at Matt, you see a curmudgeonly old man. I know you do. But back in his prime, he was an extremely good catch for a girl. Opal didn't want to let him get away."

"She loved him?" Both hands on my cheeks, I sighed.

"Yup. And I believe that he loved her too," Dad said. "I'd put money on it, as a matter of fact."

"Then why didn't they get married?" I asked, scooting closer to Dad. "Did she die?"

"No, nothing that dramatic." Dad rested his head against the railing. "Opal didn't think that Matthew loved her, so she left."

"But he *did* love her," I said. "He did."

"Well, your uncle isn't always so good at expressing his love. Do you know what I mean?"

177

"He patted my head," I said. "Like I was a dog."

"I know. And that, sweetheart, was a grand gesture for him."

"Did he go after her?" I asked. "Did he tell her that he loved her?"

Dad shook his head. "He never did."

"Why not?"

"Well, I never asked him, but if I had to guess, I'd say it was because he was afraid."

"Of Opal?"

"I don't think so." Dad leaned forward. "I think he was afraid she'd break his heart, though. Maybe he thought it would hurt less if he just let her go."

Poor Uncle Matthew. And poor, poor Opal.

"It's like *Romeo and Juliet*," I said, putting both hands over my heart and sighing.

"You haven't read that one yet, have you?" he asked.

I hated to admit that I hadn't.

The sunset was pretty. The sky never showed off more than at the very end of the day, like the sun was trying to say, "You'll miss me when I'm gone!"

Mam called through the door that we could come back in, that she had pudding for us—which was British for "dessert." That night it was actual pudding from a box mix that Uncle Matthew had brought home from the store, and I took that as another of his grand gestures of affection for us.

"I thought you girls might like it," he said when Bertha and I thanked him.

Mam never ever let us eat anything from a box mix!

Bertha took her dish of pudding to the living room, and Mam didn't take any—she was in the middle of trying to reduce a little, I supposed. Dad was already sitting in the study, trying to write a handful of words before bedtime.

That left me and Uncle Matthew alone in the kitchen for the shortest of moments. I couldn't take my eyes off him. Imagining how heartbroken he must have been over Opal made my mouth pull down in a frown.

I held it that way until he noticed.

It took him far too long to look at me, so I cleared my throat.

"What's wrong?" he asked. "The pudding bad or something?" Then he took a small bite to check.

"Oh, Uncle Matthew." I sighed. "Don't you ever think about finding Opal and telling her how you feel about her?"

He swallowed so hard that I heard the gulp from across the room.

"It's not too late, I just know it." I pushed my chair back and stood. "You should go and try to win her back."

Uncle Matthew's already wide eyes got wider, and he tucked his chin in like a turtle trying to pull into his shell.

"You know," he said, pointing at his dish of half-eaten pudding with his spoon, "this isn't so bad."

Then he rushed from the room—and from me—as quick as he could.

If the man had shown half the enthusiasm for Opal as he did for pudding, he would have been married with a couple kids.

I shook my head before taking a bite of the pudding.

It really wasn't so bad.

While nobody was looking, I snuck to the counter and spooned a little more into my dish from the mixing bowl.

thirty-five

BERTHA

Teddy's Food and More—"since 1919," the sign would like you to know—was the biggest building on Main Street in Bear Run. Dad had told me that when Uncle Matthew bought out the original owner, he'd tried to change the name to Harding's Market, but people in town had started a petition.

"They didn't want the new guy coming in and changing everything," Dad had told me.

At that point, Uncle Matthew had lived in town for ten whole years.

Still the new guy.

I wondered what that made the four of us since we'd been in town less than a month.

That morning Mam had handed me a list of things she needed from Teddy's, and I'd asked if she was sure she wanted to send the home economics dropout to get her groceries.

She'd shrugged and went out back to hang laundry on the line to dry.

I checked and double-checked the list to make sure I had everything. Elbow macaroni, stewed tomatoes, carrots, and so on and so forth. I couldn't be sure, but it looked like we'd be having goulash that night. The only thing I couldn't find was canned pineapple for the upside-down cake Mam had been dying to give a try.

Fortunately, I saw Uncle Matthew on the other side of the dry goods section, consulting a clipboard and staring down a shelf full of flour bags as if they'd just insulted his mother.

I pushed my cart toward him, zipping past a display of canned peanuts and around a pallet of boxed sugar cubes.

"Uncle Matthew," I called.

He gave a quick nod of the head in recognition and went right on glaring at the flour.

"Do you know where the canned pineapple is?" I asked, showing him the list as if to prove that I did need the stuff.

"Hm." He furrowed his brow as if trying to recall. "This way."

I followed him—gosh, he walked fast—to the other side of the store where was shelved every kind of canned fruit imaginable. Peaches and berries and pears. Even fruit cocktail. That was my favorite. Flossie's too. But she'd just pick all the little cherry bits out, so Mam hardly ever bought it except for special occasions.

"Slices or chunks?" Uncle Matthew asked.

"Golly," I said, scratching my temple. "I don't know."

"What's she making?"

"Pineapple upside-down cake."

He grabbed a can of slices from the shelf. Then he took a few steps and found a jar of maraschino cherries for me.

"Well," I said, checking my paper one more time. "They aren't on the list."

"They should be."

"Oh." I took the jar and placed it in the cart. "Okay."

"If you wait"—he checked his watch—"five minutes, I'll drive you back."

"That's okay," I said. "I don't mind walking."

"You want to carry all of that a mile?" He nodded at the cart.

"You've got a point," I said.

After the cashier tallied the total and the bagger did his job, I stood by the doors to wait for Uncle Matthew, a brown paper bag balanced on either hip. He took one of them before leading me out to his car.

In the time we'd been staying with him, I'd hardly seen him drive anywhere. He seemed to prefer walking to work and back, leaving his car parked in the one-stall garage behind his house. That morning, though, it had rained, and he'd opted to take his little Ford Shoebox out of the garage.

"It's so cute," I said when he popped the trunk for me to put the grocery bags into.

"Cute, huh?" He half smiled.

"In a very masculine way," I added.

"Huh."

It was a very short ride back to the house, and I fully expected it to be a silent trip. Uncle Matthew, though, seemed to have a different idea. Surprise, surprise.

"I know JuJu Eames," he said, glancing at me before pulling out of the grocery store parking lot.

"The Sweet Peas manager?" I asked.

"That's the one." He nodded. "Your dad tell you that?"

"No," I said. "He never mentioned it."

"I wonder why not."

"I couldn't say." I folded my hands in my lap. "Maybe he forgot."

"Huh." He stopped at the intersection and looked both ways before rolling through.

He steered the car off the straight road and onto one that twisted around trees that must have seemed too much of a bother to cut down when they'd paved the way. Uncle Matthew slowed around a particularly curvy turn.

I hadn't done a lot of driving—everything in Bonaventure Park had been within walking distance—but I knew I would be afraid of taking that road if the pavement was slick from rain or slippery with ice. Especially concerning was the giant tree—was it an oak?—at the end of the curve that was so thick no car could ever have a chance against it.

"Where'd you learn to play ball like that, anyhow?" Uncle Matthew asked.

"Like what?"

"I saw you the other day." He raised his eyebrows. "When you were playing with your sister."

"Oh, that was nothing," I said. "Just blowing off a little steam."

"You're not half bad."

"Thanks."

He pulled into the driveway, right up to the house. But he didn't get out after cutting the engine. Hands still gripping the steering wheel, face still forward, he swallowed hard.

"Anyway, we played ball together, me and Juju," he said. "At Michigan State."

"You did?" I turned toward him. "I didn't even know you went to college."

"For a year or two." He stretched out his fingers before curling them back around the steering wheel. "Justin was a good friend."

"His name's Justin?"

Uncle Matthew didn't smile easily. He didn't laugh all that often. So when he did, I was a little bit surprised.

"He wasn't JuJu in college." He released the wheel with his left hand and rubbed the back of his neck. "He was 'Just-in-Time' Eames to us. We could be down two runs in the bottom of the ninth—that means we were about to lose."

"I know," I said.

"Then Justin would step up to bat and hit a home run like it was nothing." Uncle Matthew grinned. "We used to tell a story that he once knocked the ball so far out of the park that it ended up hitting a cow in Okemos—that's about three miles from East Lansing. Maybe you already knew that."

"I didn't," I said.

"The story goes that poor cow died and the farmer sent Justin a bill." He shook his head and laughed. "Well, Justin passed that right along to the college. It was the only time we ever had steak served up in the cafeteria."

"Is that true?"

"Sure it is." He shut his eyes. "Those were good days."

I'd never heard my uncle say so much in one sitting, and I doubted that he'd talk much for the rest of the day.

"I called him this morning," he said. "Told him about you."

"You did?" My mouth went dry. "Why?"

"To brag about you." He reached into his shirt pocket and pulled out a tidy square of newspaper. "I clipped this for you. Go on, read it."

My hands were shaky, making the paper flutter a little as I read it.

WANTED!

JuJu Eames, coach of Workington's own All-American Girls Professional Baseball team "The Sweet Peas," is looking for a few good gals who can hit, throw, catch & run! Get paid to "play ball" and see corners of the Midwest you've only ever dreamed of. Tryouts THIS SATURDAY, April 12, at Judd Field in Workington, MI, starting at 9 AM SHARP.

GIRLS 15–21 ONLY!

"He's looking forward to meeting you on Saturday morning," Uncle Matthew said.

For a moment—just one—I allowed myself to dream.

I imagined myself in a Sweet Pea uniform, standing in the dugout, waiting for the announcer to call my name. How peachy to be introduced as the starting shortstop or outfielder or, really, whatever. I simply did not care what position I played.

I just wanted to be a Sweet Pea.

When the fans cheered—less for me than for the team—I'd wave. Judd Field would be sold out.

We'd line up for the National Anthem, the other team on the third base line, the Peas on first, each of us standing tall, proud to be an All-American girl.

Uncle Matthew cleared his throat, and the dream slipped away from me fast like I'd had no right to it in the first place.

"I'm supposed to start school on Monday," I said. "My mother would never allow me to try out."

"You don't think so?"

I shook my head, and he shrugged.

"I'll talk to her," he said, getting out of the car without another word and grabbing both bags of groceries from the trunk.

I sat in the car, dumbfounded, knowing that I ought to chase after him and stop him.

I couldn't imagine how Mam would react or what she'd say when Uncle Matthew brought it up to her. She'd think I put him up to it, and then I'd be the recipient of her sternest glare.

Gosh, I dreaded that glare from her silvery blue eyes. It was like being drilled into.

I got out of the car and snuck up onto the porch, listening in through the screen door.

". . . this Saturday," Uncle Matthew said.

"Matty." Mam sighed.

"She's a good player, Louisa."

I couldn't help but smile. That was as verbose as Uncle Matthew got, and he'd spent all of those words for my benefit.

"She needs to be in school," Mam said.

"The school here isn't very good."

"Hogwash."

"She'll learn more traveling with the team," he said.

"And she can do so after she's finished her schooling."

I could imagine Mam nodding once the way she did when she was done with a discussion.

And that was it. Uncle Matthew came back out onto the porch, car keys in hand.

"Don't worry, kid," he said, reaching past me and grabbing the mail from the letterbox and shuffling through the envelopes. "Huh. One for you."

He handed it to me before making his way back to his car.

Dear Bert,

First things first, I'm glad you and your folks (and Flossie) didn't get kiddie napped by the FBI or diamond smugglers or anything like that. Seriously, though, I was worried at first, seeing your windows boarded up like they are. I thought maybe the Feds had raided your house or something and booked you all.

Bobbo told me somebody threw rocks through your windows. Stinky Simon said it was just some citizen vigilante that done it. He said the police know who it was, but they aren't going to do anything about it. How do you like that?

If I find out who done it, I'll have a word or two for them. Believe me.

Second things second, we play the Monument boys again on Saturday. I'll let you know how it goes. I'm not expecting much, though. Not without our star player.

Nothing is the same without you.

Third things third, you've got to think of a code name to use when you write me from now on. Got it? At least on the envelope. My mother about jumped out of her skin when she saw there was a letter from you in our box. It's a good thing she didn't think to burn it. She just marched it out to the trash can and, lucky for me, there was just a little rotten egg yolk on the corner of it when I had a chance to sneak out and get it.

Think up something clever. But not too clever so I don't know it's actually you.

Fourth things fourth, do you need money for stationery? Don't send any more paper from a taxidermist, all right? I'm still scrubbing my hands raw after handling the last letter.

Your friend (possibly the best one you got),

Leo S.

———— Bear Run Crematorium and Taxidermy ————

Dear Leo,

Guess what! You'll never guess because it's completely bonkers. So I'll just tell you.

My uncle, Matthew Lee Harding, played baseball at Michigan State with none other than THE JuJu Eames!

Bet you didn't guess that, did ya?

As a matter of fact, I didn't know that either until just today.

Anywho, my uncle called JuJu—that's right, he has his telephone number—and told him about little old me. JuJu wants me to come to tryouts at Judd Field on Saturday! Can you believe it?

The only problem is my mother. I think you already know how she feels about me going off and playing for the Sweet Peas.

Do you think it's okay for me to pray that God changes her mind? I know that we aren't supposed to bother him with silly prayers—I heard that in a sermon one time. But I also recall memorizing the Bible verse that says we should cast our cares onto God because he cares for us.

Do you think God cares about baseball?

I'm so sorry for getting you into trouble with your mother. From here on out, I'll be an Australian socialite living in Northern Michigan. My name shall be Gladiola Von Bambinonberg. You can tell your mother that I come from old money (whatever that means) and that I plan to be your lifelong benefactor so that you can pursue your dream of becoming a synchronized swimmer.

That's all for now.

Thanks for being my friend.

Code Name: Bambi

thirty-six

FLOSSIE

We'd only been in Bear Run a little over a week. Still, that had been enough time for me to memorize the directions to the library. All I had to do was go left once I got to the end of the driveway, walk until that road ended and turn right. Then, after five minutes or so, the library would be on the other side of the street.

There wasn't a statue of a lion out front and there weren't any columns like we had back in Bonaventure Park. But the Huebert Memorial Library of Bear Run was in an old house that was painted a bright mint green color with trim in purple and pink.

It was hard to miss, that was for sure.

There was an entire section of the library dedicated just to Mr. Johannes Huebert with a painting of him on the wall and a glass case with his pocket watch and jackknife and cigarette case in it. There were even shelves full of the books that had been in his house.

None of them looked like they'd ever been cracked open, let alone read. And if anyone dared take one off the shelf, the librarian would swoop down and snatch it away, demanding that the "artifacts must be preserved."

I'd learned that the hard way the first time I was there and plopped down on the floor to read an ancient-looking copy of *The Pilgrim's Progress*.

According to Mrs. Librarian—I hadn't learned her name—some books weren't to be read. They were just for decoration.

What a waste.

That day I walked right past the Johannes Huebert display and clear to the back of the library, where the kind of books I liked were kept. There was even a comfortable chair for me to sit in while I read. I planned to pick out a book, curl up in the chair, and read until Mam came to get me.

Oh, I sure hoped she took a long time running her errands.

But when I got there, someone was already in my chair. That someone had a book held up so it covered her face. She had on a pink and green plaid skirt and black and white saddle shoes.

I looked down at my plain old Buster Browns that Bertha had handed down to me. Of course I'd forgotten to pack nice shoes in all of our hurry to get out of Bonaventure Park.

The girl in the chair had hair the color of a brand-new penny. Exactly like the girl who lived next door to Uncle Matthew's house. I checked the clock on the wall. She should have been on the bus, trundling down the road to meet her mother on the curb.

What I should have done was say hello and introduce myself. That would have been the right thing. But I, Florence Mable Harding, often did things backwards and upside down. Sometimes even inside out.

So, instead of being pleasant, I cleared my throat in the hopes that she'd notice me, apologize for being in my spot, and leave.

But she didn't seem to have heard me. She just turned the page in her book.

So I went to the shelf and grabbed a book off of it, not paying any attention to which one, and returned to the chair. I cleared my throat one more time.

The girl lowered the book just enough that I could see her eyes. She had glasses—cat-eye ones with little jewels in the corners—and the lenses made her eyes look huge. When I didn't say anything right away, she started to lift the book back up.

"Are you going to hog that chair all day?" I asked.

"I was here first," she said from the other side of the book.

"So?"

"First come, first served, I guess." She glanced down at the book in my hand. "I hope you like sad stories."

"Why?" I lifted the book and held it against my chest.

"Because that one has a sad ending."

I took a look at the cover. On it was a boy in high-water pants—which told me he was probably dirt poor and his folks couldn't get him slacks that fit properly. He held a little deer like it was a baby.

The Yearling.

I should have known that I'd pick out a sad one. It seemed to be the only kind of book I read anymore.

"Does the deer die?" I asked.

The girl lifted her eyebrows.

In a huff I put that book right back where I'd gotten it.

"I don't know what's wrong with a story ending happily ever after," I grumbled, running my finger along the spines of all the books, trying to find something more suitable to read.

"Maybe you should read *Pollyanna*," the girl said, tapping the cover of the book she was reading with one finger.

The girl on the cover of that book had on a yellow dress and carried a basket of pretty white flowers. But I didn't spend too much time looking at her. I was distracted because I'd just noticed that the girl in the chair had her fingernails painted cherry red.

Mam never allowed me to have painted nails. She said that nail polish was just like makeup. I couldn't wear either until I was sixteen years old.

That wasn't for another four and a half years!

"Have you read it?" the girl asked.

"Not yet," I answered. "Is it any good?"

"It's all right." She blinked at me over the book. "You're the girl staying at Mr. Harding's house, aren't you?"

"He's my uncle," I said.

"Why do you keep spying on my mother and me?"

"I do not." I tried for a well-I-never tone in my voice. A mixture of gasp and puff.

"Sure you do," she said. "What's your name?"

"Flossie."

"I'm Lizzie." She put out her right hand, still holding the book over her face.

I shook hands with her.

"Friends now?" she asked.

"Okay," I answered.

Then she lowered the book down past her nose and mouth. Her face looked different from anybody's I'd ever seen before. Her nose was flatter, like she was pressing it against a piece of glass. Her lip seemed like it was tugged just a little bit to one side, and a scar ran from the top of her lip to her nose. When she smiled at me, I saw that her front two teeth were crooked and her mouth uneven.

I forced my eyes to lock with hers rather than to stay fixed on the bottom half of her face.

"Still friends?" she whispered.

I could have heard wrong, but it seemed there was a little shake in her voice when she asked it again.

"Yup," I answered with as much pep as I could.

Turned out to be a little too much pep, and Mrs. Librarian shushed me all the way from the other side of the library.

Lizzie covered her mouth to catch a laugh, and I did the same.

Then she scooted over, making enough room for me to sit beside her in the chair.

thirty-seven

BERTHA

Mam hadn't tucked me in for years. But she did that Friday night because, I supposed, she felt bad for me.

A whole bunch of gals were going to Judd Field for Sweet Peas tryouts the next morning, and she'd decided that I wouldn't be one of them.

"You'll get your chance, love," she said, sitting on the edge of my bed. "There's a lot of life ahead of you. Don't be in too great a hurry to grow up."

She kissed me on the forehead—tenderness that very nearly made me start crying—and told me to sleep well.

I waited until she turned off the light and closed the door behind her to put my ball glove under my pillow for good luck.

Dad got me up while it was still dark out and reminded me to be extra quiet so that we wouldn't wake up Mam. He and Uncle Matthew pushed the car down the driveway while I steered. Once we were a good ways down the road, Uncle Matthew shooed me to the back seat and turned over the engine.

"How did you two get so good at sneaking out?" I asked, leaning forward against the front seat.

"Never mind that," Dad said. "Here. Eat this. You'll need your energy."

He handed me a banana and a hunk of cheese. It wasn't one of Mam's proper, fortifying English breakfasts, but it would do.

"Do you think Mam will worry when she gets up and we're not home?" I asked.

"I left a note." Dad glanced at me over his shoulder. "Don't worry. She won't be angry."

Uncle Matthew shook his head.

Dad may have been oblivious, but Uncle Matthew and I weren't. Mam was going to be livid.

After driving for two hours and fifteen minutes, we pulled into the gravel parking lot of Judd Field with time to spare. Uncle Matthew drove clear to the far side of the lot, pulling in under the shade of a tree just starting to bloom. Dad, ever the writer, adjusted in his seat to look at the buds.

"'The uncertain glory of an April day . . .'" he whispered.

It was Shakespeare. At least I thought so. Honestly, though, I just didn't care because, at that very moment, I was trying to control the nerves that had set my arms and legs aquiver.

"I think I'm going to be sick," I said.

"Not in the car." Uncle Matthew turned in his seat, eyes wide.

"Come on, kid," Dad said, opening his door. "Let's get some fresh air."

The morning was crisply cold, and we could still see our breath. Dad lit up a Lucky and nodded toward the edge of the parking lot. It seemed he wanted to do a lap. That was fine with me. I needed to loosen up my limbs a little.

"Did I ever tell you that I met Ty Cobb once?" he asked. "Me and Matt both."

"No," I answered. "Why didn't you ever tell me?"

He shrugged and took a puff off his cigarette. "I guess I was waiting for the right time."

We made it a handful of strides before he started talking again.

"The two of us boys believed we were destined to be Tigers," he started. "We shared a room, and every night before bed we'd work on memorizing baseball statistics. I'm not sure what we thought that would accomplish. But we did it anyway. We listened to every game we could on the radio, and whenever one of us had a spare buck or two, we'd get a couple of tickets to see them play at Navin Field."

He flicked the end of his cigarette, sending flecks of ash to one side of him.

"One time we got to the game only to find out that we were twenty-five cents short," Dad said. "One of us must have lost a quarter along the way. We were heartbroken. You've probably figured this out by now, but sometimes when a boy is sad like that, he wants to get into a fight."

"Yeah, I've learned that," I said.

More times than I could count I'd stood by, annoyed, while a couple of boys from the neighborhood duked it out over the silliest things like a scuffed-up baseball or a sideways look. Then, after the kerfuffle was over, the boys were best of chums again.

"Matt and I got into a fistfight outside the stadium, both of us blaming the other for losing the money." He laughed. "Don't tell anybody this, but your uncle is a better brawler than I am. Always was. I knew I was going to lose, but I couldn't have surrendered, either. So, I ended up with a bloody nose and a busted lip. The only thing Matt ended up with was a pair of bruised knuckles."

"He's older," I said. "It wasn't a fair fight."

"That's nice of you to say." He grinned. "My pride thanks you for the kindness."

"You're welcome."

"Anyway, we fought until he was worn out. Then we two sat on the curb and listened to what we could of the game. Just a lot of bats cracking against balls and the fans either cheering or booing. We could tell the Tigers were winning from how excited the crowd was."

He dropped the butt of his Lucky onto the gravel and squashed it into the rocks with the toe of his shoe.

"After the game was over, we waited just a little longer just in case we could catch sight of any of the players," he went on.

"Imagine our surprise when the Georgia Peach himself came out. He was so close we could have reached out and grabbed him."

I tried to picture it, two young guys—one with busted-up knuckles and the other with a bloody nose—that near to Ty Cobb.

"Always the talkative one, Matthew couldn't seem to get a word out of his mouth," Dad said, laughing. "No surprise, huh?"

"Nope."

"Well, Ty got a look at my face and started chuckling. I'm not kidding." That made Dad crack a smile. "He waved me over and handed me the hanky out of his back pocket and asked me who did that to my nose. I pointed at Matthew and Ty whistled. 'He's a big boy,' he said."

I looked over my shoulder toward Uncle Matthew's car. He'd gotten out and was making his way toward the stadium. He was at least a head taller than Dad and quite a bit broader.

"Then he said, 'If you're gonna fight a bigger boy, at least make sure you're the smarter of the two of ya.'" Dad lit up another Lucky. "How do you like that?"

"Then what happened?"

"He took his hanky back and told me to scram." Dad shook his head. "I guess he didn't want me to try to sell his old snot rag."

We were most of the way around the parking lot, and other cars were starting to drive in, other nervous girls like me, showing up to see if they had what it took to play for the All-American Girls.

"Bertha, I want you to listen to me, okay?" Dad said, stopping. I stopped too.

"You're a good player. Quite good." He pointed around the parking lot. "But some of these players are going to be better. That's just how life is."

I shuffled my feet, unsure what he was trying to say to me. If this was his idea of a pep talk, I thought he ought to stick with writing fiction.

"But, honey, you're smart. If you're going to step on that field thinking that your talent is going to carry you to a spot on the team, you've got another thing coming." He pointed at my head. "Put your foot on that baseball diamond with your wits about you and you'll be fine. Keep your mind active every single minute. Notice everything. If I know anything, it's that a manager will take a smart player over a brawny one any day of the week."

"Okay," I said, swallowing hard. "I'll try."

"That's all I can expect." He nodded toward where Uncle Matthew was, walking up to a man in a suit and tie. "Looks like he's found old JuJu."

JuJu grabbed Uncle Matthew and pulled him into a hug, lifting him right off the ground.

I expected Uncle Matthew to push him away or blush or something. But, instead, he laughed so hard and so loud I worried he might hurt himself from the exertion.

Dearest Louisa,

Good morning to you, my sweet. Upon waking this day, long before the sun dared show his face, I glanced at you and thought what a fortunate man am I to be married to one such as you. You are the very meaning of loveliness and grace.

By now you've noticed that I'm gone, Bertha with me. Matthew's with us too. And, by now, no doubt, you've done the math and figured out where we've gotten off to.

I'm sorry, honey. Our girl is a dreamer. Far be it from me to keep her from it.

Now is the time when I must rely upon your grace yet again.

We'll be home this evening. Hopefully we'll bring our girl back a Sweet Pea.

Every little bit of my love,

Will

thirty-eight

FLOSSIE

It was a rare thing, Mam getting so angry that she went to her room and shut the door. That morning, though, that was exactly what she did. But first she gave me money and told me to see if "the little gal next door" wanted to go see a movie.

Whillikers! I'd never benefited so much from Mam's temper before. I grabbed the money and scrammed before she could change her mind.

There was only one movie theater in Bear Run. And in that one movie theater was just one screen. So, on Saturday morning, it was hard to find a seat for the showing of *Snow White and the Seven Dwarfs*. Lucky for me and Lizzie, we found a couple of seats in the very front row.

We were so close I fully expected to feel a gust of wind whenever Sneezy said "achoo."

When I told Lizzie that, she giggled so hard her eyes watered.

We'd both seen it already, so we weren't too scared when the beautiful queen turned herself into an ugly, one-toothed old hag or when sweet Snow White was gullible enough to fall for the old "eat the apple and your dreams will come true" trick.

Snow White had obviously never been in Sunday school to learn that a girl should always—*always, always*—say no whenever a stranger offers her an apple.

Both Lizzie and I held our breath when the prince leaned down to kiss Snow White even though we both knew she'd wake up.

At the very end of the movie, we clapped and cheered along with everyone else, so loud that I wouldn't have been surprised if Mr. Disney had heard it.

The theater may have been small, but the kids of Bear Run were a lively bunch.

Making our way out of the theater, Lizzie and I talked about which dwarf was our favorite. She liked Dopey best.

"He's cute," she said.

"But he's not very smart," I said.

"That's all right. Because he's nice."

I shrugged and said that my favorite was Sleepy.

"He makes funny faces," I said.

"He does."

Lizzie closed her lids halfway down her eyes and made a snoring sound. We both laughed, and she covered her mouth as we stepped into the busy lobby.

She told me from behind her fist that she needed to use the ladies' room. I waited, back against the wall, watching all the people crowded in front of the concessions stand.

Who knew there were so many people who lived in such a small town?

I noticed that a handful of girls were looking at me from the other side of the room. They smiled and I smiled back. One of them waved at me, and I returned it.

Well, that was something new for me. Girls like those ones usually never gave me the time of day unless it was to tease me.

So, when the one who'd waved came my way, I got a little nervous.

"Hi," she said, sticking out her hand. "You're new, ain't you? I'm Gretel."

"I'm Florence," I said.

I thought maybe I'd save my nickname in case she turned out to be a big meanie.

We shook hands, and I was glad to find that she didn't have one of those gag hand buzzers hidden in her palm.

Maybe she wasn't as bad as I feared.

She asked me what grade I was in at school, and when she learned that I was her same age, she offered to introduce me to all the kids in class.

Golly, if all the girls in town were half as nice as Lizzie and Gretel then I'd have it made.

"Say, Florence, a few girls and I are going to get a malt." She pointed at the others. "You wanna come?"

"I'm with my friend." I glanced in the direction of the restroom. "Can she come too?"

"Oh, maybe," she said. "Who's your friend?"

Just then, as if right on cue, Lizzie came out of the bathroom. As soon as she saw Gretel, she hid behind her hand again.

"Lizzie," I called, waving my hand up over my head. "Over here."

Eyes wide, she shook her head and made a beeline for the door.

"Your friend is Lizard-Lip Lizzie?" Gretel cringed. "You should be friends with us instead."

I am far too ashamed to admit how tempting that was. It really was. All my life I'd been the one left out, and there, right in front of me, was someone offering to let me in.

I very nearly fell for it.

But then I thought of the old hag's ruby red apple.

Never take an apple from a stranger, I said in my head.

Then, out loud to Gretel, I said, "If I ever hear you call her Lizard-Lip again, I'll . . ."

But, other than the time I'd slapped Iris Markowitz, I'd never gotten into a fight and I didn't know what I would do. It didn't take much to get around Gretel, and after I gave her a little shove, she made an *umph* sound that almost made me laugh. One of the girls yelled a "Hey!" after me, but I didn't look back to see which one it was.

I just kept on going, running out of the theater and down the sidewalk with no idea where my Lizzie had gone.

200

I found her in an alley behind the bakery, sitting on an old wooden crate and with both hands cupped over her nose and mouth. There wasn't much of her face that I could see, but she'd taken off her glasses, and her eyes were red and watery.

I pulled a crate over and sat beside her.

After a couple of minutes, I got antsy—mostly because I had to use the restroom—and started to wonder how long we were going to have to stay there. Mam had told me to come back to Uncle Matthew's right after the movie, and she would be sore if I stayed gone too long.

Lizzie lowered one of her hands but kept the other up like a shield.

"You don't have to be friends with me if you don't want to," she whispered.

"Well, why wouldn't I want to?" I asked.

Lizzie raised one eyebrow at me before pointing at her scar.

I leaned back against the brick wall of the bakery.

"Those girls don't know anything," I said. "If they did, they'd be begging to get a malt with you."

"But I'd never go with them," Lizzie said.

"Yeah, me either."

We started back, and I hoped Mam wouldn't be too upset that I was a little bit later than she'd expected.

She'd understand, I was sure, if I explained to her that I couldn't leave my friend behind.

thirty-nine

BERTHA

The way the story went, Dottie Fitzgerald had come from a nothing family that lived on the wrong side of the tracks in a small farm town called Bliss, Michigan. The family home was nothing more than an old, abandoned chicken coop, and she'd grown up wearing dingy feed sacks and secondhand Buster Browns.

She didn't know anything about baseball until she was nineteen years old and somebody caught her chucking rocks through the glass windows of an abandoned house.

According to legend, she pitched those rocks like a regular old Cy Young.

That somebody who caught her was pals with JuJu Eames, who hired her on the spot to be one of the very first Sweet Peas. He taught her everything she ever needed to know about baseball.

From what I'd read, every single time she'd walked to the pitcher's mound at Judd Field—or any other place, for that matter—she was cucumber cool, never showing the slightest tic or anxiety. Nothing rattled her focus.

She played ball like she knew how good she was and didn't need to show off to make the other players know it too.

What a gal.

When I stepped onto Judd Field, I was anything but cool. More like a nauseated, jittery, bundle of self-doubt. My palms were already sweaty before I even got started. And it just got worse when I looked up into the stands and saw Dottie Fitzgerald herself sitting there, clipboard balanced on her knees.

I raised my hand to wave, but she didn't see me.

She was too busy watching a couple of girls who were already tossing a ball back and forth along the foul line.

One of the girls threw the ball far out of the other's reach. The one catching took a flying leap for it and, surprisingly, caught it. She fell into the grass, her mitt held high so anyone who might be watching would see that she'd kept a hold on the ball.

She got up off the ground and made a salute in Dottie's direction.

When I turned to see if Dottie was impressed, I noticed that she had a smirk on her face.

If I'd had to guess what she was thinking, it might have been along the lines of, "What a show-off."

Still, it had been an impressive catch.

Better than I could have done.

"Pay attention," I whispered to myself. "Play smart."

Dottie lifted her hand, thumb up, and I turned to see JuJu Eames making his way to the pitcher's mound. He nodded in Dottie's direction.

It was time to get started.

"All right, girls," JuJu yelled, crossing his arms. "Circle up."

Every girl on that field hustled from wherever they were and formed a ring around him. There were a couple dozen of us. By the looks of the others, I was one of the youngest there.

That could either be good or bad. I wasn't sure which it was.

"Who's that?" a girl beside me whispered.

She had on a baby blue cardigan with the letter "T" on it.

"JuJu Eames," I said. "The manager."

"But who's the coach?" She looked around the field.

"He is," I said. "Manager is just what they're called in baseball."

She scratched the top of her head. "Huh."

Oh boy. I didn't have high hopes for her making the team.

"All right, quiet down. Here's how it's going to work today." JuJu cleared his throat. "Each of you girls is going to have a number pinned to her shirt so we can keep track of who's who. Lorna here's going to pass those around. You might recognize her if you've been to many of our games."

Lorna Williams. How neat! She'd been pitching for the Peas for the past few years. She was good. Not the best in the league. But she did well enough.

"Once that's all set," JuJu went on, "we'll run some drills, do a little batting, play a short game. Then that's that."

Lorna handed me the number 11 and a safety pin.

"Just put that on your pocket there," she said, pointing to my flannel. "What's your name? Position?"

"Um, Bertha Harding," I answered. "I can play anywhere."

"Number 11. Bertha Harding," Lorna called toward Dottie. "Utility."

I turned, trying to see if there was any recognition from Dottie at hearing my name. But she just wrote on her clipboard.

"Don't worry about her," Lorna said. "She's just as nice as could be."

"I know." I smiled. "I met her when I was a kid."

"How about that." Lorna winked at me. "Good luck, honey."

"Thanks," I said.

"You're lucky," the girl in the cardigan said. "Your number's the same no matter if you put it on right side up or upside down."

I looked at her and allowed myself a small laugh. Her number 4 was on the wrong way and she was struggling to undo the pin.

"Need help?" I asked.

She didn't answer. Instead she dropped her hands and sighed, moving her hair off her shoulder to get it out of the way.

"Thank you," she said. "This is going to be fun, huh?"

"I guess so." I got the number put right.

"That's my grandmom up there." She nodded at the side of the stands where the other team's fans usually sat. "She saw the ad in the paper and thought, what the hay. Why not give it a try? I'm Trixie, by the way."

"I'm Bertha."

"Good to know you." She shielded her eyes and looked at the stands again. "Who've you got here?"

I squinted, finding my dad and Uncle Matthew sitting in the very first row, both of them smoking. I wondered if they were as nervous as I was.

"Those two," I said. "The small one is my dad. The big one is my uncle."

"Gosh, what a bruiser." Trixie checked her number. "Thanks again."

Dad gave me the "a-okay" sign, making a ring with his thumb and forefinger. I lifted my hand and made it flicker, hoping he'd take that as my sign that I was quaking in my boots. Then he tapped his temple.

Play smart.

I knew that was what he meant. So I nodded.

"All right, everybody got their numbers on?" JuJu asked. "Good. Take a lap. Start at home. Follow the first-base line all the way to the right field fence. Round center to left, then come back home down the third-base line. This one isn't a race. Just wanna make sure you all can go that far."

I tittered. A few other girls did too. One or two looked like they were being asked to haul bricks on their backs up forty flights of stairs.

"Well," one girl spoke up, hand in the air like she was in class, "we never had to run much in school softball club."

Bless her. The poor kid.

"This ain't school softball club," JuJu said. "Get to home, girls."

I took it easy, not wanting to spend all my energy on the very first thing. Still, I was among the first few to finish the run. A brawny girl—she had to have been as tall as Leo and just as muscular— came in right after me. Number 15. She narrowed her eyes and brushed past me, knocking me to one side as she did.

She didn't apologize.

"What was that?" I said, loud enough for her to hear me.

Usually I reserved outbursts like that for boys. When it came to boys, a girl had to stick up for herself, had to be bold. They'd never respect her if she didn't. I knew that it was different with girls.

I just didn't know what to do with bullies of the female variety.

15 didn't respond. She just went to the dugout and sat on the bench to wait for the next drill.

"We are not going to be friends," I muttered under my breath.

JuJu had us sprint to the bases, catch and throw, run different plays. We took turns at bat in no particular order, Lorna pitching to us. One girl—who had introduced herself as Weeny—had a strike zone so small even Lorna couldn't find it.

Weeny didn't even have to swing. Four balls and she got to walk to first base.

JuJu had given an impressed frown at that, and Dottie wrote something down on her clipboard.

Oh, to be a fly who could hover over Dottie's shoulder and read all the notes she was taking.

"Number 11," JuJu called. "You're up."

I stepped up to the plate, grinding the toe of my right shoe into the dirt. One good breath after another, I tried to steady my nerves and slow my heartbeat a little.

I knew better than to look up at Dad and Uncle Matthew.

I cocked the bat, ready to spring at the right ball.

When I looked at Lorna, I held my breath.

The first pitch came so fast I didn't have time to react. I just stood there like an idiot.

"Strike one," Lorna called.

As if everyone and their brother didn't already know that.

I swung for the second but missed it.

"Strike two," she yelled.

One more chance. That was it. If I didn't knock that next throw deep into the outfield, I was toast. I might as well pack up and go home.

I got myself set and watched Lorna wind up, taking in a sip of breath before the ball released from her hand. My swing sliced through the air and my body went off balance with the force of it.

There was no crack of bat and ball. Just the smack of ball in catcher's mitt.

"That's three," Lorna said. "You're out, honey."

Somebody laughed, and I didn't have to look to know that it

was number 15. I wouldn't give her the satisfaction of seeing me get upset. Calm as I could, holding in any sort of feeling I might have been having, I walked back to the dugout, setting my bat against the fence.

I felt like crying. So I clenched my teeth and breathed, hard, through my nose.

"Tough luck," Trixie said, unbuttoning her cardigan. "You'll get 'em next time."

"Golly, I hope so."

"I'm up next." She handed me her sweater. "I just hope Lorna doesn't bean me with one of those pitches."

"You'll do great," I said through my teeth.

"Thanks."

I cringed when she got to bat, her stance was so rigid, so gangly.

"Okay!" she yelled to Lorna. "I'm ready."

"You sure, babycakes?" Lorna called.

"Yup. Let her rip, tater chip!"

"All right."

Lorna wound up and gave it her all.

I flinched, thinking the ball was going to buzz right past number 4. But to my surprise—and everybody else's too—Trixie gave a swing so pretty it looked more like dancing, and she hit that ball just out of the park like it was nothing at all.

"Not half bad," Weeny muttered. "Doggone it."

JuJu took off his ball cap and scratched the top of his head. Lorna stood, wide-eyed and mouth hanging open. Dottie smiled from her place in the stands.

As for Trixie, she didn't move from home.

"Can I go again?" she asked, hopping up and down like a little girl. "That was fun!"

By the end of the day, we'd all batted five times. My second and third went much better than the first. The fourth wasn't so great, if I'm to be honest. But that fifth hit—oh, blessed miracle—was as close to perfect as I'd ever done. The ball went so high up in the air that I lost it for a second, not seeing it smack the side of the scoreboard and fall on the far side of the fence.

"That's a home run!" Lorna had yelled, clapping her hands.

We played a game where we switched positions whenever our particular team took the field. They put me in right field one inning, at shortstop the next, third base for another. But it was when JuJu told me to catch that I felt my most natural.

That entire inning felt like stepping into a pair of shoes that fit for the very first time. My thighs were sore by the second out, but it was worth it when, with a two-strike count, I wiggled my four fingers, calling for Lorna to throw a changeup that sent number 15 down swinging.

The way that girl swung—like she was trying to kill a moose—I knew she wasn't ready for a pitch coming at a slowed-down speed.

Her nostrils flared and she cussed under her breath.

I worked at not smiling.

———

At the end of the game, JuJu sent us all off to lunch, telling us to be back at two—on the dot—when he'd have a list of the girls that made the team.

I didn't know about any of the other girls, but I was far too anxious to eat. Dad and Uncle Matthew ate the sandwiches we'd packed and had the bottles of Coke they got from the little store down the street.

Dad was nice enough to get me a Vernor's. He knew that ginger ale always soothed my upset stomach.

At two o'clock JuJu met all of us girls and the folks who'd come with us at the main entrance of Judd Field. Just him. No Dottie or Lorna. Just him and his clipboard.

"Okay. I'll just read off the names of the girls who made the team," he said, not looking up at any of us. "If I called your name, I'll have you come stand beside me and then I'll give you instructions for spring training."

He cleared his throat.

I clenched my fists.

Beside me, Trixie giggled.

"Oh, the suspense is awful, isn't it?" she asked. "Like in a movie."

"Before I do that," JuJu said, "I want to say that you all played your hearts out in there today. Not a one of you is anything less than a good player. We had some tough decisions to make. If you aren't called, I do hope you'll come back and try again next year. Now, everybody take a good breath. I will too."

He did, puffing his cheeks when he let it out.

"The following girls will join the rest of the Sweet Peas for this season's games," he started. "Cecilia Trigiani."

The small girl who called herself Weeny slapped a hand over her mouth, and the man standing beside her gave her a very enthusiastic hug and a very long kiss on the old smacker.

"I knew it," he said.

"Trixie Martin," JuJu called.

"That's me," Trixie said as if it was the most normal thing in all the world to become a professional baseball player.

Her grandmom, on the other hand, started sobbing, and I couldn't tell if it was because she was happy or sad.

"Lucy Carpenter," JuJu said.

There was no outburst at the calling of that name. No clapping or surprised shouts or a girl being lifted off the ground by a proud father.

Number 15 just stepped forward with the very faintest grin on her face. It wasn't a smug smile like I might have expected.

"And last but not least," JuJu said. "Uma . . ."

I didn't hear the rest of her name. I didn't see which girl it was that stepped forward. I didn't know how everyone else reacted or what JuJu said after that.

The only thing I was aware of was the hand on my shoulder and Dad's voice.

"It's okay, Bertha," he said.

But it wasn't. It really wasn't.

I wasn't a Sweet Pea.

——— Bear Run Crematorium and Taxidermy ———

Dear Leo,

We got back from Sweet Pea tryouts a couple of hours ago. It's late. Very late. So late that even my dad is in bed. I'm at the kitchen table, nursing a broken heart.

I didn't make the team.

Ever since we left Judd Field I've been going over and over in my mind what I did wrong, and all I can really come up with is that:

1. I struck out once during batting drills.

2. I yelled (well, not loudly, but my voice wasn't sweetness and congeniality) when a girl rammed into me on purpose.

3. I wasn't good enough.

My dad's disappointed. Maybe not in me. But, still, he'd hoped so hard that I'd make it. I told him I was sorry, and he said that I didn't have to be. I am anyway.

I wish you were in the house two doors down so I could toss pebbles at your window. You could sneak out and go to the sandlot with me for a game of catch.

It wouldn't make anything better, I know. But I'd at least not feel like a complete failure.

Please don't be disappointed in me.

Bertha

forty

FLOSSIE

For the first time in my entire life, I didn't have a brand-new dress to wear on Easter Sunday. Mam said it was all right because no one at Uncle Matthew's church would know any better because they'd never seen any of my dresses before.

Still, it didn't feel like Easter in my normal, ordinary, regular old Sunday clothes.

Mam let me borrow her pearl bracelet, and that made me feel mostly better.

First Baptist Church had plenty of empty seats to pick from when we got there—Mam liked being nice and early. But Uncle Matthew led us to a pew all the way in the back of the sanctuary.

"My usual spot," he whispered.

Well, that was fine and good for him because he was tall enough to see over everybody's heads. I, on the other hand, would need a stepladder.

Mam said it was fine, though, so we stayed put.

As more and more people started filing in, I realized that it wasn't all bad, sitting in the back. From that view, I didn't miss a whole lot of anything. I was especially interested in all of the ladies and their pretty spring dresses.

Eventually Lizzie and her mother walked in. Lizzie, as usual, held her fist up over her mouth and nose. But when she saw me, she turned her hand—knuckles still hiding her face—and wiggled her fingers in a wave.

I did the exact same thing back to her.

She and her mother took a pew near the front, and I noticed that there wasn't a father with them. As a matter of fact, I never saw a man go in or out of their house.

I turned to ask Uncle Matthew about that but was interrupted by the pipe organ and everybody in the congregation standing up to sing the opening hymn.

Bertha—who had been a grump ever since she got home from tryouts—held the hymnal so that I couldn't share it with her, but I didn't have to see the words to sing along. We sang "Holy, Holy, Holy" at least once a month back at our church in Bonaventure Park.

Full of confidence, I sang at the top of my lungs. The problem was that, instead of singing "casting down their golden crowns around the glassy sea," what came out was "crashing down their golden clowns around the grassy bee."

Bertha glanced at me and smiled. Then she covered her mouth, her shoulders shaking and eyes watering. At first I thought she was crying. But then I realized that she'd gotten a case of the giggles. It was catching, because she got me started too, and hard as I tried, I couldn't quite hold it in. I thought I might burst.

"Girls," Mam scolded.

"I'm sorry," I said.

At least I tried to say it. But it came out with a chortle, and I fell to the pew, sticking my head between my knees in the hopes of making it stop. I sucked in breaths until I got myself calmed down.

Then, sitting up, I made the mistake of looking at Uncle Matthew. He had his jaw clenched and was holding the pew in front of him for dear life. When he noticed me watching him, he started snickering and rushed out of the sanctuary.

Well, that just got me laughing all over again.

"Out," Mam whispered. "The both of you girls."

"Sorry," Bertha chuckled, grabbing my hand and dragging me out behind her.

It was a good thing we'd been sitting in the back row.

We didn't grab our coats on the way out the front door of the church, and the chill of the morning knocked the giggles right out of us. Oh, my tummy hurt from all the laughing.

Uncle Matthew was sitting at the top of the steps, and he grinned at us.

"Hi," he said.

"I'm sorry," I said, hopping down the steps one by one. "I think I got us all in trouble."

"You did," Bertha said, sitting down next to Uncle Matthew. "But I sure needed that."

Since the day before, I'd been told more than once by Mam that I wasn't allowed to say one word to my sister about not making the team. And I hadn't. But it had been like trying to hold in the giggles just a few minutes before. Completely impossible. I just couldn't stop myself.

"Are you sad you didn't make the team?" I asked.

Uncle Matthew made the kind of face that said "there she goes again."

"Yeah," Bertha said. Then she sighed and let her shoulders droop. "I guess it just isn't my year."

"But what happened?" I kicked the step with the toe of my shoe. "Did you make a lot of mistakes?"

"Not really." Bertha curled her fingers into her palms and used her fists to tap her knees. "The others were just better than me."

"I don't believe that," I said. "I can't imagine anybody being better at baseball than you."

"Well, that's awful nice of you, kid."

It was. I knew it. And it was just the kind of thing that a sister was supposed to say.

After a few more minutes, Uncle Matthew said, "We ought to . . ." and then tilted his head toward the door.

We wandered back inside, the three of us, and slid into the back pew beside Mam to listen to the sermon. Dad showed up just a minute or two later.

In a book or a movie, Bertha would have made the team. Not

only that, she would have been the star player and she would have been the one who scored the point that would win her team the championship. Then she would have gotten the "Best Player of All" award—or whatever sports people called those things.

And then she would have gotten the handsome man she was in love with.

And if we'd been a work of fiction, the three of us would have walked into the sanctuary at the exact moment when the preacher would say the very perfect thing to encourage Bertha to keep trying, to never give up.

Something like, "They that wait upon the Lord shall renew their strength; they shall mount up with wings as eagles; they shall run, and not be weary; and they shall walk and not faint."

I'd memorized that in Sunday school the year before.

But Bertha hadn't made the team. And, when we took our seats, the pastor was in the middle of telling the congregation that the downstairs men's room was closed until further notice.

"We have, it seems, a leaky commode." Then—in a subject change that gave us all sore necks—he lifted his hands in the air, a full smile on his face, and declared, "Today we celebrate!"

I didn't know why, but it made me want to catch the giggles all over again.

forty-one

BERTHA

Chip's Mercury was in Uncle Matthew's driveway when we got home from church, and I didn't know if Flo was happier to see him or the books he'd brought her from home. She ran to him, wrapping her arms around him and the bag at the same time.

It was probably a tie.

Peg made her way to me, saying, "There she is," and giving me a giant smile. She linked arms with me like we were old girlfriends. "I can't wait to hear all about yesterday."

Oh boy. They hadn't heard.

"We tried to make it for church," Chip said, shaking hands with Dad first and then Uncle Matthew. "But we had a flat before we even got to Lafontaine."

"Charles changed the tire all by himself," Peggy said.

How sweet of her to be so impressed.

"Well, you're here now and I'm glad," Mam said, going up on her tiptoes to kiss Chip on the cheek. "I think you're an inch taller than you were a week ago."

"Oh, I don't know about that," he said.

But he stood a little straighter after she said that.

"Well, I need to get dinner on." Mam headed toward the front door. "Girls, I'll have you set the table, if you would please."

"Hold on, Bertha," Chip said, crossing his arms and leaning back against the side of the house.

I waited until everybody else was inside.

"What's up?" I asked, shoving my hands into the pockets of my coat.

"How did it go yesterday?"

His eyes were bright, brows raised, smile big. He expected good news.

I wrinkled my nose and grimaced. I didn't have any good news to give.

"Ah. Too bad." He winced. "Maybe next year?"

"Oh, I don't know." I lifted one shoulder in a shrug.

"What do you mean, you don't know?" He pushed off the side of the house. "You gave it one try. Just one. You ought to go in there and ask Dad how many times he sent in a manuscript before it got accepted. I can tell you this, it wasn't just once."

"I know."

"Remember that box he used to have in the old apartment?"

I did. It was an ancient wooden cube that we always pretended was an old treasure chest full of gold doubloons. Chip and I had harangued Dad for years to let us see what was inside and he always put us off. When he finally gave in, we'd been disappointed that it was just full of paper. One hundred forty-seven pieces of paper, to be exact. Each one a rejection. Most were from magazines, others from agents, and then there were a bunch from editors who weren't interested in his first novel.

We knew there were one hundred forty-seven because we'd counted them.

Dad had called them his collection of battle wounds and badges of honor.

When we asked which of the letters were wounds and which badges, he'd told us they were the same thing.

"What did he say about those rejections?" Chip asked, crossing his arms.

When I didn't answer right away, he nudged me and said my name.

"That they forced him to get better," I muttered.

"And?"

"That they gave him a chance to try again," I mumbled.

"So get better and try again," he said in his kindest voice. "But, whatever you do, don't give up so easy."

He turned on his heel and went inside, declaring once through the door that, "Something smells good!"

I stayed on the porch another minute or two, thinking about what Chip had said.

Somehow, I had to get better. I'd find a sandlot in Bear Run and beg the boys to let me play. Maybe the high school had a girls' softball club I could join. If they didn't, maybe I'd just have to start one.

If worst came to worst, I'd have to get Dad and Uncle Matthew to play catch with me in the backyard.

One way or another, I'd get better. Then I would try again.

I wouldn't give up.

Not ever.

Well, maybe I'd give up when I was too old and feeble to play. But I figured I had plenty of years before that happened.

I pulled the screen door open for myself, once again following in my brother's footsteps.

Get better and try again. Don't give up.

Doggone if he wasn't right.

Drat.

I hated it when Chip was right.

forty-two

FLOSSIE

When Peggy and Chippy first started going steady, I'd wish on every first star of the night that they'd break it off. When I'd told Bertha that, she'd laughed and then told me that I wasn't very nice.

Well, it wasn't my job to be nice.

All my wishing came to nothing, though, because they stuck it out and ended up getting married. The only reason I wasn't frowning in any of the wedding pictures was because Bertha had promised to give me a nickel for every time I smiled and there was a cute little teddy bear at Richmond's Department Store that I'd been saving up for.

I'd smiled enough to get the bear and a green gingham bow tie for around his neck.

I named him Kenneth.

When we left Bonaventure Park, I decided that I was too old to bring that bear with me, so he stayed on my bed to be packed by the movers.

I hadn't told anyone, but I missed him.

So, when Peggy pulled Kenneth out of her purse, I decided that, despite all her flaws, my sister-in-law was peachy keen.

They hadn't brought us too much. Mostly things that Mam was worried would get broken if left to the movers.

"I can't be sure they'll take good care of my dishes," she'd said when giving Chippy a list of things to bring over the phone a few

218

days before. "And your father would like William Shakespeare, please."

William Shakespeare had lived on the shelf in Dad's writing shed for years. Well, it was just an old plaster bust of him. Mam had gotten it at a church bazaar for a good price because one of his earlobes was missing.

Dad claimed that he did his very best writing under the supervision of Mr. Shakespeare, and I wondered if that was why he'd spent more time staring at his typewriter the last week or so than typing on it.

After lunch while us ladies put away the leftovers and did up the dishes, the men lugged boxes in from Chippy's car. Most of it they took down to the cellar where it would stay until we found a place of our own.

William Shakespeare went directly to the room where Dad had set up his typewriter.

I followed behind him, peeking in to watch him place the bust on the shelf under the window, angling Shakespeare so as to hide his broken ear.

Then he plopped down into his chair behind the card table he was using as a desk and pulled a stack of envelopes from his jacket pocket, opening them one by one. Once done reading them, he put them to the side of his typewriter.

One of them, though, took him longer to read. Either that or he read it a couple of times. He rubbed his forehead and sighed a bunch. Finally he took off his glasses and rested his head on the table until Mam called him to come have his dessert.

I hopped across the hall and into the bathroom, closing the door. I counted to thirty before leaving and sneaking back to his makeshift office where he'd left the letter—folded up and back in its envelope—in front of the typewriter.

It was from Mr. McClinton, the smarmy man.

It was none of my business, but I read the letter anyway.

"There you are," Chippy said from the doorway. "Come on. It's time for dessert."

"Oh." I jumped and dropped the letter.

"What are you doing?" He stepped into the room. "You aren't reading Dad's mail, are you?"

It was no good trying to lie to Chippy, so I didn't even try. I just held the letter out for him to read too.

He did, his smile dropping instantly.

"Loyalty doesn't count for anything anymore," he muttered. Then he handed it to me and said, "Put it back where you found it."

"Shouldn't we tell Mam?" I asked.

"That's not our job, kiddo." He fiddled with his wedding ring, turning it round and round on his finger. "Leave that up to Dad. Got it?"

"Yes."

"Promise me that you won't tell anybody about that." He nodded at the letter. "Promise me, Flossie."

"Okay." I swallowed. "I promise."

I fit the paper back into the envelope and set it where it had been. Chippy nodded at me once before taking me by the hand and leading me to the dining room.

"Found her," he said, all the charm he could muster in his voice. "I think I deserve a reward."

"Being a good brother is reward enough," Peggy said, winking at me.

Dad didn't touch his cake.

After Chippy and Peggy left for the long drive back to Bonaventure Park, I was down in the dumps. And when I was feeling blue, nothing cheered me up as much as sneaking a little bit of something sweet. It was my lucky day because I knew for a fact that there was still nearly half a cake leftover in the kitchen.

I, of course, didn't plan on eating all of it.

I could have, but I wouldn't.

That was too risky, and I did not need to get in trouble with Mam.

Just the smallest little bit. That was all I'd need. Enough to taste but not so much that anyone would miss it.

I waited until Dad had turned on the radio and Mam had picked up a piece of needlework she'd wanted to get to before I made my sneaky entrance to the kitchen.

But, drat! I was foiled! Just when I was tiptoeing my way into the kitchen, Uncle Matthew was making his way out the back door, a crate of glass bottles in hand.

"Oh," he said, eyes wide.

"Uh," I answered, returning his look.

"I was just . . ." He looked at the crate.

"What's that?" I asked, crossing the room.

"It's, well," he stammered. "It's alcohol."

"You drink booze?"

I added a little gasp at the end of the sentence so that he'd know how scandalized I was.

"Not much." Then he scowled. "I am an adult, you know."

I frowned at him.

"Why are you taking it outside?" I asked.

"So nobody gets into it."

I dropped my mouth open. Did he think that *I* was going to sneak it?

All I ever wanted to sneak was some cake. That was it. I was just about to tell him that, but Mam came in, embroidery hoop in hand. She glanced down at the crate Uncle Matthew still had and sighed like she'd never been so relieved in her life.

"Oh, Matthew," she said. "Thank you."

He nodded once before ducking out the back door.

McClinton Literary Agency
To: William S. Harding, author

Dear Mr. Wm. Harding,

We regret to inform you that Paramour
Productions has canceled the contract to adapt
your novel This Working-Day World into a full-
length feature film. In their communications
with us, they cited the morality clause of
the contract in which it states that the
signee (William S. Harding) shall not engage
in activities, public or private, that could
impact the reputation of Paramour Productions
and their partners.

According to them, your alleged involvement
in the Communist Party disqualifies you from
working with them.

As such, the full amount agreed on in regard
to payment will not be made.

Your publisher, Relf and Morten, retains the
subsidiary rights.

It is with regret that we also inform you
that, due to recent allegations against you,
the McClinton Literary Agency has chosen to
part ways with you professionally. You are,
essentially, no longer our client and are free
to find another agency to handle your literary
endeavors.

The appropriate paperwork dissolving our
working relationship will be forthcoming.

Thank you for being a loyal client for all
of these years.

With great regard,

Mr. Roger McClinton

P.S. Will. I'm sorry about this. I truly am. Business is business, though. I've enclosed an article from The Publishers' Weekly News about this unfortunate development.

This isn't the end of your career. Just a bend in the road. Best luck.—R

The Publishers' Weekly News
Wm. HARDING: NEWEST ADDITION
TO THE BLACKLIST

Bestselling novelist William S. Harding's novel *This Working-Day World* had been optioned for film production with a projected release date in late 1953. Producers were reportedly eyeing such Hollywood stars as James Stewart and Lauren Bacall to headline the cast.

However, according to an industry insider who asked to remain unnamed, the contract between Paramour Productions and Mr. Harding is to be canceled.

Neither Mr. Harding nor his literary agent, Mr. Roger McClinton, could be reached for comment.

forty-three

BERTHA

Monday morning was the start of the Harding girls getting back to life as normal. Only in a different town up north and at a school where we didn't know anybody. Well, I didn't know anyone. Flossie had the little girl next door for a dear, devoted friend.

Lucky ducky.

Mam fed us a stick-to-your-ribs breakfast of eggs, sausage, toast, tomato slices, and baked beans—"The very thing the queen eats every morning," she'd claimed—and made sure we looked mostly presentable before sending us off to wait for the school bus.

"Bertha, love," she called after me just before I pushed open the screen door. "May I have a word?"

Flossie pursed her lips into a tight little "oh" and used her sing-song voice to say, "Someone's in trouble," so quietly that Mam wouldn't hear it. Good thing she scurried her little self out the door, otherwise I would have given her a little shove.

Facing Mam, I took a breath and held it. She'd hardly said anything to me since I got back from Workington late Saturday night, and I just knew she was upset with me.

I couldn't blame her, really.

"I know you're disappointed," she said, standing with her hip against the edge of the counter. "About the tryouts, I mean."

"I guess so," I answered.

I glanced out the door to see if the bus was coming. It wasn't. Flossie and her friend stood together at the end of the neighbor's driveway, both of them looking at a book that the other girl held in her hands.

"I know it's scary, starting over," Mam said. "But maybe you'll make a friend or two."

"Maybe."

The bus chugged its way down toward our road and slowed for the turn.

"Bertha," she said.

"Yeah?" I glanced back at her.

It wasn't usual for Mam to have heavy-looking, dark bags under her eyes or for the rest of her face to seem so pale. Even the pink she always had in her lips was faded. I was just about to ask if she felt all right, but before I could, she smiled.

"You best be off," she said.

My first few days at Bear Run High didn't necessarily go to plan. For one, I had a heck of a time trying to work the combination on my locker and no one seemed especially interested in helping me find all of my classes.

On the third day I was frantically trying to read *Walden* so I could write a five-page report on it that was due in American Literature on Friday. The teacher hadn't had a lick of sympathy for me, a transfer student, who hadn't had the last month to do the assigned reading.

The fourth day was a slog, I was so exhausted from staying up all night reading Thoreau's thoughts about his life as a hermit in the woods.

Then, on Friday, I was in what Dad called a "mood most foul" because the literature teacher wouldn't accept my paper because I'd typed it instead of writing it by hand.

Had I been Flossie I would have screamed before collapsing in a heap of melodrama on the floor.

Instead I'd asked for a pass to the ladies' room and saved my tears for once I was locked in a stall.

Making new friends was the very furthest thing from my mind.

What was the closest thing?

How much I missed Bonaventure Park and playing baseball on the sandlot with the boys. I missed my room back home even if I'd had to share with my kid sister. I wished that everything would go back to the way it had been before.

But I knew that would never happen, and that made my stomach ache.

Most of all, though, I worried that Leo had given up on me. I hadn't heard from him in too long.

forty-four

FLOSSIE

My first week and a half at my new school had gone better than I could have expected. Sure, I only had one friend. But with a friend like Lizzie, who needed anybody else? I didn't even mind too much that she was better at math than I was.

She, at least, wasn't a show-off about it.

I'd kept my nose clean for eight whole days of school and didn't get in trouble once.

Well, that streak broke on the Thursday of my second week when the teacher—his name was Mr. Hinkley—wrote on the chalkboard that the United States had never lost a war.

Well, I couldn't help myself. I stuck my hand in the air and told him that his fact was erroneous.

I was proud that I'd thought of using that particular two-dollar word.

He scowled at me like he wanted me to be quiet, but I charged on, explaining that America hadn't, as a matter of fact, won the War of 1812. Nobody had. That was what Dad had told me, and he was always right about such things.

One thing led to another and I ended up sitting with my nose in the corner for being "a disrespectful girl" and had to stay inside during recess to write "I will not question my teacher's authority" a hundred times.

When I got home that afternoon, I hid in the pantry and bawled my eyes out beside the shelf of maple syrup. On any normal day I might have twisted the cap off one of those bottles and taken a swig or two. But that day I was as down in the dumps as I'd ever been.

I was too out of sorts for all that sugar.

I couldn't even enjoy the simple pleasures of life anymore!

Just the thought of that made me start crying even harder than I already was. When no one found me in my despair, I wailed just a little bit louder in case they were looking for me.

Thank goodness it only took me boo-hooing a couple of times before Mam opened the door.

"What in heaven's name?" she said, reaching up and pulling the cord to turn on the overhead bulb. "Flo, whatever is the matter?"

"I miss Chippy, Dad got fired by his agent, everybody thinks we're Communists, and I got in a teeny-tiny little bit of trouble at school," I sobbed. "Besides, I feel sorry for Bertha because she's not good enough to be a Sweet Pea!"

"Oh, dearie me." Mam shut the door behind her. "Life has its many burdens, doesn't it?"

I rubbed my eyes.

She lifted the hem of her apron and wiped my face.

"We are descended from Vikings," she whispered. "Did I ever tell you that?"

I shook my head.

"Would you like to hear about it?"

I nodded.

"Your father's the storyteller. Still, I'll give it a go if you won't expect too much of me."

"All right." I sniffled.

"A thousand years ago and a little bit more, the Danes invaded Northumbria."

I thought that was a good start and climbed up on the stepping stool in the corner of the pantry to listen.

"They crashed into the shores in their *langskips*—that's Norse for battle ships—and roared their way into every village they came to, demanding fealty or else promising sure and fierce death."

"Is this a scary story?" I asked.

229

"Nay, lass." Then, after considering, "I'll leave out the scary bits."

"Thank you."

"You're welcome." She reached up and straightened a bottle of syrup. "The story your nan told me when I was young was of a boy by the name of Bran—he would be your extremely, very-great-grandfather. Now, Bran was taken during one of the raids, carried off by the Vikings. They made him a slave, putting him to labor on a ship."

"What happened to the rest of his family?" I asked.

"I said that I'd leave out the scary stuff."

"Oh."

I tried not to let my imagination fill in what Mam didn't say.

"Now, Bran was a strong lad, he was," she said. "But he was just as smart as he was brawny. He'd work himself bone-tired all the day long and at night lay upon his pallet, the wide and starry sky above him as he devised a means of escape."

Mam went on a little longer than she needed to, telling me what kind of work the Vikings had Bran do—swabbing the deck, tossing the gunk out of the chamber pots, and so on and so forth. Dad never got lost talking about unimportant details like that when he told a story.

I didn't tell her that, though. I wouldn't have wanted to hurt her feelings. Besides, I wanted to find out if Bran ever figured out how to get free of the Vikings.

"Along with Bran, the Viking earl had carted off a young girl from another village. Each day, no matter if clear or stormy, whether the work be hard or light, the lass sang her heart out, songs of fair days and easy loads," Mam went on. "One day, Bran asked her how she could sing under such a burden as slavery. She smiled at him and said 'twas all that kept her alive."

"What was her name?" I asked.

Mam frowned and knit her brows.

"I don't know. Is it important?"

"Of course it is."

I didn't say that Dad always named every character no matter how important or unimportant they were.

"Hm. Well, I don't know it."

"You can make one up," I said.

"No. I don't think I can." She sighed. "Anyway, the girl told Bran that, though her life was hardscrabble, there was yet good in it, if only she could strain to see it."

I looked at Mam. She looked at me. I waited for her to finish the story. She didn't say another word.

"And then . . ." I said.

"Oh, I forgot," she said. "The end."

"That's not the end of the story."

"Yes, 'tis."

"But you didn't get to the part where he found a lifeboat and stole it off the side of the ship and paddled his way back to England to find his family," I said. "You have to let him win."

"Ah, I see." She put a finger to her right temple. "He didn't gain his freedom, though."

"No, no, no. Mam, you have to let the hero win. That's how stories work."

"I'm afraid not."

"Dad always lets the good guys win."

"Maybe in the stories he tells *you*," Mam said. "But not in all of the ones he writes."

I crossed my arms. "So, Bran didn't end up a free man?"

"I'm sorry, no."

"Did he at least fall in love with the girl who doesn't have a name?"

"Again, no." She put up her finger. "Even if he had been freed and made his way home, he wouldn't have found his family. They were long dead. The Vikings had seen to that."

"Mam," I whined.

"Oh, that was the scary bit I'd left out before." She bit her thumbnail. "Ah. He did sire a child with the Viking earl's daughter which, as it turned out, didn't exactly please the earl."

I tilted my head.

"Then Bran died," she said. "Dear me, I'm not good at this."

She wasn't. But I was glad she'd figured it out so I wouldn't have to be the one to say it.

"The point is," she said, "every living soul finds difficulty from time to time. Some of it light, some of it too heavy to bear. And sometimes we don't understand the ways of God through our suffering, but we have little more to do under the weight than trust that we don't carry it alone."

She bit her bottom lip.

"Flossie, my love, you carry none of this by yourself," she said. "We all have our portion of the burden, but God has the lion's share. Trust that, dear heart. I pray you'll come to trust it."

Even in the dim light of the pantry, I could see how tired Mam looked, like she hadn't had a full night's sleep in a very long time.

"How about you and me have a cuppa?" She offered me her hand. "Then you can help me get supper around."

I let her lead me out into the kitchen. She let me have an extra butter cookie with my tea, so when she asked me to peel the potatoes, I didn't put up a fuss.

At supper I sat beside Dad, watching as he spread mustard on a slice of rye and then dropped it onto the cuts of leftover Easter ham.

"Did you know that I'm descended from Vikings?" I whispered to him.

"Ah, your mother told you the story of Bran, did she?" he asked.

"Yes." I leaned closer to him. "Is it a true story?"

"Aren't all stories?"

"You know what I mean." I wrinkled my nose at him. "Was Bran real? Did all of it really happen?"

"I don't know." He used the mustard knife to cut his sandwich in half. "But it doesn't have to be real to be a good story."

"It's not a good story."

"You don't think so?" he asked.

"No. It doesn't even have a happy ending."

"Many of the best stories don't, Flossie."

"Like *Of Mice and Men*?" I said.

He touched the tip of his nose and said, "Bingo," leaving a dot of mustard behind.

Part Four

The lie of the American dream—the lie we all bought at some point or another—was that we were masters of our own fate.

Work hard, mind your manners, help old ladies cross the road, eat your spinach, say your prayers. That's the way to win the day, get the girl, earn your ride into the sunset.

What we didn't know was that we couldn't strong-arm the American dream into coming true. We mastered nothing. Not one blessed thing.

From *The Thousand Natural Shocks: A Novel of America* by William S. Harding

forty-five

BERTHA

In the years following Dottie's abrupt departure from baseball, there were dozens and dozens of articles in the local newspapers. Speculation about where she'd gone, interviews with former teammates, stories that added to the myth that she had become.

I'd read every single one of them.

They were each preserved in a scrapbook that the movers had brought with all of our other things—dressers and boxes of books and various housewares—over the weekend.

One of the stories that I liked most was about the time when a fan from the other team started to heckle her. He'd yell whenever she wound up to pitch, saying that she had bad form or that she didn't know what she was doing and that she was all around horrible at baseball.

Somehow he didn't rattle her for seven whole innings.

But it was during the eighth, when he yelled something at Mickey McRae—third base for the Peas—saying that she ought to quit playing ball and pursue a barefoot and pregnant life that Dottie had finally had enough.

She dropped the ball, threw off her glove, and walked off the field. She climbed the chain-link fence between the diamond and the grandstand and told the fellas sitting next to him that they'd better scram.

Then, as the story went, she sat down, crossed her legs at the ankles like she'd learned in the etiquette classes the league had made all the girls attend, and asked him what made him think that he could talk to a lady that way.

What a gal.

Dottie had been fined five dollars for what the team owner had called "a stunt." The entire team—including JuJu, the chaperone, and the bus driver—split the fine so they'd all contribute a quarter.

At the very bottom of that story was a quote from JuJu Eames.

"Everything we do," it read, "we do as a team. That's the Workington way."

I'd decided to take the long way home from school that day. So, instead of riding the bus, I found a trail that took me through the woods, past a little creek, and over a set of train tracks. I was no Girl Scout—a fact I was reminded of whenever I tried to figure out which way was north or which green leafy thing was poison ivy—but I did enjoy walking in the forest every once in a while. If nothing else, it was quiet.

Along the trail were all of these little white flowers that looked almost like daisies. They had little yellow centers and pretty petals. But even I knew it was a little too early in the year for daisies.

I picked a handful of them for Mam and made my way back to Uncle Matthew's house.

A green Chevy was parked in the driveway, and a man I'd never seen before sat on the front porch.

"Hello?" I said, hesitating before making my way up the walk.

He stood when he saw me and took off his cap.

Maybe, I thought, he was one of Uncle Matthew's friends.

Then I thought again. Uncle Matthew didn't have friends. Or did he?

"I'm Tony," he said. "I'm a bus driver."

"Oh," I said, making my way to the porch. "If this is about me not taking the bus home from school, I'm sorry. I didn't know I'd get in trouble."

"I'm not *that* kind of bus driver." He laughed. Then he pointed at the flowers in my fist. "Those for me? You shouldn't have."

"I, uh," I stammered.

"Just kidding," he said. "I know those aren't for me. Sometimes people have a hard time getting my jokes."

"Ah." I nodded and tried for a laugh. "Ha."

"That's generous of you." He nodded toward the door. "Say, Dottie's inside talking to your folks."

"Who is?" I asked. "Oh. This a joke."

"It is not."

"Then who's here with my parents?"

"Dottie. You know. Dottie Fitzgerald." He swatted a bug from in front of his face. "From the Sweet Peas."

"Why's she here?" I asked.

"Well, she's here to get you."

I gasped—Flossie would have been so impressed—and put a hand to my forehead.

"Surprised?" he asked.

"Uh-huh" was all I could eke out.

Then I rushed up the porch steps and into the house, tiny white flowers still clenched in my hand.

There in the living room, sitting on one end of the blue couch with my parents on the other end, was Dottie Fitzgerald. Mam had been in the middle of saying something but stopped. All three of them looked up at me.

Dad and Dottie smiled.

"Hey there, doll face," Dottie said. "You sure grew up, didn't ya?"

I nodded.

"Ah," Dad said. "You found some bloodroot."

"I what?" I asked.

He pointed at my hand.

"They're for Mam," I said, crossing the room and handing them to my mother.

"How sweet. Thank you," she said, getting up. "I'll get them in some water. William, don't you have work to do?"

"Right," Dad said, standing and nodding at Dottie.

When he passed by me, he squeezed my hand and gave me a wink.

Once they were out of the room, I put both hands on my hips then crossed my arms then tried to find the pockets of my skirt only to remember that this one didn't have any. I sighed and cleared my throat and cracked my knuckles.

"Have a seat, would ya," Dottie said. "You're making me nervous."

I sat on the other end of the couch.

"I met Flo just a little bit ago." She grinned. "Quite a character, that one. Just how I imagined her from your letters."

"I didn't know you got them," I said.

"Yeah, I did." She folded her hands in her lap. "Sorry I stopped writing back. I didn't know how to tell you."

She inched up the hem of her long skirt so I could see the braces on either sides of her knees, running all the way down to her ankles.

"Kind of hard to slide into home with these things on," she said, knocking on the leather strap that went around her right calf.

I didn't have to ask to know what happened. I'd been in school with a handful of kids with braces just like those. Polio was a nightmare.

"I'm so sorry," I whispered.

"You didn't give it to me, did ya?" She laughed. "Don't worry, honey, it doesn't bother me like it used to. Sure I get mad some days when I can't get around by myself. But I've made my peace with it, I guess."

"I can't imagine anything worse."

"I can." She smiled. "I'm still alive and kicking. Well, maybe not kicking so much anymore."

"But you can't play baseball."

"Baseball isn't life, Bert," she said. "It's part of it. A darn good part of it. But it's not all there is to live for."

In the quiet that lasted between us for the next few moments I heard the slow clacking of Dad's typewriter and Flossie singing up in her room. When I heard the clanking of dishes from the kitchen, I knew that Mam was preparing to serve supper.

"You've got a spot on the team if you want it," Dottie said.

"But I . . ."

"Do you want it or not?" She lifted her eyebrows.

"I didn't make the team," I said. "I wasn't good enough."

"Sure you were." Dottie lifted her hands, palms up. "We just didn't have the right position for you. Sometimes that's all it comes down to, sweetie."

I opened my mouth to ask all sorts of questions. What had made me good enough? What made them choose the other girls over me if I was so good? What position did they have in mind? Had Uncle Matthew pulled strings with JuJu Eames to make him change his mind? And on and on.

I just couldn't figure out how to get any words out of my mouth.

"Lorna threw a fit when she found out that we'd sent you home," Dottie said. "She refused to get on the field that first day of spring training. She's cornered JuJu at least once a day, making her case. She wants you on the team, honey."

"But why?" I asked.

"She said she trusts you." Dottie licked her lips. "When a pitcher can trust her catcher, babydoll, that's gold."

"She really said that?"

"She really did. I wouldn't lie." She made an X over her heart. "So, what do you think?"

"My mother . . ."

"Honey, I wouldn't ask you without getting your folks' permission first," she said. "I'm a little bit smarter than that."

I heard Mam call up the back stairs for Flossie to come help her set the table.

"Are you staying for supper?" I asked.

"That sounds nice." She narrowed her eyes. "Are you going to ride back to Workington with me and Tony?"

No one had ever told me how terrifying it was when a dream actually came true.

I peeked my head into the kitchen to see if Mam needed any help with anything just as she was handing Flossie a stack of linen napkins and a handful of spoons. She looked up at me and took in a deep breath.

"Mam," I said. "I . . ."

"Flo, be a lamb and finish up the table," she said, cutting me off. "Then go keep Miss Fitzgerald company."

Flossie rushed off, jumping at the chance to talk to someone famous, I was sure.

Mam turned and stirred the pot of soup she'd, no doubt, had simmering all afternoon.

"What made you change your mind?" I asked.

She lifted the wooden spoon out of the soup, tapping it on the edge of the pot four times.

"Did I ever tell you why I left England?" she asked, putting a lid on the soup.

"No."

"I'd been in love with a lad named Scott." She glanced at the door Flossie had just gone through. "Don't tell your sister. She'd be scandalized."

Mam flashed me a grin.

"Your secret's safe with me."

"Scott promised over and over that we'd get married one day when he'd saved up enough money to support me." She rolled her eyes. "I was a silly girl with silly dreams, and I believed his every word. The trouble was, he'd made the same promises to a girl the next village over."

"What a crumb," I said.

"Turned out that he and that other girl had to get married." She leaned back against the counter. "Do you know what I mean by that?"

"I think so," I answered.

"It broke my heart, and the only thing I could think to do was run away." She shook her head. "I didn't want you leaving home the way I did. But when Dottie was talking to us just now, I realized that you're different. You aren't running away from anything. You're running to something. And that's entirely different, isn't it?"

"I've wanted to be a Sweet Pea my whole life," I whispered.

"I know, love." She reached for me, pulling me near. "You make me so proud."

When she let me go, she reached into her apron pocket, pulling out an envelope addressed to me.

"From Leo," she said.

Dear Bert,

I know you wrote to me about how you Hardings were gone for good, but I guess I didn't believe you. Not until I seen the for sale sign in your front yard. Maybe I should stop thinking of it as your yard now. That's going to take some time to get right.

There's been a few families who have come by to look at the house. Some of them even have a couple kids. Not a one of them looks like he'd know a thing about baseball.

None of them will be close to as great as you are.

I miss you, Bertha.

Gee, it's too bad that JuJu Eames needs glasses so bad that he couldn't even see what a great player you are. He'll regret it, believe me.

Is there some ball team you can play on there? I sure would hate for you to get rusty while you wait to try out for the Sweet Peas next spring. It won't be the same as when you played with us. Course it wouldn't. But something's better than nothing.

Take care, Bert. Don't forget about me.

Love,

Leo

P.S. They started putting up posters for prom. You'll never believe it, but old Stinky Simon himself asked Violet Lancaster to be his date! She said she would! Wonders never cease, huh?

P.P.S. I wish I could ask you to the prom. We'd have a heck of a time, you and me.

——— Bear Run Cremation and Taxidermy ———

Dear Leo,

Sorry that my handwriting is so sloppy. The fact is, I'm writing this as fast as I can (it won't be a long note, that's for sure) in between packing my bags and losing my ever-loving mind over what just happened.

What happened?

Dottie Fitzgerald came all the way to Bear Run to offer me a spot on the team!

I'M GOING TO SPRING TRAINING!

You read that right, my friend. Your best girl is officially a Sweet Pea!

Sometime I'll tell you about all of it. Everything. But for now, I'll just say that you've got to find a way to come to one of my games.

Pretty please.

I'll make sure you have my address there as soon as I can. But first I have to have supper with Dottie, the bus driver named Tony, and my family.

I might be too excited to eat!

Your favorite All-American Girl,

Love from,
Bertha

P.S. If you end up deciding that you absolutely, positively have to go to prom, do me a favor, would you? Have a blast.

P.P.S. Just don't have so much fun that you forget about little old me.

243

forty-six

FLOSSIE

We were having what Mam called "London Particular" for dinner, but split pea soup by any name still smelled—and tasted—disgusting. I thought it should have been called "Mouthful of Mud."

The stuff was so thick that I could stick my spoon into the middle of it and it would stay upright, standing at attention.

But Dottie Fitzgerald said it tasted better than her mother's recipe, and Mam beamed.

"Don't you tell her I said that," Dottie said, pointing her spoon Bertha's way. "She'd twist my ear."

"I wouldn't dare," Bertha said.

"Does your mother still live in a chicken coop?" I asked.

"Florence Mable," Mam sputtered, covering her mouth with her napkin.

"Oh, golly, Dottie," Bertha said, turning red. "I'm sorry."

"I'm not sorry about it," Dottie said, winking at me. "The kid's right. I grew up poorer than a worm. As a matter of fact, my first pet was a worm because my father said that was the only kind of critter we could afford to feed."

I waited to laugh until she did because I was polite.

"That old chicken coop is long gone, though," she went on. "My folks live in a nice little place in Toledo now. My dad works at the zoo."

"What does he do there?" Dad asked.

"Feeds the worms," the man named Tony said, so straight-faced I believed him.

But then Dottie laughed again and called him a kidder.

The grown-ups talked about grown-up things like when the baseball season would start and how many games Bertha would be playing in. Or something like that. I didn't listen. I used the time when they were distracted to pick cubes of Easter Sunday ham out of my bowl and sneak them to Sully, who was smart enough to sit on the floor at my feet.

When I sat up from dropping half a dozen chunks of meat to the cat, I realized that Dottie was watching me. She put a finger to her lips as if to say that my secret was safe with her. Then she filled her spoon and lifted it in a toast before shoving it into her mouth.

I disliked that soup with every inch of myself. But I ate the rest of it, trying not to make a face with each bite I took.

Never in my life had I been inside a chicken coop. I wasn't near brave enough to be in a room full of birds for fear that they'd peck at me. But the ones I had seen didn't look big enough for a whole family to live in.

I didn't even think Mam would have been able to get a place like that clean.

Poor Dottie Fitzgerald.

I even wiped the bowl clean with my bread.

⌣

I stood on the porch, holding Sully and watching as Bertha said goodbye to Mam and Dad outside Tony's car. Mam kissed her cheek and held her hands, getting one last look at her before she left. Dad shook Tony's hand after the two of them lifted Bertha's things into the trunk.

When he hugged Bertha, he closed his eyes.

As soon as he let go of her, she glanced at me and lifted her hand in a wave. Then, almost running, she came to me and wrapped her arms around both the cat and me.

"Take care of Mam and Dad," she said. "I'm going to miss you."

"I know you will," I said.

Sully mewed, and Bertha loosened her hold on us.

"Have the very best summer, Flo," she said.

"You too." I smooshed my face into the top of Sully's head. "Don't forget about me."

She pushed her mouth all the way to one side of her face and squinted her eyes.

"How could anyone forget you?"

Was there any sister in the world half as good as mine? I wasn't sure how that was possible.

"We'll take good care of her," Dottie Fitzgerald called out the rolled-down window of the truck. "Cross my heart."

We stood on the porch until the car was out of sight, Mam, Dad, and me.

RULES OF CONDUCT FOR PLAYERS
of the WORKINGTON SWEET PEAS

1. *Players will wear feminine clothes (i.e., skirts, dresses, blouses) at all times when in public. No slacks, jeans, short pants allowed.*
2. *Hair must be kept clean, tidy, and long. Short haircuts are discouraged.*
3. *Lipstick must be worn at all times.*
4. *No smoking in public.*
5. *No drinking hard liquor at any time. Dainty alcoholic beverages permitted only after games and may only be imbibed by ladies twenty-one years of age or older.*
6. *Absolutely no coarse or foul language.*
7. *All dates must be approved by the team chaperone.*
8. *No jewelry may be worn during games or practice. No exceptions.*
9. *Players must be in their rooms (whether in hotel or host's home) no later than two hours after the end of game. On days when no game is played, curfew is strictly at midnight.*
10. *Absolutely no friends, relatives, or other guests in the team dugout at any time.*
11. *Uniform skirts may not be more than six inches higher than player's kneecap.*
12. *On travel days, players must arrive at the bus no later than thirty minutes before scheduled departure. Girls who miss the bus will be responsible for the cost of other transportation.*
13. *Absolutely no fraternizing with any member of rival teams. This includes players, coaching staff, chaperones, bus drivers, and bat girls. Friendly*

conversation is permissible but only in public spaces.

ANY GIRL WHO BREAKS THE RULES WILL BE FINED $5 FOR THE FIRST INFRACTION, $10 FOR THE SECOND, AND SUSPENDED FOR THE THIRD.
Coaches and chaperones have the authority to impose fines and suspensions at their discretion.

forty-seven

BERTHA

Tony pulled up at the entrance to Judd Field. He was going to drop Dottie and me off and then deliver my things to the house where I'd be staying.

"Thanks, sport," Dottie said to him. Then to me, "Looks like we got here just in time to catch the end of practice."

I checked my watch. It was quarter until nine at night.

"They go late, huh?" I asked.

"We go until JuJu says we're done." She shoved open her door. "You think you can help me out, doll?"

Dottie fit her arms into the crutches while I held them and only needed me to help her a little bit to get up and out of the car.

"It's the gravel that makes it tougher," she said. "Otherwise I'd be okay on my own."

"I know you would," I said.

"My darn pride." She took a deep breath. "It's hard to accept help, you know?"

"Yup." I dropped my hand from her elbow. "But you don't have to be embarrassed about it with me."

"Well, you're a gem. An absolute diamond." She winked at me. "Come on and meet the girls."

They were at the end of their second week of spring training— all the girls were circled up by home plate, looking roughed up and dirty—and it wasn't lost on me that I would be far behind them

249

the next morning. Number 15, Lucy, rolled her eyes when she saw me, like she didn't think I deserved to be there.

Maybe I didn't.

"JuJu," Dottie called. "Look who I found hitchhiking on the side of the road."

"Well, I'll be," he said, hands on his hips. "You caught yourself a catcher."

"Yes indeedy." Then she nudged me with her elbow. "Go on over and say hello to the gals, honey."

"Are you sure I should?" I said.

"Sure I'm sure." She bumped me again. "Go on. They won't bite."

Well, Lucy might.

I was sure I saw her snarl as I hustled over to join the circle.

Trixie grinned like a gator—all teeth—and waved me over to stand beside her. I stepped in between her and Mariposa Rodriquez. I'd have known her and her sister Ava anywhere. I'd been watching them in the outfield for three seasons.

"The Bird and the Butterfly," the announcer always called them.

I clenched my fists trying not to let myself act starstruck. Then I swallowed hard, trying not to feel intimidated to be standing, right there, beside the Butterfly herself.

As a matter of fact, I knew who most of those girls were. Back at home I had a program from last season that nearly all of them had signed.

"All right, girls, that's Bertha," JuJu said, nodding at me. "She'll be catching along with Viv."

"Happy to have ya, Bertha," Viv said.

"Glad to be here," I said.

"You know Lorna," JuJu said.

"Hi, sugar," Lorna said.

JuJu went around, introducing everybody. There were the other pitchers, Nancy and Iris. Then Goldie on first, Amy on second, and Mickey on third. The shortstops Ruby and Weeny. Of course Trixie and the Rodriquez sisters in the outfield.

"Last is our center fielders," JuJu said. "Astrid Jackson. And you remember Lucy Carpenter."

I nodded.

Lucy turned her face toward the dugout and spit.

When we were in Workington for practice and home games, we'd all stay with folks who lived near Judd Field. I got put together with the other rookies—Weeny, Trixie, and Lucy—at a house just a quarter mile away.

"So we can walk," Trixie said, skipping along the way.

Lucy trudged ahead of us, ball glove hanging from her fingers.

"She's not real friendly," Weeny whispered to me.

"Huh." I shrugged it off.

I wasn't eager to be friends with Lucy. That was true. But I sure didn't want to be her enemy either.

"She's real strong, though." Weeny shook her head.

"I believe that," I said. "Say, what ever happened to the other girl?"

"Oh, Uma?" Weeny made a tsk sound. "She left last week. I guess she didn't want to be away from her mother."

"That's too bad."

"Yeah. She was a pretty decent first baseman," Weeny said. "She's just a kid."

"How old is she?"

"Fifteen, I guess." She lowered her voice. "Between us, I think Lucy scared her off."

That wouldn't have surprised me in the slightest. Still, I didn't say anything. I did not want to stoke any embers against another girl. I'd seen how that went at school.

Besides, Dottie had warned me on the way from Bear Run that it was best to leave that sort of gossip alone.

"Don't get caught up in it," she'd said. "All it'll do is wreck the team from the inside."

Trixie caught up with Lucy and chatted at her the rest of the way.

"That girl," Weeny said. "Trixie? She could make friends with a hungry mountain lion."

The streetlights popped on, one by one, as we got closer to the end of the road.

Dear Dad, Mam, Flossie, and Uncle Matthew,

I made it to Workington! My first day of practice is tomorrow, bright and early—yup, even on a Saturday morning. I get to wear the catcher gear for the first time. It'll be strange to play with a set of bars on my face.

While we're in Workington we're staying with the nicest lady named Mrs. McFadden, who has been to every single Sweet Peas home game . . . and some of the ones they've played away. She's a big fan. When I first met her, she told me that she only wished she was younger when they started the All-American Girls league because she would have loved to play.

Trixie (that's one of my roommates) says she's afraid Mrs. McFadden would break a hip if she tried to slide into base now. The woman (Mrs. McFadden, not Trixie) has got to be at least eighty years old!

Mrs. McFadden puts up the rookies each year. This season there are four of us and I think we'll mostly get along. One of the girls might be a little harder to get to know than the other two, but Trixie and I have decided that we're going to be kind as can be to her.

Weeny (that's another of us rookies) said Lucy (the more difficult one) is a hard nut to crack.

But Trixie and I are determined.

Like I said, it'll be an early morning. I need to get some sleep.

Write me back, please.

With love,

Bertha

forty-eight

FLOSSIE

Saturday morning, just after breakfast, Mam and Dad left to go for a drive. There was a house for sale on the other side of town that they wanted to look at. I didn't ask to go along, and they didn't offer. Adults liked things like that. I, on the other hand, got too bored.

"You're going to be okay all by yourself?" Dad asked, keys in hand.

"Of course," I said, nodding at the crate of *Nancy Drew* books next to the couch.

They'd been Bertha's and she'd told me that I could read them while she was away playing baseball.

"All right." Dad kissed the top of my head. "Enjoy your reading."

I would. I knew it.

As soon as they were out the front door, I settled in to start reading my very first Nancy Drew mystery.

It didn't take very long before the story got a little spooky. Then, not long after that, I started to feel a little on edge. Soon enough, I was hearing creaks that I was sure had come from the servant's stairs and bumps that could only have come from the attic.

"It's just your imagination," I whispered to myself. "There's nobody here."

Then came a thunk that at first made me jump and hide my face behind the book. But when I thought about it, it sounded a lot like Sully hopping off a bed upstairs.

"Silly kitty," I said.

It was just the cat. Right?

A couple of months before, Bertha had read *Jane Eyre* in school and told me that it was about a woman who fell in love with a man only to find out that he was already married! And his wife's name was . . . oh . . . I could not remember it.

Anyway, the man—Mr. Richardson, I thought—kept his mad wife locked away in the attic.

And Jane Eyre married him anyway!

I wouldn't have thought Uncle Matthew was the kind of man to hide a mystery wife in his house somewhere.

I thought I probably should check anyway.

So I got up, putting the book on the coffee table with the greatest of care, and grabbed the nearest weapon I could find.

Just in case there was a wild woman up there, waiting for a curious girl to come along and set her free.

It was the baseball bat that Bertha had found in the cellar. Dottie had told her she wouldn't need it, the Sweet Peas had plenty to share.

I held the bat out in front of me like it was a sword and started up the stairs.

"Bertha's bat," I whispered to myself. "Bertha's baseball bat. Batty Bertha bats balls."

When I was nervous I liked to jibber jabber to myself. It calmed me.

"Batty Bertha . . . Batty Bertha lives in the attic!"

That was it! I'd figured it out. Mr. Richardson—or whatever his name was—had locked his wife Bertha in the attic. That was why my sister had told me about that strange little book. Because the other woman had her same name.

I chuckled a little bit and moved along down the hallway.

That was when I noticed that the door to Uncle Matthew's room was open an inch or two. And the clunking sound was coming

255

from in there. Clunking and a strange caterwauling that could only have come from the Sultan of Swat himself. Dumb cat.

Now, I was under strict instruction to never, never, ever go into Uncle Matthew's room. No matter what.

"We've done a good enough job invading his space as it is," Mam had said. "Leave him that room to himself, love. Don't even ask to see inside. He's one who needs his privacy."

I wanted to follow that rule. Honest to goodness I did. But I also wanted to shoo Sully out of there so he wouldn't tear Uncle Matthew's curtains to shreds or leave a very unwanted surprise under the bed.

So, I pushed the door open.

As soon as I did, Sully zoomed out, bolted down the hall, and clambered down the stairs.

Good gravy. He must have been in what Bertha always called his berserk moods.

I could have left right along with him. I should have made my way back to my book. It would have been the right thing to close the door tight first.

But, since I was already in the room, I thought I might as well look around. Just for a minute.

"I won't touch anything," I said, as if making a promise to the room itself.

Uncle Matthew's bedroom smelled like cigarette smoke and Old Spice and was just as spare and boring as the rest of the house. I very nearly lost interest. But then I saw that he had one picture stuck in the space between the glass and frame of the mirror over his dresser.

It was a picture of him wearing a very nice suit and tie, his arm around the waist of a woman.

A very pretty woman with dark, curly hair.

"I promise that I'll put it back," I whispered, grabbing the picture and turning it over.

Oh boy. Was I ever glad that I did. Because on the back was a note in neat penmanship.

"My Matthew," it read. "My heart is yours if only you will ask for it. Love, your Opal. May 25, 1937."

I clucked my tongue and put the picture back where it belonged. She could have been my auntie. Too bad.

I walked my fingers across the surface of the dresser, letting them hop over a loose penny or screw. They stopped at a flyer, the kind that people might hang up on the library corkboard. Paper clipped to the flyer was a note that asked Uncle Matthew to "Please display at Teddy's. Tx.—S."

I traced the big letters across the top of the page.

Bear Run Civic Theatre presents:
AS YOU LIKE IT

A play by William Shakespeare
Open Auditions May 10 at Huebert Play House!
All Ages Welcome (Must be able to read!).
Come prepared with a <u>memorized</u> monologue.

All ages? I was that age! And I could read. Quite well, as a matter of fact.

This was my chance. Fame at last!

forty-nine

BERTHA

On my first day of practice as a Sweet Pea, it was clear that everyone except me knew what they were doing. I would have given my left pinky finger to go back and start spring training with the rest of them.

I was always the slowest, the worst at batting practice, the one who had to ask at least two questions when JuJu gave us directions for a drill, and it never failed that I was the one who let the team down.

The first half of my second day wasn't a whole lot better.

It was as if I signed the contract and instantly lost any ability to play ball.

And every time I made a mistake or dropped a ball or anything like that, I could practically feel Lucy glaring at me.

I didn't deserve to be there. She thought so, and I was starting to believe it.

I was beginning to think Uma had been the smart one, leaving early on.

JuJu blew the whistle, calling us all over right before we were to break for lunch. I found a gap in the circle between Trixie and Lucy. Lucy took two big steps away from me as if my horrible playing was contagious.

"Pretty good this morning, girls," JuJu said. "Some of the ladies from the First Reformed Church have lunch for you in their fellowship hall. It's a couple blocks away. Be back here after and we'll work on fielding. Dismissed."

The girls started toward the gates where the bus was idling. Trixie linked her arm through mine and pulled me along.

"Don't worry, Bert," she said. "You'll get the hang of things. I just know you will."

"Harding," JuJu called.

"Oh no." I groaned. "I'm getting canned, aren't I?"

"No." Trixie made her voice deeper. "Nope. JuJu's just gonna give you a pep talk is all."

"You're sure?"

"Of course I am." Trixie let go of my arm and gave me the gentlest little shove toward JuJu.

I swallowed hard.

"You wanted to see me?" I asked.

"Let's you and me play catch." He nodded toward the outfield. "Head on out. I'll be right there."

I jogged to right field and slid my hand into my glove. With my right pointer finger I traced the petals of the daisy burned into the leather.

It wasn't a catcher's mitt. Didn't have the padding that I'd need to keep Lorna's pitches from bruising the meat of my hand. I just couldn't get myself to switch over to the one Viv offered to share with me.

Dottie said she'd come up with something to add cushion if I really insisted on wearing that one.

"You ready?" JuJu asked, jogging into the outfield.

His glove looked like it was older than he was and as if it had done some hard living over the years. I didn't doubt that it had.

He stood about the distance away from me that first base is from second—just about seventy feet—and lobbed the ball at me. It traveled in a high, slow arc that I would have had to work to miss.

259

I threw it back to him, putting a little elbow grease on it so he'd know I wasn't weak.

Then he lobbed his throw back at me.

I chucked it.

He tossed it.

The knot in my stomach loosened, and a tiny little spark took its place.

JuJu Eames didn't think I could handle it. He doubted me.

So I took a step back. For each throw he eased at me, I took another back, back, back. And for every step back, I added heat to what I sent back at him.

He tossed to me underhand. Underhand. I could have screamed. Not only that, he'd placed it so I'd have to run for it, closing the distance I'd stepped away from him.

If he was trying to tell me that he'd made a mistake bringing me all the way from Bear Run to be on the team, then he had a heck of a way of saying it. I was just about to let loose the humiliation I'd been holding back for two whole days.

I threw one more time. That one was perfect, I could tell as soon as it left my hand. Fast and straight and with just the right amount of English on it. I wondered if, when it cut through the air, it made a little *zing* sound.

The ball smacked against JuJu's glove, and he allowed just half a smile.

"There it is," he said, closing his mitt over the ball and walking toward me.

"There's what?" I asked.

"Lorna said you were a fighter." He pointed at me. "I just needed to see it for myself to believe it."

"Oh." I blinked hard. "You aren't sending me home?"

"Nope." He walked past me. "Come on. We're late for lunch."

I tried not to trot along behind him like a puppy. But his legs were so long, and I had to take two steps for each of his single strides, so it was hard to look dignified walking with him. Thank goodness the church was close so I wouldn't have to prance with him for too long.

We got to the doors, and JuJu stopped before stepping inside. He turned to me and gave me a stern look.

"You walk in there like you belong," he said. "Do you understand me?"

"Yes, sir," I mumbled.

"You're a Sweet Pea," he said. "Now and always."

He pulled the door open and nodded for me to go in first.

At the end of practice Dottie told me that I needed to try on my uniform.

"I guessed at your size," she said, leading me into the locker room. "The socks and cap are on the bench there."

"Thanks." I grabbed them and the uniform and waited for her to turn around so I could get changed.

The green of the fabric was the color of grass after a good soaking rain, and the yellow of the patch was like the center of a daisy. I stepped into the dress and pulled it up so I could slide my arms through the sleeves. It was a little big in the chest when I fit the buttons through their holes, but I thought that would allow for more movement.

Once I'd buckled the belt and pulled up the socks, the last thing to do was put on the cap. After a full day of practice my hair was a mess, and I wondered if I'd ever be able to look pretty while playing ball.

"All right," I said.

Dottie turned to see me and put one finger in the air—*wait a second*.

"I forgot," she said, pulling a tube of lipstick from her pocket. "You ever wear this stuff?"

"Not if I can help it."

"Well, I'll do it for you this time." She looked me over. "But you're gonna have to practice. Hold your lips like this."

She parted hers, and I tried doing just that.

"All right," she said once she was done. "Pretty as a picture. Go look at yourself in the mirror."

It wasn't a clear image of me. The mirror must have been around when Mr. Judd himself was born a hundred years before. It was cloudy. But what I could see was a bleary reflection of me in Sweet Pea green.

I didn't know that I'd ever looked so much like myself.

Workington Dispatch
April 26, 1952

FRESH FACES FOR THE SWEET PEAS

Justin "JuJu" Eames Gearing Up
for Best Season in Years

by Al Rogers

Spring training has sprung for our girls, the Workington Sweet Peas! Fan favorite Lorna Williams retains her position as starting pitcher even after rumor that she was being scouted out by the management of the Grand Rapids Chicks.

Thanks for sticking it out with us, Lorna!

Lorna and the rest of the Peas veterans welcome four rookies this year. Lucy "Lucky" Carpenter of Bath, Michigan, joins Astrid "Star" Jackson at center field. Cecilia "Weeny" Trigiani of Detroit will be at shortstop with Ruby "Slippers" Lennox. Trixie Martin of Sault Ste. Marie, Michigan, is in the outfield with "the Bird and the Butterfly" sisters Rodriquez. And, a late addition, "Big" Bertha Harding of Bear Run will catch with our own Viv Marlowe.

"At the start of every season I'm more and more hopeful that this will be the year for the Sweet Peas to make it to the playoffs," Justin "JuJu" Eames told me after Wednesday's training. "This year I'm looking forward to some great games."

Dottie Fitzgerald, former pitcher for Workington, said that this group of girls plays "with as much heart as you'll see anywhere."

What a group of gals!

See the schedule below for a list of Sweet Peas games at Judd Field! Come and watch them all.

And, as always, let's root, root, root for the home team!

fifty

FLOSSIE

I told Lizzie about the play auditions that Monday on the bus ride to school. Then again at recess. Once more when the teacher left the room and we were all supposed to be finishing our arithmetic work. At the end of the day she told me she would think about it.

Think about it? What was there to think about? Who in the world wouldn't want to be center stage with all eyes on her as she delivered a soliloquy written a thousand years before by the greatest playwright in the history of humanity?

When I'd asked her that, Lizzie told me that William Shakespeare hadn't lived a thousand years ago.

"He was born in 1564, Flossie," she said.

"How do you know that?" I asked.

She tapped a finger against her forehead. "It's like the Encyclopedia Britannica up there."

Oh, please.

On Tuesday, I asked her how she'd known when William Shakespeare was born, and she told me that she'd already seen three of his plays and that it had been written in the program.

"And no, Miss Flo," she said, "I haven't made up my mind about auditioning."

Wednesday and Thursday Lizzie stayed home sick and Friday she was awfully quiet on the bus, so I didn't bring it up.

I still had a lot to learn about being a friend. But one thing I knew was that I didn't like it when Lizzie was sad. Mam had told me that the word for how I felt was called empathy. As in, "Oh, love, you're finally learning a little empathy."

Over the weekend I sat on the end of my bed and tried to read a copy of *As You Like It* out of an enormous collection of Shakespeare's plays that Dad said I could borrow. I couldn't make heads, tails, arms, or legs out of any of it! I kept having to trudge myself downstairs to ask Dad what words like *bequeathed* and *pr'ythee* and *roynish* meant.

Every single time Dad pointed across the room at where he kept old Merriam-Webster.

And all of that was before I got halfway through the first act of the darn play!

I wondered if William Shakespeare really was as great as everybody seemed to think he was. After all, how good could a writer be if everything he wrote was so doggone hard to understand?

I gave up on Sunday afternoon. I lugged that oxen of a book back down to Dad and clunked it on the card table desk. That, as it turned out, wasn't such a grand idea because the flimsy old table nearly buckled under the weight.

"Whoa there," Dad said, looking up from his typewriter. "Easy."

"William Shakespeare was a lousy writer," I said, crossing my arms.

Dad glanced up at the bust of Mr. Shakespeare. "Careful. You'll hurt the old guy's feelings."

"You can't fool me." I pointed at the plaster statue. "I know that's not his real head."

What I didn't say was that, for years, Bertha had me convinced that the Harding family owned William Shakespeare's mummified skull just to give me the heebie-jeebies.

"Why do you think it's lousy?" Dad asked, pointing at the book.

"Because it's gobbledygook," I said.

He picked up the lighter from beside his empty coffee cup and fiddled with it, flipping it open and flicking the wheel to make a flame to shoot up. Then he closed it and did the whole thing all over again.

Each time, I got more and more annoyed with him and with Mr. Shakespeare.

"*As You Like It* is about . . ." He paused, thinking. "Well, it's a complex plot."

I scrunched up my face. "See what I mean? Nonsense."

"Not entirely." He dropped the lighter and made a tent with his hands, bouncing his fingertips off each other. "I suppose it all boils down to this—no one escapes difficulty. Nobody. But when it comes, we have a few choices to make. We can become angry, bitter, hard-hearted. Or we can look our troubles right in the face and decide that we won't let them steal our hope."

Dad stopped talking then. He stopped moving. The only part of him that twitched was his left brow. His eyes, though, got the closed-off, faraway look he always had when an idea took to seed in his brain.

I looked up at Mr. Shakespeare's plaster face once before grabbing his massive book off the card table and taking it back up to my room.

Then I stormed back downstairs for the dictionary.

I was going to need it.

Part Five

It's family legend that my very-great-grandmother read the tea leaves before sending her son on a ship called *Mayflower*. What she saw in the dregs at the bottom of her cup told of suffering, hardship, strife.

Still, despite her warnings, sonny-boy got on that boat.

I've never put much stock in such things as palm reading and crystal balls and tarot cards.

Poppycock and balderdash all.

I imagine, though, if it were true, if she could see the future in the pinch of broken leaves of *Camellia sinensis*, had she seen the joy and beauty that was to come along with the grief?

From *Where the Wild Thyme Blows*
by William S. Harding

fifty-one

BERTHA

Every Sweet Pea had to be on the team bus with her backside in a seat by six o'clock sharp. No exceptions. Tony was going to pull out of the parking lot at that time no matter who was missing. Even JuJu.

That meant that we all had to be up and going at five in the morning.

I'd been dreading that very early alarm all week long.

But when it rang, we rookies woke up to the smell of bacon, which took a little of the sting off. Even better, we stumbled into the kitchen to find dear Mrs. McFadden flipping pancakes.

"Good morning, girls," she said. "Get yourselves some coffee. These will be done lickety-split."

I was sure that Mrs. McFadden put something extra special in the coffee to make it taste so good. I sank down into the kitchenette chair and took long sips, sighing with gratitude each time.

Weeny about collapsed, laying her head on the table next to her coffee cup. Trixie, on the other hand, didn't seem to need the caffeine at all. She was already talking a mile a minute. She was so excited.

Then there was Lucy who, instead of pouring herself coffee, went straight to the cupboard and grabbed five plates and brought them to the table. Then she went back for the silverware and napkins. I took just one more sip of my coffee before getting up to help.

I could have been wrong, but I was pretty sure that when I caught Lucy's eye, she gave me the tiniest little hint of a smile.

The neighborhood was quiet that early in the morning, and there was only one dim streetlamp on the corner to offer us light. Mrs. McFadden had insisted on walking us to the field and linked arms with Lucy to steady herself down the porch steps and just kept holding on to her.

She slowed us down a little, but that was all right. We'd all been too nervous to wait long to leave after having our breakfast. We had plenty of time to get there.

But then she stopped in the middle of the sidewalk when we'd only made it halfway there and let go of Lucy, motioning for us all to huddle around her.

"Girls, I want to tell you something. Put down your bags and come near," she whispered. "The four of you are special."

She said that last word—special—like it was the very best thing she'd ever said.

"I've had dozens of rookies stay in my home over the years, so I know special when I see it." She met eyes with each of us before going on. "Would you think it was silly of me if I told you that I pray for the Sweet Peas?"

"Oh no. That's not silly at all," Trixie said. "I think it's wonderful."

"Thank you, dear," Mrs. McFadden said. "I prayed for you before I ever met you. And now that I know your names, I will pray for you for the rest of my life."

Weeny blinked fast a bunch of times, and I couldn't tell if that was because she was moved to tears or was still working at waking up.

"This season may be difficult." Mrs. McFadden dropped her eyes.

We all knew what she meant. We'd heard the mumblings among the other players, we'd read the articles about how, unless the

Sweet Peas had a winning season, this could be the last year for the team.

"But I believe with everything in me that God sees when we do good things in this world," she went on. "And, yes, baseball is good."

She pointed toward Judd Field.

"I've seen more joy there during hard times than I can say." She smiled. "Don't get tired of doing good, girls. There's blessing in it if we don't give up."

Trixie grabbed my hand on one side and Weeny's on the other. I took Mrs. McFadden's and she held Lucy's. Even though she curled her lip, Lucy followed along and clamped her hand on Weeny's.

"We don't give up," Trixie said.

"I'm happy to hear that." Mrs. McFadden squeezed my hand before letting go. "We'd better shake a leg. I'd hate for you girls to miss the bus."

We picked up our suitcases and duffels and purses—everything we'd need for a full week of games on the road—and headed toward the field.

When we got there, we found a parking lot full of folks from Workington, there to send us off. My watch said that it was ten till six. They all must have gotten up as early as we did. It made my heart beat a little faster.

Then it started pounding when Lorna climbed up on the front bumper of the bus and yelled, "Hey there, ladies and gents! Lookie, lookie! It's our rookies! Come on, girls, and meet your fans!"

I'd never in my life heard people cheer so loudly that early in the morning.

"What just happened?" Weeny asked, her eyes clear for the first time since we got up.

Workington Dispatch
May 9, 1952

GAME DAY AT LAST

by Al Rogers

After a long and snowy winter, it's time for our "Girls in Green" to play ball yet again! Tonight they face the Grand Rapids Chicks and tomorrow there's a doubleheader against the South Bend Blue Sox.

They'll be on the road all week, so take a day trip to cheer on the Sweet Peas as they try to best the teams in Rockford, Battle Creek, and Fort Wayne.

I'll report back about the games—all wins, we hope!

We'll see you when we come back to Workington next Saturday for our first home game of the season.

See the full season schedule on page 4.

fifty-two

FLOSSIE

Lizzie and I stood in the library side by side, looking up at the portrait of Mr. Johannes Huebert that hung on the wall. I couldn't remember ever having seen anyone with a nose that sharp before.

"I bet he could cut meat with that schnoz," I said.

"What's a schnoz?" Lizzie asked.

"A nose." I nodded at the picture. "He's got a pointy nose. Didn't you ever notice?"

"I guess not." She lifted her hand and covered her face. "I think it's a nice nose."

"But it looks like a beak." I laughed. "Don't you think he looks like a bird?"

"I'm going to find a book."

She scurried away from me.

That was one of the things I liked about Lizzie—she was serious about reading.

"Wait for me," I called after her.

Of course, I kept my voice down as much as I could. We were in the library, after all.

But Lizzie didn't wait. I might have run if the librarian hadn't just peeked out at me from behind a shelf, glaring in my direction over her reading glasses.

She, too, was serious about reading. I wasn't sure I liked her nearly as much as I did Lizzie, though.

Her eyes on me, I made a point of taking it slow down the row toward where the novels for children were kept, flashing her my best smile as I passed by.

Surprise, surprise. She smiled back.

I guess wonders never did cease.

As soon as I was out of her sight, I rushed along until I got to the chair where Lizzie sat, that old copy of *Pollyanna* held up over her face.

I grabbed *Little House on the Prairie* and waited for Lizzie to make room for me on the chair. She didn't right away, so I cleared my throat so she'd know I was there.

She just turned the page.

"What gives?" I asked, crossing my arms.

Lizzie didn't answer me.

I noticed that the red nail polish on a few of her nails was chipped.

"Are you mad at me?" I asked, reaching out and tapping her on the shoulder.

She moved the book so that it was between her face and mine like a shield.

"What in the world, Liz?" I humphed.

That was when I heard her sniffle.

"I'm not sure that I want to be your friend anymore," she said.

"Quit kidding around." I swallowed. "You are kidding. Aren't you?"

I crossed my fingers, hoping that she was.

She lowered the book to just below her eyes. They were red and watery, but they were hard too.

It was the same look I'd made—or tried to make—at the bullies who sang the Little Baby Bumpkin song to me or chased me around the playground, yelling about me being a Commie. When I'd shot that glare at them, it was because I wanted them to think they couldn't hurt me even though they already had.

"Did I do something wrong?" I asked.

"If you think Mr. Huebert had a funny nose, then what must you think of mine?"

She lowered the book so I could look at her face. I glanced at her nose. And my tummy did a flip-flop. Not because I thought her nose was ugly. That wasn't it at all.

My stomach hurt because it made me nervous to think that I could have ever said something that hurt her feelings.

"I don't think about your nose." I took a deep breath. "I used to, I guess. But then I sort of forgot."

"You forgot that I have a nose?" She narrowed her eyes.

"Well, no," I said. "I just forgot that it was different is all."

"I wish I could forget."

She said it so quietly I very nearly didn't hear it.

I knelt next to the chair, resting my hand on the arm. Had it been any ordinary moment of my life, I might have opened my mouth and let out whatever words my brain thought up first. But my being quick to talk had gotten me into enough trouble already that day.

"Be slow to talk and quick to listen," Mam was always telling me, advice I couldn't recall ever taking.

It couldn't hurt to give it a try for once.

"I wish I looked normal," Lizzie said. "And I wish that I wasn't afraid that people will think I'm ugly."

She knocked away a big, fat tear that rolled down her cheek.

"I wish I didn't have to cover my face." She swallowed. "And I wish my dad wasn't uncomfortable around me."

She buried her face in both hands and sobbed. She even got the shoulder shakes and made hiccupping sounds. I knew they were real and not just for attention because Lizzie never did anything for attention.

"Do you want me to hold your hand?" I asked.

She nodded and lowered one of her hands.

"I'm sorry that I hurt your feelings," I said.

"I know you are," she said.

"Still friends?"

"Yup."

When I got home, Laura Ingalls Wilder under my arm, Mam's jaw dropped and I worried for a minute that there was a giant toad on my head or something.

"Well, look at you, Flossie," she said, bending and tugging at the hem of my dress. "I don't think you'll be able to wear this frock anymore."

"Why?" I asked, glancing down to see much more of my leg showing than was appropriate. "Did you shrink my dress?"

Mam stood upright, eyes full of laughter and a smile to match.

"No, lass." She put both hands on my cheeks. "You grew."

"I did? When?"

"Seems like you're taller since breakfast."

"That's not possible," I said. "Is it?"

"Sure is, love," she said. "You're growing up right before my eyes."

I squared my shoulders and straightened my spine. Then I glanced down and asked, "Mam, do you think I need a bra now?"

I did not understand why that made her laugh so hard.

fifty-three

BERTHA

Mickey kneeled on the seat in front of me and Trixie, crossing her arms on the back of it and grinning down at us.

"First game, girls," she said. "How ya feeling?"

"Nervous," I said.

And at the same time, Trixie squealed, "So excited!"

"Wanna hear about my very first game?" Mickey snapped her gum. "Course you do. So, I was just fifteen and a little too big for my britches. Wasn't I, Dot?"

"Still are," Dottie said from a couple rows up. "And those britches better be covered up by a skirt once we get to Rockford."

"Yeah, yeah." Mickey rolled her eyes for Trixie's and my benefit. "Anyway, it was the first season for the league, 1943 was, and everybody was still trying to figure everything out. We was all told to put on a show for the folks. Well, I wasn't all that pretty—"

"Oh, I don't believe that," Trixie cut in. "You're awful cute now."

"Aw, you're just being nice, Trix." Mickey swatted her hand in front of her face. "I don't care about that stuff anyway. Thing was, I had to think of another way to entertain the fans other than batting my lashes or swinging my hips."

"I never told you to do that," JuJu said from his seat behind the driver.

"Well, maybe *you* didn't," Mickey called over her shoulder. Then, back to us, "Anyway, I knew if I was ever gonna make it in

277

the league, I had to figure out a way to get the fans to sit up and take notice of me."

Trixie leaned forward, eyes wide as if she was watching a movie.

"So, when it came to our first game—we was playing the Peaches, by the way—I scoped out the girl on Rockford's team that got the most attention. Hands down, it was Dottie."

"Our Dottie?" Trixie asked.

"Nah. There's lots of Dotties in the league," Mickey said. "This was Dottie Kamenshek. They called her Kammie sometimes, but that's neither here nor there. What matters is, that particular Dottie is a showman. She'd drop into the splits right in the middle of the game to catch a ball. It was amazing."

"Oh, wow," Trixie said. "Do you think she'll do that today?"

"She's not on the roster this year," Mickey said. "Anyway, she hit a triple and ended up on third base."

"You should probably also mention that it was one of the prettiest hits you've ever seen," Dottie said. "Kamenshek is the best there is."

"Yeah, yeah." Mickey sighed. "So, she gets to my base, and I says something about her being real good at playing up to the crowd. She ignored me. Acted like I wasn't even there. How do you like that?"

"What did you do?" Trixie asked, voice dreamy like she was completely entranced.

"Well, I didn't have much choice, did I?" Mickey said. "I had to show her what I was made of. I couldn't let her be the only hotshot on the field."

"Wrap it up, Mick," JuJu said. "We're almost there."

"So, next time a hit came my way, I slid my feet—one in front, one in back—and dropped myself into the splits." She nodded.

"Wow," Trixie said.

"Problem was, I got myself stuck down there and it took half the team to get me back up."

"I guess that's one way to get attention," Lucy said from the seat behind us.

At that, Mickey threw her head back and laughed.

278

JuJu waited to come into the locker room until Lorna went to give him the "all clear," letting him know we were all dressed and ready. When he did, he added one more green uniform to the bunch of us.

Dottie came in behind him, not in an official uniform but in a skirt made of the same fabric and a sweater set to match.

Viv shushed us all and shooed us to the far side of the room, nodding for us to sit on the bench.

JuJu took off his ball cap and scratched his scalp before putting it back on. He paced in front of us, hands on hips. If I hadn't been nervous before—which I had been, and how—all this going back and forth would have done the trick.

Thankfully, he stopped after half a minute and turned toward us.

"I've been thinking of what to say to you before this game," he said. "I know you all want me to give inspiring speeches like Mrs. McFadden's."

He turned toward Dottie and said, "We should've brought her along."

"You'll do fine," Dottie said, nodding him on.

He took a deep breath, pointing at us girls down the line.

"You all go out there today and play with as much heart as you have all spring training." He swallowed. "And remember, when you get on that field, you aren't girls."

"We're ladies," Trixie said, putting her fist in the air.

"Well, I was going to say you're Sweet Peas," JuJu said.

"Oh, sorry." Trixie dropped her hand.

"Let's try that again." He moved his hand in the air in front of him like he was erasing a chalkboard. "When you get on that field, you aren't girls. What are you?"

"Sweet Peas!" Trixie yelled.

"That's right," JuJu yelled back at her. "What are you?"

"Sweet Peas!" a few more girls joined in.

"Tell me again." JuJu put his arms out at his sides.

279

"Sweet Peas!"

We did this back and forth, and each time my heart beat faster as we yelled louder and louder. Each time I looked into a different set of eyes. This was my team. Each of us belonged right where we were.

Last of all, I met eyes with Lucy. She shifted her eyes away from me like I didn't even exist. Her voice was deep—nearly a growl—when she said, "Sweet Peas."

On the way out of the locker room, Lorna put her arm around my neck.

"Ready for the time of your life, sugar?" she asked.

"I'm not sure I'm up for this," I answered.

"Better get up to it." She snapped her gum. "We can't do it without you, Big Bee."

Then she grabbed my hand and ran with me out onto the diamond. With her free hand she waved over her head at the cheering fans. They may not have been our fans, but they were there for a show, and that was just what Lorna was going to give them.

"Come on, honey," she said. "Let's us show 'em what you got."

I lifted my left arm up and waved my glove in the air, glancing around at all the folks who'd come out to watch the game. Strangers every single one.

Well, that was until I got to a couple of mugs sitting smack-dab in the middle of the seats on the first-base side.

Dad and Uncle Matthew had made the trip down from Bear Run.

I dropped my hand without taking my eyes off my father, the only one in the entire place who really mattered to me just then.

He cupped his hands on either side of his mouth and yelled what I was almost certain was, "Go get 'em!"

On my way to the dugout, I traced the daisy shape imprint on my mitt.

———————— 28th Street Motel ————————
Grand Rapids, Michigan

Leo,

Our first game was a heartbreaker. The Peaches beat the Sweet Peas 4–1. I wish I could say that one run was my doing. Alas, I cannot. Credit belongs to Lucky Lucy for that one, and I'm sure she plans on being smug about it for the rest of the evening.

Unlucky me has to room with her and the two other rookies for the night.

The good to come out of the game was that my dad and uncle came to watch. I even got permission from Dottie to go out to dinner with them afterwards. Gosh, was it nice to see the two of them.

Say, how are you? Baseball season must be in full swing (ha ha) at school. You're playing, aren't you? I'm sorry I won't get to make any of your games this year. I am hoping, though, that maybe you can make a couple of mine when we play at home.

Just in case you needed it, I sent you a schedule earlier this week. Did you get it?

I'll try and write you after every game. Dad gave me a whole book of stamps while he was here. Write back to me, would ya? At the address I gave you before, care of Mrs. McFadden. I won't get them until I'm back in Workington, but I'd like to hear from you anyway.

Love and hugs,

B

fifty-four

FLOSSIE

Every year Bonaventure Park Junior High put on a production of *A Christmas Carol*. Chippy got to be Ebenezer Scrooge all of his three years, which had put some other kids' noses out of joint. It had been more than fair, though. Chippy was aces at acting. When he woke up on Christmas morning, Chippy's Scrooge cried for joy. They'd been real tears and everything.

Bertha was just on the stage crew—she hadn't even tried out for a part!

When it was finally my turn last December, I waffled over which role I wanted. For one, there was the beautiful Belle, who Scrooge had pined over. Then there'd been Mrs. Cratchit, who had a handful of lines. Or the Ghost of Christmas Past, who got to wear a white nightgown with sleeves that looked like bells.

So dramatic!

Miss Lange, though, had decided that she knew just the part for me. I hadn't been given a choice at all.

I had to play Tiny Tim.

"You're the only one in the whole school who is small enough to fit into the costume," she'd said. "Don't you feel special?"

No! I hadn't felt special.

I'd felt cheated.

What young lady wanted to play the part of a sickly little boy?

Not me, I knew that.

I'd thrown an absolute fit and Miss Lange had called home to tell Mam all about it.

Lucky for me, Dad had answered the telephone.

He always had been the more reasonable parent.

"You know," he'd said. "I just thought of something."

I was, at that moment, standing against the wall and pouting, hoping that he'd thought of a way for me to never have to go back to school.

If only I could have been so lucky..

"When I was a kid, your uncle and I went to the movies," he said. "*Peter Pan* had just come out. Do you know who played Peter?"

"No," I had grumped.

"A lady by the name of Betty." He'd slapped his hand on the arm of his chair. "What do you think of that?"

"Really?" I'd asked.

"I would not lie." He'd crossed his arms. "Flo, the part of Tiny Tim doesn't just require someone who is small of stature. The role needs someone who can really act like a sick little boy. You'll have to put a lot of work into it, honey. But I know you'll knock everybody's socks off."

I, of course, had.

Dad told me that when I hobbled on my crutch to center stage and said, "God bless us, every one!" there wasn't a dry eye in the whole theater.

Somehow I'd managed to talk Lizzie into coming with me to the play auditions. And, since she was there, I told her she may as well try out.

"What could it hurt?" I asked, handing her a pen so she could put her name on the list under mine.

She rolled her eyes before taking the pen and signing "Elizabeth Nelson" under my "Florence Mable Harding."

Then we found a few chairs against the wall to sit in while we waited for our names to be called.

Five minutes passed. Then seven. And in that time no one else passed through the theater lobby except for the janitor with his push broom.

"Excuse me, sir," I said.

"Yeah?" He looked up.

"Do you have the time?"

I felt so grown-up and sophisticated when I asked that.

He lifted his arm and shook his sleeve down so he could see his watch.

"Nine o'clock," he said. "On the dot."

"Thank you."

He nodded at me before pushing his broom across the floor and down the hall.

"What time are auditions?" Lizzie asked, dropping her hand from in front of her face.

"Ten," I answered.

"Well, no wonder nobody's here yet." She slumped her shoulders.

"I wanted to show the director how serious we are." I sat up straighter in my chair. Then I handed her a piece of paper that I'd written my monologue on. "Here. Help me practice my lines."

She held the page so I couldn't see the words.

I got out of my seat and recited my lines with all the gusto I could muster. Especially the "I do frown on thee with all my heart; And if mine eyes can wound, now let them kill thee!"

Dad had helped me memorize them, giving me an idea of the best way to say all of the words, even the ones I didn't know the meaning of.

When I finished, Lizzie clapped for me and smiled.

"You're a shoo-in," she said.

—— From the Desk of Florence Mable Harding ——

Dear Chippy,

I got a part in *As You Like It!* You have to promise that you'll come see me. Bring Peggy too ~~if you want~~ please. I just don't want you to get your hopes up, thinking that I landed the starring role. I, alas, am not Rosalind. I'm not even Phoebe or Audrey.

I am, however, a sheep. Well, me and my friend Lizzie too.

We don't have any lines. But we do get to bleat whenever we follow Audrey around.

Please say you'll come!

Everyone is okay here, I guess. We miss you and Bertha. And Peggy too.

Love,

Hopsy

Workington Dispatch
May 12, 1952

FROM DISAPPOINTMENT TO TRIUMPH!
by Al Rogers

After a few tough losses in Rockford and South Bend, our Sweet Peas tasted victory for the first time this season, upsetting the Chicks of Grand Rapids when rookie Lucy "Lucky" Carpenter hit a grand slam at the top of the ninth, putting the Peas at an advantage. Then our own Mickey McRae, not to be shown up by a freshman player, followed it up with a homer.

Grand Rapids wasn't able to get a run in the bottom of the ninth thanks to Lorna Williams's expert pitching and the skilled fielding of the Rodriquez sisters.

It's anybody's guess if they can win again when they go to Battle Creek and Fort Wayne to end their week on the road.

If they can, they'll have a better record than the Tigers for the season thus far.

Maybe we can talk Red Rolfe into letting our girls play the Detroit boys sometime. Seems our gals could teach them a thing or two.

The Sweet Peas play at Judd Field this Friday against the Kalamazoo Lassies. Come one, come all!

fifty-five

BERTHA

Amy—our second baseman—had a habit of getting ready real quick for a game so she could sit and read while the rest of the team scrambled around looking for socks and hairpins and cleats. Everybody else was frantically trying to get their lipstick on just so, and Amy would be turning pages, calm as could be, ignoring all the fuss around her.

It was exactly the kind of thing that Flossie would have done. Who could have known how much I would miss that girl?

"Why's she always doing that?" Weeny whispered to me, nodding in Amy's direction.

"What?" I asked. "Reading? Well, I guess she likes to."

"My ma always said too much reading'll burn your eyes out." She used her teeth to separate the ends of her bobby pin and stuck it into her hair.

"I don't know about that." I stepped into my uniform.

It was amazing how fast I'd grown accustomed to getting dressed in front of all those girls.

"It's true," Weeny went on, grabbing a powder compact from her bag. "Just think of everybody you know that reads all the time. They're all half-blind. They gotta wear glasses. I'm not wrong."

I glanced over at Amy just as she pushed the wire rims up her nose.

"Well, they're not getting burned out, exactly," I said.

"Uh-huh," Weeny said. "You know what I mean, though."

Amy pulled her knees up on the bench and rested the book on her thighs, and I got a glimpse at the cover. I couldn't hardly believe it. There on the dust jacket was my dad, glowering back at me.

My jaw dropped, and Amy looked up from the book.

"Hey, I've been meaning to ask you something," she said, pointing at the picture of Dad. "Any relation to you?"

"Oh, uh," I started, not entirely sure how to answer.

All the other girls talked about their families. They'd say what their dads did for work and the best meal their mothers cooked. Mickey's dad sold Fords down in Indianapolis, and Ruby's folks lived in the Smoky Mountains. Trixie lived with her grandparents, and Lucy always talked about her mother's sour cream raisin pie.

I'd told them a thing or two about Flossie—they were all eager to meet my kid sister—and my English-born mother. Both Iris and Nancy had been disappointed to find out that my handsome brother was already hitched.

But I'd kept mum about my dad.

Not because I didn't miss him. Not because I was ashamed of him.

I just didn't want to bring him up on the off chance that someone on the team had heard of him.

I wanted to be an All-American girl. I couldn't very well be that if everybody thought I was a secret Commie.

When I was growing up, I'd thought the very worst sin in the entire Bible was when Judas betrayed Jesus for a handful of coins. The second worst was when Peter had denied knowing him at all because he'd been afraid.

My father was no Jesus. Still, I thought it would be a deep and dark sin if I denied William S. Harding as my dad.

Maybe it was more important to be a good daughter than a good American.

I crossed my arms and nodded.

"Yeah," I said. "He's my dad."

Amy hopped up off the bench and I flinched, worried for a

second that she was going to haul off and punch me or yell in my face or something like that.

Instead, she stood in front of me, her eyes wide as hubcaps, and gave me a grin.

"You're not pulling my leg, are you?" she said.

"Nope."

"Neat!" She turned. "Hey, Goldie! You'll never guess."

"What?" Goldie asked, bent over to tie her shoe.

"She'll never guess," Amy said to me. "She's a big fan. I think her favorite is . . ."

She screwed up her face, thinking.

"Say," Amy called back over to Goldie. "What's your favorite Harding book?"

"Golly, I dunno," Goldie said, straightening up. "Maybe *A Strange Eventful History* or *This Working-Day World*. Why?"

"Bert's his daughter!"

"Swell." Goldie rushed over and lowered her voice. "You know, I don't believe any of what they're saying about him. No siree Bob."

"What's he like?" Amy said.

"He's nice," I said. "Real nice. And funny. He drinks so much coffee my mother's worried his heart will burst."

"What else?" Amy held the book against her chest.

"Well, he writes in a shed in our backyard . . ." I stopped myself and cleared my throat.

The two girls waited for me to go on, but I was too choked up to talk for what felt like forever.

"Aw, honey," Goldie said. "You miss him, dontcha?"

I nodded.

"Yeah, we all miss our dads, don't we, Amy?"

"Yuppers," Amy said.

"Hey, girls," Lorna yelled. "Get decent. JuJu's wanting to come in."

"Nuts," Goldie said. "I've gotta get my lips on."

She joined the rest of the girls, busy getting last-minute touches done.

That was when I noticed Lucy standing with her shoulder

resting against one of the lockers not three feet from us. She scowled at me and adjusted her ball cap.

"Good luck," I said.

"Don't need it," she said.

"I was just trying to be nice." I crossed my arms. "You don't really make it all that easy."

"Why should I?"

fifty-six

FLOSSIE

Miss Somerville—the director of the play and the high school English teacher—had told Lizzie and me that we didn't have to be at every practice. But what kind of actresses would we be if we skipped out? I would have bet five whole dollars that Doris Day never missed a single practice, and where did that get her? On the silver screen. That was where.

So, Lizzie and I stuck around, reading or playing cards in the wings until we were needed which, as it turned out, wasn't a whole lot. The play was two and a half hours long, and Audrey and her sheep were only on stage for ten or fifteen minutes of it. Still, we wanted to show how dedicated we were to our art.

Besides, Mr. Sawyer—the man who played the part of Touchstone—owned the bakery in town and always brought a whole tray of goodies for the cast during rehearsals.

The longer we stayed, the more cookies we could eat.

We were no fools, Lizzie and me.

We'd go out on stage and say "bah-bah" a handful of times and get rewarded with a treat.

And when the high school boy who played Orlando complained that there were never any chocolate chip left—we never touched the oatmeal raisin—Lizzie and I would tiptoe into a shadow so he'd never suspect it was us who'd eaten all the good ones.

By Thursday—the last rehearsal of the week—Miss Somerville gave up on trying to send us home. And, when Duke Senior didn't show up for practice, she came backstage and handed me a script.

"I need you to read his lines," she said.

Well, I didn't hesitate for a second. I rushed out to the center of the stage, perched on the fake boulder where Duke Senior delivered his lines from, and took a deep breath.

At the top of my lungs, I yelled the first lines of the speech. "Now, my co-mates and brothers in excelsior—"

"It's supposed to be 'exile,'" one of the foresters said.

"I know that," I sneered.

"Just skip ahead," Miss Somerville said, rushing to me on the stage and putting her finger halfway down the speech. "Start there."

"Okay," I said, sighing.

"And you don't need to yell." She wrinkled her nose. "We can hear you fine."

I looked down at the lines, remembering how Dad had told me what they meant, sentence by sentence. Word by word.

The script shook a little in my hands, but I willed myself to say the lines with a steady voice.

"Sweet are the uses of adversity . . ."

"That means," Dad had said, *"that life gets difficult sometimes. It knocks you down. But that's not an altogether bad thing."*

"Which, like the toad, ugly and venomous, wears yet a precious jewel in its head."

"Some people used to believe that toads had gems in their heads," Dad had told me. *"And that they had the magical power to heal sick people."*

"And this our life, exempt from public haunt, finds tongues in trees, books in the running brooks, sermons in stones . . ."

"Now that we're away from the hustle and bustle, we have the time to learn from the world around us."

"And good in everything."

"There's always a silver lining." Dad had said that with a smile.

"I would not change it."

By the end of the speech, I'd somehow climbed up the boulder so I was standing on top of it, both hands over my head in victory.

I half expected a standing ovation for my performance.

Instead, all I got were confused looks from the men who played the roles of loyal subjects to the duke. That and the guy closest to me—the man who was playing Amiens—had stuck a finger in his ear, moving it around like he'd heard a very loud boom.

"Happy is your Grace," he said, "that can translate the stubbornness of fortune into so *quiet* and sweet a style."

"Come," I said, reading my script. "Shall we go and kill us venison?"

As a rule, I didn't go into the pole barn behind Uncle Matthew's house. The first reason was that it was dark. What little light did leak in through the gaps in the panels made scary-looking shadows. Secondly, Uncle Matthew had told me that mice lived in the loft and that one had fallen on his head one time when he was out there. I did *not* want that to happen to me ever, ever, ever. And thirdly, it smelled funny out there, and I had a sensitive sniffer.

Strong odors made me sneeze.

Dad, however, had no such qualms—that, by the way, was one of the words on the list for the school spelling bee I intended to win later in the spring. He'd been writing out there all week long because that was where the movers had put his desk. He'd even relocated Shakespeare's head, saying he didn't want "Old Bill" to miss him while he was working.

According to Dad, he'd gotten more writing done in that old barn in a handful of days than he'd accomplished since we arrived in Bear Run.

So, when Mam wasn't adequately impressed with my retelling of the performance I gave that afternoon during play practice—a distracted "that's nice, love" was the best I could get out of her—I decided to tell Dad instead.

Before leaving the kitchen, though, I waited until Mam's back was turned and grabbed a couple bottles of Coke to take with me.

He'd dragged his desk to be directly under the one hanging light-bulb in the whole building. Mam worried that it wasn't enough light for him and that he'd hurt his eyes. Dad, though, said it was just right.

Dad wasn't typing when I got to the barn. Instead, he was leaned forward in his chair, elbows resting on his thighs, something that looked like a postcard in his hand.

I opened my mouth to announce my presence, but then shut it quick when Dad used his thumb knuckle to wipe under his eye. Mam would have wanted me to turn around and let him have some time to himself. She'd told me before that men wanted to be left alone when they were sad. Even if that was true, my gut told me to go to Dad anyway.

Phooey on what he might have wanted. Being alone wasn't what he needed, I was sure of it.

So, I opened my mouth to offer some comforting words.

Unfortunately, what came out was, "Are you crying?"

He glanced at me and made a grunting sound that I thought was supposed to be a laugh.

"No," he answered.

Even in that dim old barn I could see that his eyes were red. Despite my love of the truth, I decided not to scold him for the lie.

Instead, I held out a bottle of Coke.

"For me?" he asked, putting the postcard facedown on his desk and getting up.

"I forgot a bottle opener," I said.

He patted his pockets—jacket, shirt, pants—until he found his jackknife. It took him a few tries to find the hook-shaped blade.

"Viola!" he said.

"It's voila."

"Sure." He grabbed one of the bottles, popping off the top. "Already smarter than dear old dad, huh?"

I shrugged. I couldn't argue with him.

He opened the second Coke and nodded me over to his desk.

"I'll get you a chair," he said. "That is, if you'd like to imbibe with me."

Never in a billion years would I admit to him that I had no idea what that word meant, so I just nodded and smiled before taking a sip of my pop.

Dad put his bottle on the desk—without a coaster, which Mam would have cringed at—and threw a canvas tarp off the wingback chair that used to be in our living room, pushing it across the dirt floor.

We sat in our chairs, Dad and me, and he rolled his near to me so that we were face-to-face. Then he tipped his bottle toward me, and I clinked mine against his before we both took a drink.

He made a satisfied sigh and said, "The All-American drink."

"Dad, what makes something All-American?" I asked.

"You know, I have no idea."

"Me either."

I swung my legs back and forth while I took another sip, liking the way the pop tingled when it went down my throat. Dad put his elbow on the edge of his desk and rested his chin in his hand, watching me.

"Flo, I lied to you," he said.

"I know you did," I said.

"Every man in the world cries from time to time." He bit his bottom lip. "We tend to hide when our eyes get leaky, though."

"Why?"

"Well, I guess because we're afraid."

"Of what?"

"We're afraid of people thinking that we're weak," he said.

I balanced my bottle on my knee.

"Why were you crying?" I asked.

He sighed and then grabbed the postcard off the desk. Then, when he turned it toward me, I saw that it wasn't a card, it was a picture.

"Is that him?" I asked, inching up to the edge of my seat.

"Amos," Dad said.

In the picture Dad held Amos, supporting the small head with his big hand. The two of them looked into each other's eyes, both smiling.

"He was laughing," Dad said. "All I was doing was making this *buh-buh-buh* sound, and he'd laugh like I was Bob Hope. I think we sat there for half an hour, me doing the noise and him giggling."

Dad propped the photo up against his typewriter and then grabbed a Lucky Strike from the pack on his desk. He didn't light it.

"I don't remember him," I whispered.

"You were young."

I looked down at my bottle of Coke. Half-empty. Half-full.

"I'd change it," I said.

"What's that, Flossie?" He leaned forward.

"I'd change it." I swallowed. "Duke Senior said he wouldn't change it, being exiled and betrayed."

"Why do you think he wouldn't?"

"Because all of that helped him see the good in the forest."

"That's right," he said. "I would agree with old Senior most of the time."

"You would?" I asked.

"Sure." He glanced at the unlit cigarette and tucked it back into the pack. "For instance, this whole communism thing. It wasn't fun, huh? We were in some hot water there for a little bit. I'm still not sure what's going to happen with this book I'm writing."

He thumped the stack of papers beside the typewriter with his knuckle.

"But, you know, I'm not sure I'd change it," he said.

"Why not?"

"Because it brought us here." He lifted his hands. "I went for a walk today, and although I didn't find a toad with a gem in its head, I did take a minute to listen to the way the leaves rustled in the wind and how the little creek babbled along. And I did find a stone, as big as a softball, that I'm sure is full of crystals inside. I'd have to break it to find out, though."

"Wow. Can we bust it open?"

"Maybe later, sweetheart." He cleared his throat. "Anyway, I never would have taken that walk if Mrs. Sanders hadn't said those things about me or if that angry man hadn't smashed in our windows. I saw all of the good in the woods because it was a whole lot brighter when compared to the bad."

I looked from Dad to William Shakespeare to the picture of Amos.

"Would you change what happened to Amos?" I whispered.

"Of course I would." He swallowed. "I'd do almost anything to have him back."

My bottle made a clunking sound on the edge of the desk when I set it there. The chair skidded just a little when I got up. Dad hugged me back when I put my arms around him.

The evening paper's front page had two pictures on it, side by side. One was of Mrs. Sanders wearing a pillbox hat and clutching a handbag as if her life depended on it. The other photo was of Dad at a book signing from years before.

Over those pictures the headline read:

SANDERS ADMITS: "I LIED!"
Harding Cleared of All Suspicion

Dad told Mam to stop making supper even though she'd already chopped all the carrots and potatoes for her casserole.

"We're going out," he said. "Put on your nicest dress, Lou."

She put the knife down on the cutting board when Dad pulled her to him and spun her around the kitchen while he sang "Into Each Life Some Rain Must Fall." She joined in on the part about the coming sunshine.

When Uncle Matthew peeked his head in to see what was going on, I tugged his sleeve.

"I know you can dance," I said. "Dad told me so."

He shrugged before offering me his hand with the flick of a wrist.

I counted one-two-three-four in my head so I wouldn't miss a step. Uncle Matthew, though, seemed to be able to move his feet without even giving it much thought.

That day, in that moment, when Uncle Matthew spun me around and my skirt flared at my sides, I could believe there was good in most things.

Bear Run Gazette
May 15, 1952

SANDERS ADMITS: "I LIED!"
Harding Cleared of All Suspicion

ASSOCIATED PRESS: Unlikely Communist Marjory Sanders has once again made a shocking revelation. Previously, the widowed housewife accused several of being in league with the Reds. Recently, however, she has recanted, saying that her testimony was coerced.

"My client was told that she would not face incarceration if she gave the names of others guilty of the same crime of which she was accused," Sanders's attorney, James Stephenson, said in an official statement. "She did not believe that any of those she named would suffer indictment or harm. She rattled off the first dozen names she could think of."

One of those names was bestselling, award-winning author William S. Harding, previously of Bonaventure Park, Michigan.

Mr. Harding has, according to the House Un-American Activities Committee (HUAC), been cleared of all suspicion.

"Never a doubt in my mind," said Roger McClinton, Harding's literary agent. "That's why I never wavered in my devotion. Will is, perhaps, the best American novelist of our time."

Sources close to McClinton revealed that the agency recently cut ties with Harding over the affair.

Mr. Harding could not be reached for comment.

fifty-seven

BERTHA

We'd bested the Fort Wayne Daisies. It was almost too good to be true. The short of it was that we'd gotten just one run more than they did. I thought that was a more heartbreaking loss for them than if we'd beaten them by a landslide.

The long of it was that we'd been down by five at the top of the ninth. It seemed a foregone conclusion that we were going to lose.

Weeny was first at bat, and just before she stepped up to the plate, she turned to all us girls in the dugout and made her face serious as a badger and said, "Girls, I smell a comeback."

Then, by some miracle of physics, the smallest girl on our team knocked the first pitch that came to her just beyond the reach of the outfielders, earning her a home run.

Next up was Goldie, who got a double, and then Ruby with a single. Ava struck out and Amy got a walk—which loaded up all the bases. I went next and only managed to hit a single.

When Trixie struck out, I worried that we'd never make it.

But then Lucky Lucy stomped her way to the plate and held that bat like she wanted to club the stuffing out of the ball.

That was exactly what she did. Well, the innards of the baseball didn't really come out. Still, she whacked it so far out of the park that all the kids who took off after it came back disappointed when they couldn't find it.

Lucy jogged around the bases in no hurry, like she wanted to really enjoy that moment of greatness.

She had deserved it.

When I offered her an "attagirl," she rolled her eyes.

When JuJu patted her on the back, she lowered her head and grinned as if to say, "Aw, shucks."

She was a bulldog to me, a puppy with JuJu. It just didn't make any sense to me at all.

That was neither here nor there, however, because just moments after Lucky's triumph, Astrid struck out, ending our chance of getting a better lead on the Daisies.

She dragged the end of the bat in the dirt behind her when she shuffled back to the dugout.

"I'm sorry, gals," she said. "I swear, I'll make it up to you somehow."

But JuJu, not wanting to leave anything to chance, put Ava and Mariposa—the Bird and the Butterfly—and old Lucky in the outfield. That left Astrid benched along with Trixie and Weeny.

"Lorna's pitching," JuJu said.

"Come on, Big Bee," Lorna said.

My stomach lurched. It should have been Viviane when the stakes were high as they were.

I shook my head.

"Trust me?" Lorna asked. "Grab your glove. Let's go."

I suited up, shaking so hard that I struggled with the buckle of the chest protector. Trixie and Weeny came to my rescue. Dottie came around the front of me, leaning heavily on her crutches.

"Guard home with your life," she said. "Got it, honey?"

I nodded.

Then she slid her arm out from one of her crutches and handed it to Weeny so she could reach up and cup my cheek.

"Bert?" she said. Then, with sparkling eyes and a wide smile, "Have fun, all right?"

I pulled the catcher's mask down over my face and made my way to home. All the nerves fell off as soon as I locked eyes with

301

Lorna and flashed her the signal for a fastball, inside—one finger down, then four.

The first hitter made it to second base. When the second batter was up, the first—a girl they called Squeaky—stole third. Good thing Lorna struck out that second hitter.

Squeaky stood on third base, getting ready to run when the third girl got up to bat.

The batter hit a pop-up that Amy caught, no problem.

Two outs. We were so close.

While the next hitter made her way to the plate, I met eyes with Lorna, and she winked at me.

"Ready, Bert?" she called.

"Sure am," I answered, holding up my glove.

Lorna threw a ball, then one strike, then another ball, and I knew she was trying to throw Squeaky off balance a little bit.

The batter got the fourth pitch, hitting a grounder, and took off running to first. Lorna bolted for the ball, grabbing it and lobbing it to me in what seemed like one fluid motion, like ballet.

I had to hop for it but caught it just before Squeaky, sprinting at me down the third-base line, slid into home, leg extended and cleats pointing right at my calf.

It was going to hurt.

And, gee whiz, it did.

I thought for half a second that Squeaky had broken my dog-gone leg, and I stayed on the ground, coughing on the dust the two of us had kicked up, waiting for the ump to make his call.

"Out!" he yelled.

Then all I could see was Lorna's face and all I could feel was her pulling me to my feet. She grabbed the bars on my mask and shook, yelling that we'd done it. We'd come back. We had won!

A whole line of Indiana boys had gathered in the lobby of the hotel, waiting for us Sweet Peas to get cleaned up so they could ask a few of us out for supper. Of course, Dottie went ahead of us and informed them that they'd need permission from her before escorting any of her girls for the evening.

"No funny business," she said. "And have the girls to the hotel by ten at the very latest. Understand me, boys?"

"Yes, ma'am," a couple of them answered.

I was surprised when one of the guys—a good-looking one too—stepped up to me, took the fedora off his head, and said, "What do you say, cutie pie? Have supper with me?"

"No thanks," I said. "I've got plans."

"With another fella?"

I shook my head. "I'm eating with my friends."

"Oh, I see." He winked at me. "You got a guy at home, do ya?"

"Why do you say that?"

"Well, why else would you turn down a date with me?"

"Do you think that's charming?" I asked.

"Is it?" He sidled up to me. "I think I deserve an explanation why you won't let me buy you dinner."

"She doesn't owe you one darn thing," Lucy said, glaring daggers at him. "She said no, so scram."

"What?" the guy said. "You sweet on her or something?"

"Mister, I can't stand the girl." Lucy scowled. "But what I hate more than her is a guy like you. Now get."

He put his hat back on and said, "All right, all right."

"And don't go sniffing around any of the other girls," Lucy said. "They're all too good for you."

He slunk off, leaving the hotel altogether.

"Hey, thanks," I said.

"Yeah." Lucy pulled at the waist of her skirt, straightening it out.

"You have dinner plans?" I asked. "A couple of us are going to the diner a block over."

She huffed. "Fine."

"Come on, Big Bert," Mickey called from the other side of the lobby. "You too, Lucky."

Lucy made a sound like a growl but slouched her way to the door. I stuck by her side. She'd said that she couldn't stand me

303

and that she hated me, but I still felt like I owed her a little kindness at the very least.

Mickey had a whole group of us following behind her like she was our mama duck. She didn't seem to mind at all. Lucy and I took up the rear. The other pairings chattered along the way. The two of us, however, didn't say anything.

Well, that was, until within sight of the diner.

"Your dad's a writer, huh?" she asked.

"Yeah."

"Huh." She scratched behind her ear. "That why JuJu let you on the team after all?"

"What are you saying?" I asked.

"I'm saying you got cut from the team, then all of a sudden, you get added on."

"I got this spot because that other girl quit."

"There were better players they could have called up to take Uma's place." She scrunched up her face and lifted her hands. "You don't think your rich, famous dad had anything to do with that?"

"For one, we aren't rich." I closed my eyes. "We don't even have our own house anymore, if you really need to know. And my dad's not famous. If anything, he's infamous."

"What are you talking about?" Lucy took a step closer to me.

"Not long before tryouts, my dad was accused of being a Communist," I said. "It's not true. Still, we had to move all the way across state to live with my uncle because people were threatening to burn our house down."

Lucy looked at me sideways.

"If ever my dad were to use his so-called fame to get me onto a team, it wouldn't be now, I can tell you that." I stepped closer to her. "I'm on the team because I belong here. That's it."

I met her eyes and didn't flinch, as much as I wanted to.

"I guess I just thought everything came easy for you," she said.

"Yeah, well, it hasn't."

I walked past her toward the diner, my leg still smarting from the run-in at home.

Workington Dispatch
May 16, 1952

THE SWEET PEAS COME HOME!
by Al Rogers

Boy, what a game the Peas had against the Daisies, stomping them in the very last inning. I yelled myself silly when Big Bertha stopped the efforts of Fort Wayne's Squeaky Jean at home to win the game.

No doubt Bertha's got an impressive bruise to remind her of her heroism.

I'll bet she'll even show it to you at Sunday's double-header against the Kalamazoo Lassies at Judd Field. We'll get the game started at 1:00 p.m. So, go to church, eat your roast as fast as you can, but leave some room for peanuts and Cracker Jacks.

And don't forget to wear your Sweet Pea greens so the girls will know you're there for them.

It's the Workington way!

fifty-eight

FLOSSIE

Mam was the kind of woman who believed that it was a grave sin to miss out on church for any reason. There was no snowstorm too heavy or head cold too stuffy that would keep her separated from the Sunday morning worship service. The trouble was, Dad said, if we went to church before heading to Workington, we'd be late for the game.

"It's a doubleheader," Uncle Matthew had reminded him.

That was when I learned that sometimes teams played two games back-to-back. That was eighteen entire innings of watching girls run around and swing bats.

I was going to have to pack an extra book. And an umbrella.

The rain was coming down hard that morning.

We bustled around, getting ourselves dressed and ready for church. Mam and I even packed a lunch for the four of us—Dad, Mam, Uncle Matthew, and me—to eat on the car ride.

But when Dad came down for breakfast in his usual Sunday morning clothes—just his pajamas and bathrobe—Mam threw her hands in the air.

"Why aren't you dressed?" she asked.

Uncle Matthew excused himself from the table, carrying his toast with him out of the room.

"Tell you what," Dad said. "You and Flossie ride there with

306

Matt. He'll get you there in time for Sunday school. I'll get there in time for the sermon."

"William." She sighed. "Why must you make everything so difficult?"

"Honestly, Lou, I don't know what's so difficult about it." He took his seat and waited for her to pour him his coffee.

She didn't.

She just walked out of the kitchen, shaking her head and muttering to herself.

"You should come to Sunday school," I said, pushing the baked beans Mam had served me to one side of the plate. "Do it for Mam. Please."

"Not you too," he said, picking up the morning paper.

I nodded and got up from the table.

The percolator was heavier than I'd expected it to be, and I worried that I'd spill the coffee when I went to pour a cup for Dad. But I did it without so much as a single drop getting away from me.

"Hey," Dad said, patting my arm once I'd finished. "You're better to me than you ought to be."

"I know."

Then I planted a kiss on his cheek.

The man sitting in the pew directly in front of me smelled like he'd soaked in a tub full of cologne for twelve hours. It was so strong it made my eyes sting, and whenever I took a breath during the hymns I started coughing.

Mam handed me a mint from her purse, but it didn't help. As a matter of fact, nothing did. I looked over at the window, wishing somebody'd get up and crack it open. Even just an inch.

In the middle of the sermon, I coughed again, that time nearly gagging.

"Go get a drink of water, love," Mam whispered.

She did not have to tell me twice.

There were two drinking fountains in the church building. One between the restrooms—those were the closest to the sanctuary—and one in the basement near the kitchen. That one had the coldest water, so I decided on that one.

Besides, if I went to that one, it wouldn't matter how loudly I slurped because there wouldn't be anyone around to hear me or tell me to quiet down.

The cool water felt good on my throat after all of that coughing, even if the musty air in the basement didn't do much for my cologne-itchy eyes.

I didn't hurry back upstairs but wandered just a little bit, peeking my head into the fellowship hall and the room where they kept shelves and shelves of old, dusty books by men named Wesley and Calvin.

There wasn't anything in there that interested a girl like me—not a novel in the whole bunch!—so I didn't stick around in there too long.

When I finally made my way back up the steps, I saw there was a police officer standing against the wall, hands clasped in front of him and waiting patiently. I smiled and he smiled back at me.

I walked right up to him and whispered, "If you want, you can take my seat in the back row."

"Oh, that's okay, honey," he said, his voice quiet.

"It's probably for the best." I wrinkled my nose. "The man sitting in front of me is . . ."

Then I waved a hand in front of my nose.

The policeman smiled.

"Is it Mr. Ritsema?" he asked.

I shrugged.

"Do you know Mrs. Harding by any chance?" he asked.

"Yes," I answered, perking up. "She's my mother. Would you like to meet her?"

His face got very serious. "Well, if you could point her out to me . . ."

I didn't know if it was the way the smile fell from his face so fast or if the cologne fumes were stuck in my nose, but I got dizzy all of the sudden.

"Officer," I said, "I don't feel so good."

"Why don't you sit down, honey," he said, steadying me and leading me to a chair in the corner. "You said your mother's in the back row?"

I nodded.

He stepped into the sanctuary, then right back out again, Mam following behind him. She rushed toward me.

"Are you unwell, Flo?" she asked.

"I don't know," I said.

She fanned me with her bulletin and thanked the policeman for getting her.

"Mrs. Harding?" he said.

"Yes." Mam straightened.

"I'm not here because of her." He glanced at me. "I'm afraid, ma'am . . ."

He hesitated, and Mam told him to go on.

"I'm afraid there's been an accident."

fifty-nine

BERTHA

Dottie Fitzgerald had only ever pitched one perfect game in the season she played for the Sweet Peas. I wasn't sure if it was true or not, but legend said that the game in question was on her little sister's birthday and that Dottie was in a hurry to get back home so she could see her blow out the candles on the cake.

A cake that her mother had bought with money Dottie had sent home the week before.

They were playing in South Bend, Indiana, a three-hour drive if she really got on it.

So, she'd struck out every single hitter, the ball passing by each one like they weren't even there.

She hadn't stayed for the standing ovation the Blue Sox fans gave her. She just hopped in a car she'd borrowed from one of the other players and sped away.

Later, when asked in an interview why her folks hadn't just brought the little sister to South Bend to see the game, Dottie reportedly said, "I never play so well when my family's there to watch me."

I'd long wondered if the same would be true of me.

From the letters that had come to Mrs. McFadden's while I was on the road, I'd gathered that my whole family was coming to the games that afternoon. Even Chip and Peggy wrote to say they'd be there.

Leo, though, had written to say that, much as he'd like to, he just wouldn't be able to get away.

"Who are you most excited to see?" Trixie asked while we walked to the ball field.

Well, I walked, she skipped.

"I don't know," I said.

"My grandmom is coming." She put a hand to her heart. "I can't wait to hug her neck."

We turned the corner, and there in the parking lot was a car I would have known anywhere. Nobody else I'd ever known had gotten a mint green Chevy from her folks at Christmas. Nope, that was only something that could happen to Peggy.

And there she was, standing next to the car, hands over her head, waving like she was trying to take off.

"That's my sister-in-law," I said.

"What's she got in her hands?" Trixie asked.

Pom-poms that just so happened to be the exact same green as the Sweet Peas uniform. That was just like Peggy to think of.

What a gal.

Chip came around the car and stood next to her, hands in his pockets.

I could have cried, I was so happy to see him. Instead I took off running.

But, as soon as I reached halfway across the parking lot, I stopped dead in my tracks because the back door of the mint green Chevy opened.

I dropped my baseball glove.

Thank goodness Trixie had trotted up right then and picked it up for me.

"Oh, who is that?" she asked.

"Leo," I whispered. Then I yelled, "Leo, you big lug! I thought you couldn't come."

"Surprised?" he asked.

Boy, was I ever.

I ran at him, throwing the full force of my body against him, and he didn't hardly budge.

"I wouldn't have missed this for the world," he whispered.

"But how?" I asked, pushing away from him. "You didn't sneak out, did you?"

"Nah. I guess my ma's not as hysterical about you no more." He lifted one shoulder in a shrug. "She knows where I'm at."

"Hey, Sis," Chip said.

"Am I ever glad to see you," I said, hugging him and Peggy at the same time. "You two are a sight for sore eyes."

"That color is perfect on you," Peggy said.

"Thanks." I stepped away from them and looked around the parking lot. "Mam and Dad here yet?"

"Not yet." Chip crossed his arms. "You know Mam. She probably stayed at church until the very last amen."

"Yeah, you're right." I glanced in the direction of the stadium. "Say, I better get inside. Wish me luck."

"Good luck," Peggy said, hopping and shaking the pom-poms.

Leo nodded once and then winked.

Gosh, it was good to see them.

———

JuJu had us stand single file on the first baseline, and the Kalamazoo coach had his girls do the same on third, all of us players making a V while we waited for the playing of the National Anthem.

I put my hand over my heart and glanced up to where Chip, Peggy, and Leo were sitting. They'd put some space between them to save spots for the others. But those seats were still empty.

They'll be here, I repeated over and over in my head.

Halfway through the song, I saw Mrs. McFadden standing by our dugout, wringing her hands and working her mouth like she was bothered by something. I probably wouldn't have thought anything of it, except that she was looking directly at me.

At the end of the song, I flinched when the fans all started to cheer.

"Play ball," the umpire yelled.

I headed for the dugout only to see JuJu talking to Mrs. Mc-Fadden. Then Dottie joined them. All three kept their eyes on me.

I rushed to get my catcher's gear on. Lorna and I were starting, and I always had a hard time with the darn buckle. I didn't have a minute to waste.

"Bert," JuJu called.

"Getting my stuff," I said back.

"Viv, you're starting with Lorna," he said. "Bert, I need you over here."

I took a deep breath and let Viviane take the mask out of my hands.

"Bertha?" JuJu said.

There was something in the way he said it that very nearly broke my heart. It was too kind. Too tender.

"Yeah?" I choked out.

"Come here, honey," he said.

I did, stepping out from under the overhang of the dugout and into the brightest day we'd had in weeks. There was just the slightest wind, and it made the branches of the trees on the far side of the field move in such a pretty way.

"I'm so sorry," Mrs. McFadden said before putting both hands over her mouth.

"Bert," Dottie said, squinting up her eyes. "Sweetie, it's your dad."

sixty

FLOSSIE

I was nine years old the first time I saw *A Little Princess* starring Shirley Temple. It had been one of the movies the theater in Bonaventure Park had played on a Saturday, and I'd sat through it twice on the same day, I'd loved it so much.

Then, for my tenth birthday, Chippy had gotten me a copy of the book and I'd cuddled up on the couch to start reading as soon as I'd torn off all the paper.

I hadn't even bothered opening the rest of my presents.

When I got to the very end of the book, I marched my way up to Chippy's room and insisted that he'd gotten me a faulty gift.

"Well, what's the matter with it?" he asked.

"The ending's all wrong," I said, putting on a deep pout. "Sara Crewe's supposed to find her father in the hospital. He's supposed to have been alive all along even though she thought he was dead. He doesn't die in the movie. He shouldn't die in the book."

I stomped, and Sully scampered out of the room with a groan.

"Maybe the movie's wrong," Chippy said.

"How dare you?"

And with that, I'd stormed out of his room and buried myself under all my bedclothes so I could bawl my eyes out in peace.

It took me days—entire days—to get over Captain Crewe's death. It had felt so wrong to me. Like I'd been cheated right along with Sara.

That was how I felt when the policeman told Mam that Dad . . . I couldn't even bring myself to think the word.

It was the wrong ending. It wasn't how it was supposed to go.

Dad was supposed to drive the car to church and sneak into the pew after all the hymns were sung for the day. Then, after the final prayer, we would go to the baseball game. They would watch Bertha play, I would get a box of caramel corn. We would leave after the game, driving all the way back to Bear Run so I could get to bed on time. I had school the next day, after all. I'd planned on bringing my autographed program to show my classmates, and they would all be so jealous of me, the sister of the best player on the team.

Mam would cook and clean her day away as usual, Uncle Matthew would go to work at Teddy's, and Dad would go out to the barn to write.

Dad wasn't supposed to take the corner too fast, losing control on the rain-slick street and hitting the tree. That wasn't what should have happened.

Once we got back to Uncle Matthew's house, I went from room to room, closing my eyes whenever I stepped in through the doorway, hoping and praying—begging God—to let my dad be sitting at the table or standing at the window or working the crossword puzzle in front of the radio.

But whenever I opened my eyes, he wasn't doing any of those things. He wasn't there.

Sara Crewe from the movie had nuzzled her face into her father's neck and asked him over and over to hold her close.

I wrapped my arms around myself.

sixty-one

BERTHA

Chip didn't cry when Amos died. Not right away, at least. It wasn't because he didn't care or that he wasn't as heartbroken as the rest of us. He was. There was no doubt about it.

But those first few weeks he kept his hands balled up into fists and his jaw clenched. Maybe he didn't know what to do with so much sorrow. Maybe he was afraid if he lost control of himself, he'd never regain it again.

So he kept himself busy. He made meals—ham sandwiches became his specialty—when Mam was swallowed by the grief. He read bedtime stories to Flossie. He mowed the grass so much that he wore bare patches into the yard.

A few months after Amos passed, I overheard Mam tell Dad that Chip had finally "let it out." In the process he'd broken a few slats in the backyard fence, he'd kicked them so hard.

Dad had told her that, for boys, sometimes mourning turned to rage.

My brother didn't cry when he found out that Dad died. He bustled Peggy and me to the car, but not before finding someone to collect my things from the locker room and arrange a ride back to Bonaventure Park for Leo.

Good old Tony volunteered for both tasks.

Chip drove as fast as he dared all the way to Uncle Matthew's.

After the drive—it was so long, so impossibly long—we pulled into Uncle Matthew's driveway and Mam stepped out onto the porch, grabbing hold of the railing for support. Chip barely waited until the car stopped before throwing it into park and getting out, rushing to her. I followed close behind.

I remembered right after Chip and Peggy got married, how Mam had worried that her boy wouldn't need her anymore.

"He will, Lou," Dad had said. "A boy always needs his mother."

Chip put his arms all the way around her and she lifted her free hand to put it on his back. His shoulders heaved up and down and he sobbed so loud I almost couldn't bear it.

"Bertha, love," Mam said, reaching for me. "I'm so sorry."

"Me too," I said.

She hooked her arm around mine and pulled me near.

"Your sister . . ." she started. "She . . ."

She didn't finish, and I took in a sharp breath.

"Flossie?" Chip asked. "Was she with him?"

"No. No." Mam shook her head. "She was at church with me."

"Thank God," Chip said.

"She needs you." Mam looked between the two of us. "Both of you."

Chip nodded and wiped his eyes with the back of his wrist.

"Where is she?" I asked.

"The pole barn." She let us go.

Chip hesitated before leaving the porch.

"I'll stay with her," Peggy said. "Go to your sister."

I still had my cleats on, and they made a crunching sound in the gravel walk to the barn. Chip stopped just before we reached the door and grabbed my hand.

His eyes had welled up again and he blinked hard.

"Ready?" I asked.

He nodded.

Flossie was sitting in Dad's chair, pulled up to his desk and staring at the bust of William Shakespeare.

"Flo?" I whispered.

She didn't turn toward us, so Chip sat in the old wingback chair right next to the desk.

"Hey." He reached for her arm. "We're here."

I knelt on the floor next to him.

Pushing against the edge of the desk, Flossie swiveled in the chair to face us. Her eyes were red and her hair a mess. She sniffled and scowled at me and Chip.

"Why can't I change this?" she asked. "I want to change this."

Chip leaned forward.

"I would change this," Flossie said.

"Me too," he said.

He grabbed Flo's chair and dragged it closer to him so he could get a hold of her. She let him pull her onto his lap and didn't wriggle away when I put my arms around both of them.

I held on tight to my brother and sister, afraid to let go.

Bear Run Gazette
May 19, 1952

BESTSELLING AUTHOR DEAD IN TRAGIC ACCIDENT

ASSOCIATED PRESS: Author William S. Harding has died in a car crash in Northern Michigan. Law officers close to the case say it was a tragic accident.

Mr. Harding was in the process of writing his ninth novel, *Flight of Angels Sing*, which was originally scheduled to release in the fall of next year. In recent months, the publication has been delayed. Still no word on whether or not the publisher will proceed with the novel and/or who would be slated to finish the manuscript.

Longtime editor of Wm. Harding, Dean Sleiman, said of the author's passing, "Will was, for my money, the All-American writer. This is a tragedy for the literary world, for America, but most especially for his family and those who treasured him as a man."

Mr. Harding had recently been cleared of suspicion regarding accusations that he had formerly belonged to the Communist Party.

CONT on page 3

sixty-two

FLOSSIE

Peggy brought me a new black dress that she'd bought at a department store in town, and Mam tied my hair in a ribbon that matched the lace of the collar. Bertha polished my shoes, and Chippy brought me a cup of tea. Uncle Matthew gave me his arm when we got to the church, and Lizzie snuck into the pew that was supposed to be reserved only for family.

It was all right. There was room enough for her.

All day I sat still when Mam asked me to and stood when the minister told the congregation to. I ate the food people gave me and let strangers pat me on the head even though it gave me the heebie-jeebies when they did. I said thank you when someone told me they were sorry and saved up all of my loudest crying for when we got back home and I could lock myself in my room.

Days passed. A week went by. Chippy and Peggy stayed for a while and then needed to get home to Bonaventure Park. Uncle Matthew went back to work at Teddy's. Mam started making breakfast in the mornings even if she sometimes forgot and set a place for Dad. Bertha went for long walks in the woods, and Lizzie came over to tell me how play practice was going.

"Miss Somerville wants you to know that you can still be a lamb," she said. "If you want."

I wasn't sure about that.

I wasn't sure about anything.

A couple of times a day I went out to the pole barn, no longer afraid of the dark or the mice in the loft, and sat at Dad's desk. Sometimes I went through the drawers, finding treasures like Indian head pennies or little pieces of paper he'd scribbled ideas on.

Half the time I couldn't read his handwriting.

The other half of the time I had to work to puzzle out what it was he'd been trying to say because, put together, the words I could figure out didn't always make a whole lot of sense.

Some days, when I knew nobody would walk in on me, I sat and talked to William Shakespeare's head, pretending that he was Dad.

It was nuts, I knew that. And sometimes it only made me miss Dad more. But it also made me feel better, even if just for a minute or two.

That day, a whole month after Dad died, I went out to the barn after lunch. School was out for the summer, and I was bored sitting around the house with nothing to do. Well, I could have done chores, but the pole barn seemed like a more interesting option.

"Hello," I said to Mr. Shakespeare.

He greeted me with his usual empty stare.

"Not very talkative today, are you?" I pulled out the desk chair. "That's okay. I'm not either."

Before I sat down, I straightened a stack of papers that Dad had left disheveled next to his typewriter. Under them was a photo album with a slip of paper hanging out the top.

Show to Flossie, it said in Dad's handwriting.

I set the loose papers on the seat of the chair and picked up the album. I flipped through it. I'd seen some of the pictures before. Us kids when we were little, standing in front of the fountain at Belle Isle in Detroit. Him and Mam on the day they got married. Our school pictures—most of mine snapped while I was in the middle of saying something to the photographer.

Then there were others that were new to me. One of Mam when she was little, standing on a cliff that I knew was somewhere in England. Him and Uncle Matthew when they were boys, arms around each other. One with Mam holding baby Amos, Chippy, Bertha, and me looking down at him.

The slip of paper marked the very middle of the album, and when I turned it over, I saw more writing.

> *I wouldn't change the way Louisa smiles at me after I kiss her. I wouldn't change the sound of Chip playing piano or the way Bertha comes to life with a baseball in her hand. I wouldn't change Flossie's courageous spirit. I wouldn't change the way it felt to hold Amos for the short time I was able.*
>
> *I can't change the pain, but I can fight to remember the good in everything.*

There was more, but I couldn't read because my eyes were blurry.

I took the album, sneaking in through the front door and up the stairs so that I could hide it in my room, a treasure I was sure Dad had meant to be just for me.

———

I'd gotten up in the middle of the night to use the bathroom. When I stumbled back to bed, I noticed out the window that there was a light on in the pole barn. I didn't even throw on my robe or slippers. I didn't hesitate for a second.

I ran all the way down the stairs, through the house, and out the back door. It slammed closed behind me and I cringed, hoping that it hadn't woken anyone up.

I wasn't exactly sure what I'd expected once I got there. I did, though, entertain the thought for a second that maybe—oh, please let it be true—I'd dreamed up the whole thing about Dad's accident. That his funeral had just been part of the nightmare. That I'd go out to the barn to find him typing away, a cigarette half-finished and resting on the ledge of his ashtray.

When I got just inside the door, I skidded to a stop.

It was Mam.

On the floor around her were half a dozen boxes full of the stuff from Dad's desk. Even Shakespeare peeked out from the top of one of them. The stack of pages that were Dad's novel were gone from the desk, and I hoped that Mam had kept them in order.

All that was left was the typewriter and the single piece of paper Dad had left in it at the end of his last writing day.

"Mam?" I said, taking a step toward her.

She twirled around, hand on her chest.

"Good heavens," she gasped. Then, after seeing it was just me there, "What are you doing out of bed, love?"

"I saw the light."

"How about I warm up some milk for you?" She wiped under her left eye. "Would you like that?"

Even though I didn't care for warm milk until it was mixed with cocoa and lots of sugar, I nodded anyway. It would be nice to sit in the kitchen with just her for a little bit.

She reached for me and we both stepped forward, closing the distance between us. Once she got her arm around my shoulder, she led me to the door of the barn, not remembering until we stepped outside that she needed to put out the light.

"I'll do it," I said. "You can go ahead and start the milk."

"All right."

She pulled her cardigan around herself and started toward the back porch.

I rushed into the barn and pulled up the flaps on each of the boxes Mam had packed, hoping to find Dad's unfinished novel. It wasn't in any of the boxes on the floor, and I puffed out my cheeks. Doggone it.

I turned to William Shakespeare and said, "Where did she put it?"

When he didn't answer—which, of course he didn't—I pulled the chair out from under the desk and—viola! as Dad would have said—there on the seat was a shirt box with Mam's handwriting in marker.

Flights of Angels Sing.

I grabbed it and held it to my chest before pulling the cord to turn off the light.

On my way out of the barn, I patted Shakespeare on the head.

"I'll be back for you," I said.

I stopped when I got halfway to the kitchen door and looked up. It would have been nice, maybe even poetic, were it not for the clouds that covered up all of the stars.

But the sky was overcast and I couldn't do anything to change it. So, I went inside.

Mam glanced at the box I'd carried in with me.

"I didn't want it to get lost," I said.

She nodded and poured warm milk into my cup. Then she made a cuppa for herself. Chamomile. I was glad she hadn't offered any to me. It was like drinking tree bark unless it was thick with sugar.

"Do you know where your father got that title?" she asked.

I shook my head, sipping my milk.

"It's from *Hamlet*." She sat and leaned an elbow on the table. "Horatio says it as Hamlet's dying."

"Hamlet dies?" I asked.

"He does." She looped her finger through the ear of her cup. "Most everyone does in that one."

I glanced out the window toward the pole barn, thinking about what a sad, sad man William Shakespeare must have been to write plays with so many people dying in them.

"As Hamlet's fading, Horatio says, 'good-night, sweet prince, and flights of angels sing thee to thy rest.'" She grabbed a hanky from the pocket of her skirt and held it under her eye. "I'm sorry."

"For what?" I asked. "For crying?"

She nodded. Then she covered both eyes with her hand so I wouldn't be able to see. But her lips pulled out of shape and her chin shook.

"I'm sorry, Flossie." She folded her arms on the table and rested her forehead on her hands. Her voice was thick because she was crying. "I'm just so very sorry, love."

I got up from the table so fast that I knocked over my cup of milk.

"Oh shoot," I said. "Shoot, shoot, shoot."

Mam lifted her head and, seeing the spill, got up and reached for the hand towel on the cupboard.

Leave it to her, she had the puddle mopped up in no time.

sixty-three

BERTHA

I worked for a couple of hours most weekdays at Teddy's Food and More, bagging groceries and stocking shelves. Every once in a while, when we were especially busy, Uncle Matthew let me man a checkout line. It was fine work and the people who shopped there were friendly.

But it was a sad substitute for playing with the Sweet Peas.

Once or twice a week I'd get a letter from Trixie or Weeny begging me to come play. They wrote that they missed me.

I missed them too. All of them. Even Lucy.

I couldn't leave my family, though. It wouldn't have been right.

So I passed the time by working all day at the store and listening to Tigers games on the radio every evening. Leo wrote more often, which was a nice distraction. Once or twice a week I walked through the cemetery after work and stood beside Dad's grave.

It had been a month since his accident and the hurt of losing him was just as strong as the first day. I suspected that I would miss him every day for the rest of my life.

I punched out of work on Monday just before noon and hung up my apron. But before I got out the door, Uncle Matthew called for me to come into his office.

"Close the door behind you," he said, not looking up from his clipboard.

I did as he asked, but not without a twinge of anxiety.

"What's wrong?" I asked.

"Nothing." He glanced up. "Oh, I didn't mean to worry you. I'm sorry."

"It's all right."

"I just wanted to tell you that you can't work here anymore."

"Are you firing me?" I crossed my arms.

"Sort of," he said. "But . . . well . . ."

He didn't finish his sentence. Instead, he pulled an envelope from his shirt pocket and handed it to me. The note inside was just two sentences long.

Matt, my best pitcher says she's going to quit if Bertha doesn't come back. We need her.

JuJu Eames

"I can't go back." I said, still looking at JuJu's messy signature.

"Sure you can."

"But Mam . . ."

"Your mother'll be fine without you for a couple months," Uncle Matthew said. "Your sister too. I'll see to it."

"Will you let them stay with you if I go?"

"Course I will." He grinned. "As long as they'd like."

"I just don't think . . ."

"Bertha, sit down." He nodded at the seat in front of his desk. Then he took the chair next to mine. "It's rare, somebody getting a chance like you've got. You know that?"

"I guess so," I said.

"I've never been one to have big dreams," he said. "But Will, he had plenty for the both of us."

"He always wanted to be a writer, didn't he?"

Uncle Matthew nodded. "And an explorer and a fireman and a movie star. Like I said, he had plenty of dreams."

I smiled to think of Dad as a little boy who believed that anything was possible.

"Your grandfather didn't understand him," Uncle Matthew

said. "He didn't like that your dad seemed always to have his head in the clouds. I guess I felt the same way until I got a copy of Will's first book."

"Did you read it?" I asked.

Uncle Matthew cringed. "I tried."

"Don't feel too bad. I've only read one."

He grinned and then glanced down at the floor. "Your dad was really proud of you."

"He was proud of all us kids," I said.

"Yeah." Uncle Matthew met my eyes. "But right now we're talking about you."

I clenched my teeth and blinked real fast in the hopes of keeping the tears from breaking loose. It was more for his benefit than mine. The poor man. No matter how much crying he'd been witness to over the past month, he still hadn't grown accustomed to it.

I had come to suspect that it had more to do with our tears breaking his heart than making him uncomfortable.

Somebody knocked on the door, and Uncle Matthew told them to wait five minutes.

Then he put his hand on my shoulder, and one tear forced its way out and rolled down my cheek.

"He wouldn't have wanted you to quit," he said. "Not if you still wanted to play."

He got up from his seat and went around to the other side of the desk, pulling another envelope out of the center drawer.

"I have one ticket for the bus to Workington." He hit the envelope against the palm of his hand. "It leaves in a couple hours."

He held it out toward me.

"It's yours if you want it," he said. "You'd make it just in time for tonight's game."

"I really should ask Mam before I take that," I said.

"She'll tell you to go."

"How do you know that?"

"Because she's the one who bought this ticket."

Mam had my Sweet Peas uniform pressed and on a hanger, waiting for me when I got home. That eased away any little doubt that still remained in my mind that going back to Workington was okay.

"I've packed a little something for you to eat on the bus," Mam said, nodding at a basket on the kitchen counter. "Nothing special, mind. Just a morsel or two."

I peeked into the basket, glad to see that, along with a sandwich and a thermos of what I suspected to be tea, she'd put in a tin of butter cookies. I would have to guard those with my life so Flossie wouldn't snatch them when I wasn't looking.

"Thank you, Mam," I said.

She glanced at me over her shoulder.

"You're welcome."

"Not just for the food." I took a step toward her.

When she turned toward me and smiled, I reached out and pulled her to me. She held me back as tight as she could.

"Thank you," I whispered.

For the bus ticket and for ironing my uniform. For getting out of bed every morning to brew tea and fry eggs for my sister and me—even on the days when the grief must have been heavy enough to crush her. For insisting that we hold hands when we prayed before supper and for getting us to church every Sunday even when we couldn't sing the hymns without bawling our eyes out.

For letting us see her mourn Dad even though it was uncomfortable for her to show emotion.

And for loving me enough to let me go. Just for a little bit.

I didn't tell her all of that—I couldn't have without dissolving into a puddle of tears—but it seemed she understood.

"You're welcome, sweet," she said.

Then the kitchen door creaked open and Flossie came charging in, Lizzie following close behind her.

I let go of Mam, who turned away from my sister to wipe under her eyes.

"You're still here?" Flossie asked, squinting up at me.

"Yup," I said. "Hi there, Liz."

"She prefers Lizzie."

Lizzie looked at me and shrugged.

"When are you leaving?" Flo crossed her arms.

"Are you in a hurry to get rid of me?" I asked. "Won't you miss me?"

"Yes and not really."

"Florence," Mam said, eyebrows raised.

Flossie rolled her eyes and shuffled over to me, wrapping her arms around my waist.

"Of course I'll miss you," she said. "You're my one and only sister. Well, except for Peggy. But that's not the same."

"I'll miss you too." I leaned down and kissed the top of her head. "Make sure Uncle Matthew brings you to a game or two. Okay?"

"Ugh. Do I have to?" She groaned. "Baseball is boring."

"I'll buy you some Cracker Jacks."

"And can I bring a book?" she asked.

"Sure. Why not?"

Then she looked up at me, a wide grin on her face.

It was the biggest smile I'd seen on her in a month.

How someone so small could hold so much sorrow and so much hope at the same time was beyond me.

I didn't understand it.

Still, it was good.

No one met me at the bus station in Workington. Why would they have? They didn't know I was coming. Fortunately, Uncle Matthew had paid me for my last few days of work in cash. Also lucky for me, there were a couple of cab drivers waiting for folks to cart around.

I got into the one closest to me and asked him to take me to Judd Field.

The cabby looked at me in his rearview mirror.

"Hold on," he said, turning in his seat. "You a Sweet Pea?"

"Yes," I answered.

"Big Bertha?"

"That's me."

"You playing tonight?" He didn't wait for me to answer before facing forward and putting the taxi in gear. "We better get you there pronto."

It was a good thing that the drive to the ballpark wasn't very long. The way that man drove—whipping around corners and swerving to pass slow-moving cars—I worried I'd get woozy.

When he pulled up to the entrance of the stadium, I asked him how much I owed.

"Nothing this time." He glanced at me over his shoulder.

"You sure?"

"Yup." He nodded. "Just glad to have you back."

"Thanks," I said.

"That's fine." He winked at me. "You better get in there."

I grabbed my bags and my uniform and rushed toward the locker room.

The first to see me was Trixie, who squealed and skipped over to me, alerting the rest of the team to my arrival. All the girls surrounded me, hugging me and asking if I was back for good and telling me how glad they were to see me.

Well, all of the girls except for Lucy.

She stayed in her spot, warming the bench on the other side of the room. That was fine. We might never become friends. But we were teammates, so we'd have to figure out a way to get along.

I lifted my hand to wave at her and she nodded back. She didn't scowl. It was a start at least.

The crowd of girls around me parted when Dottie came in to announce that JuJu was on his way for the pregame talk.

"Look who's here," Weeny said.

Dottie's smile was one of the warmest I'd ever seen. She put all of her weight on one crutch so she could reach one hand out to me. When I got to her, I had to remind myself not to hug her so hard it would knock her over.

"I'm so glad to see you," she whispered into my ear before letting me go. "You better get changed. And quick. I'll have you added to the roster if you're up to playing."

"Are you kidding me?" Lorna called from her locker. "Course she's up to it!"

I got into my uniform and put my lipstick on all while Lorna quizzed me on pitch signals to make sure I still had them memorized. I did. Then I tied my cleats while Dottie read the batting order.

By the time JuJu joined us in the locker room, I was all suited up in the catcher's gear and ready to go.

"Well, look who showed up," he said, hands on hips. "Good to have you back, Bert."

"Thanks," I said.

"All right, girls." He nodded toward the bench, and we all scrambled to get a seat. "In case you forgot, tonight's game is against the Kalamazoo Lassies."

A couple of the girls booed and a few others groaned.

"All right. All right. Simmer down," JuJu said. "We all remember how bad they whooped us last time."

"So much for a pep talk," Mickey called out.

"I'm getting to the pep part." He put up his hands in surrender. "But first I've got to get through the straight talk part."

"Alrighty." She crossed her legs. "Go on, sir."

"They beat us ten to zip," he said, holding up his clipboard with the statistics from that last game. "That ain't great, girls. And that's nobody's fault but our own."

Trixie pulled her mouth in an exaggerated frown.

"But, you know what?" He grabbed the paper, tearing it out from under the clip, and wadded it up, hurling it toward the trash can. He, of course, made the shot. "I don't care about that game. That was weeks ago. We're going to forget about that game. All right?"

"That's more like it." Mickey clapped her hands.

"We're playing a brand-new game today." He crossed his arms, the clipboard against his chest. "And I don't care how far behind we get in runs, we're coming back. I want us to be up at the end of every inning. Got it?"

"Got it!" Trixie yelled.

"Now, get out there and win." He nodded, stepping to one side so we could run out to the field.

"Bert," he said when I passed him. "Go get 'em."

"Will do, Coach."

We were down by one at the bottom of the eighth inning when I got to bat. As if by instinct, I looked up into the grandstand where Dad and I sat at the first Sweet Peas game we went to. Some other folks were sitting there. The same people who had been there every other time I checked during that game.

I swallowed hard and got myself set.

I swung at the first pitch, hitting nothing. There couldn't have been a more unsatisfying feeling in all the world than cutting through air. The second pitch zipped right by me too.

Stepping back from the plate, I let myself take a breath.

Without thinking about it, I looked back up to that spot in the stands even though I knew Dad wouldn't be there.

What I'd missed all those other times was a little girl two rows down from where we'd sat. That little girl was in a green dress with a matching ball cap on her head. A worn-out glove—far too big for her—was on her left hand.

"Hey there," I said, pointing up at her. "You in the green dress."

The man sitting next to her—I imagined he was her father—pulled her onto his lap and whispered, pointing at me.

She gave me a shy smile.

"You like baseball?" I asked her.

The girl nodded.

"This next hit? It's for you, all right?"

"All right," she called back at me.

I nodded and then stretched my neck, turning my head from one side to the other.

That was when I saw a bunch of daisies growing out of the dirt near the backstop.

I hit the next pitch. It didn't go out of the park, but it was enough for me to get to second base.

I was halfway home.

EPILOGUE

FLOSSIE
WINTER 1968

William Shakespeare looked on as I turned the knob on Dad's old typewriter, rolling the very last page up and out. Leaning back in my chair, I read the last few lines. They'd need finessing, but they were written and that felt good.

I was exhausted.

I got up out of my seat—a different one than Dad had used all of his novel-writing years. That one was murder on my body, especially in the state I was in. I pressed a hand against my lower back and groaned.

My husband neglected to come running to see if I was all right, so I moaned a little louder.

"You okay?" he asked, glancing from my face to my very round, very big belly. "Is it time?"

"Yes," I nodded my head, tearing up.

"Oh. Oh." He rushed out of the doorway and down the hall, calling behind him, "Where's the bag you packed for the hospital?"

"Honey," I said, lumbering across the room. "I'm not in labor."

He popped his head out of our bedroom.

"You aren't?"

"No." I held up the paper. "I finished the novel."

His face lit up. Bless him.

The longest my dad had ever taken to write one of his books was, according to Mam, five years. He'd put one year into *Flight of Angels Sing* before he died, leaving the second half undone.

It had taken me sixteen years to finish it.

Admittedly, my first attempts went as well as one might expect from a twelve-year-old. Those early drafts—thank goodness—no longer existed, burned in Uncle Matthew's fireplace years ago.

As I kept trying, though, I got better.

At least I hoped Dad's remaining loyal readers would think so.

Nathan made sure I had my coat on even if I couldn't button it up anymore. He even got on one knee to tie the laces of shoes I couldn't see when I looked down.

A regular old Gilbert Blythe, my husband.

"You want me to go with you?" he asked.

"I'm fine, love," I said. "I promise."

He carried the manuscript box out to the car and kissed me before I pulled out of the driveway.

"Be careful," he said.

"I usually am."

The drive from our little house in Lafontaine to Bonaventure Park was just over thirty minutes. Nathan had pointed out that there was a perfectly good post office just two blocks away from home. He'd also made sure I knew that he thought it was madness for me to be gallivanting about so close to my due date.

It was silly, but I couldn't bring myself to mail the manuscript off from any other place than the town where Dad wrote the very first words.

Nate had done his best to understand.

I parked on the street. The closest I could get was a spot in front of the library—half a block from the post office. I waited for traffic to clear before getting out of the car.

Most things had changed in Bonaventure Park since the Harding family left in 1952. Many of the older buildings had been demolished in the name of revitalization. Ugly, square, cement structures took their place. Where the old soda fountain had been was now the location of a McDonald's. The park where Bertha had played ball with the boys was turned into an apartment complex.

But Archie—the lion, not the man—still stood guard in front of the library. I patted his nose when I passed by.

Just as I got to the post office, I felt Baby moving about, something that always took my breath away. Particularly with a well-placed foot to my ribs.

Even then, feeling my baby move was good.

I would not change it.

They walked to the edge of the property, and she held his hand, even though she was too old for that anymore.

"Does the story have a happy ending?" she asked.

"I can't know for sure." He kicked at a tuft of dirt. "But I know it's good."

A toad hopped out of the tall grass. The father stooped to pick it up.

The daughter was too afraid to touch it.

The toad blinked up at her, his eye green as an emerald.

—From *Flight of Angels Sing* by William S. Harding and Florence Harding-Jones

AUTHOR'S NOTE
AND ACKNOWLEDGMENTS

During the early days of social distancing in 2020, I read a book called *A Good American Family: The Red Scare and My Father* by David Maraniss in which a family living in Detroit endured accusations of involvement in the Communist Party. I guess I was halfway through my reading of it when a friend of mine (hi, Andy Rogers!) tweeted about a book called *The Incredible Women of the All-American Girls Professional Baseball League* by Anika Orrock.

I remember pausing and thinking, *Hm. What's more American than baseball? What's less American than Communism? What would happen if I put them together in a story?*

Imagine my delight when I realized that the Red Scare in Detroit lined up with one of the years of the All-American Girls Professional Baseball League.

While there was no team called the Workington Sweet Peas in the AAGPBL (and, as a matter of fact, no city called Workington in the State of Michigan), there were teams like the Grand Rapids Chicks, the Kalamazoo Lassies, and the Racine Belles (to name a very few). These teams featured players from all over the Midwest, girls who played every bit as well as their male counterparts. The eleven years of the AAGPBL (1943–1954) made a difference in the world of women's athletics that girls around the world enjoy to this day.

If it hadn't been for women like Marilyn Jenkins and Marie Zeigler, Jo Kabick and Betty Whiting, I may not have had the opportunities I did as a student athlete.

The women who dared to play baseball like the guys—only in short skirts and lipstick—get the first of my heartfelt thanks. Most of them are gone now. It's my hope that this story will help to carry on their legacy. Please take the time to learn more about them at www.aagpbl.org.

This novel took longer to write than originally planned. We can all thank Flossie for that. She and Bertha were worth the extra effort. Many thanks to my editors, Kelsey Bowen and Kristin Kornoelje, for the gift of time to make this story all it needed to become.

My appreciation to Tim Beals for being the best agent a girl could hope for.

Hugs and shenanigans to my friends from Fiction Readers Summit. You are a community unlike any other. It's pure joy to belong to #TeamFiction with you all.

Much gratitude to the folks at Full Circle Coffee for keeping the lattes and the encouragement coming on some of the most intense writing days.

My friends are generous with their pep talks and kind enough to check on me often as I'm in the thick of writing. There isn't enough ink and paper in this book to list you all. Just know that I hold you in my heart. And I owe you coffee.

Love to my kids. Being your mom is the very greatest.

Kisses to my Jeff. You make this possible.

To you, faithful reader, who reads every word—even the acknowledgments—you keep this work worthwhile. Thank you.

And to the God who inspires my heart with goodness, all glory to you.

Turn the page

for a sneak peek at another artful novel from Susie Finkbeiner

AVAILABLE NOW

Revell
a division of Baker Publishing Group
www.RevellBooks.com

Available wherever books and ebooks are sold.

one

JUNE, 1967

When God created the world, he only afforded Michigan just so many good-weather days. He caused the bookends of the year to be winter and the months between to be warm enough for the earth to almost thaw before it was to freeze solid once again.

And somehow, in his infinite wisdom he had chosen to call it good.

In the deepest of winter, I often questioned the soundness of mind that made my ancestors think that Michigan was a good and fine place to settle. But it was in spring, when the whole world came back alive and I forgot the cold, that I swore to never leave my home state. Leaves turned the forests back to green, and flowers speckled bright red and yellow and orange across the lawns and fields. Purple lilacs bloomed on the bush below my bedroom window, smelling like heaven itself. Finches molted tawny feathers to show off their brilliant goldenrod. Robins returned with their trilling song, and just-hatched chicks peeped from their nests, discarding pretty blue shells on the ground.

Every year it caught me by surprise, the return of life to Fort Colson. But by June I'd fallen into the routine of longer days and leaving my jacket at home, letting the sun warm my bare arms.

I certainly would have liked to enjoy the sunshine. Instead, I stood looking out the big window of Bernie's Diner, dripping washrag in hand, wishing the view was of something other than the five-and-dime across the street. It was the perfect day for sitting on a dock, dipping my toes into the waters of Chippewa Lake.

Old Chip. That was what my brothers and I called it. Where we all learned how to swim and row a canoe and catch fish. Growing up without Frank around hadn't been a walk in the park. But having a mother who was unafraid of getting muddy and hooking a worm on the line made it a little bit easier. Especially for my brothers.

The sound of clattering pots or pans from the kitchen snapped my attention back to my job. I wrung the extra water from my rag and scrubbed down the tabletops, wiping away the breakfast crumbs to make way for the lunch plates. A couple of girls I knew from high school walked along the sidewalk past the diner window, wearing minidresses and bug-eyed sunglasses that seemed all the rage that year.

Using my knuckle, I pushed up my plastic-framed glasses and hoped they wouldn't notice me. Bernie's dress code only allowed white button-up shirts and slacks—no jeans. On my own I was a certifiable L7 square. The uniform didn't help matters at all.

The girls looked in through the window. Sally Gaines with the perfectly coiffed auburn bouffant and Caroline Mann with her diamond engagement ring sparkling in the sunshine. Sally's mouth broke into an impossibly perfect smile and she waved, her fingers wiggling next to her face.

I knew that it was not meant for me. As far as girls like Sally and Caroline were concerned, I was less than invisible. I didn't even exist.

Turning, I saw my brother behind the counter, lowering a crate of freshly washed glasses to rest beside the Coca-Cola fountain. The glasses clinked together, but delicately, sounding just a little bit like chimes.

"You have an admirer," I said, stepping away from the window.

"Great," he said, thick sarcasm in his voice. Not looking up at the girls, he took one of the glasses and put it under the fountain, pulling half a glass of pop for himself. "They're good tippers at least."

"For you." I watched him take a few drinks of the Coke before moving on to setting the tables with silverware wrapped in paper napkins. "I don't have the advantage of flirting with them."

"You've got a point," he said. "I am charming."

"And I'm a nerd."

"Nah, you're peachy keen."

"Well, thanks." I looked back to where the girls had stood. They were already gone.

"I have my meeting today," Mike said, finishing off the last of his pop. "The one I told you about."

"When?"

"After lunch. Bernie told me I could leave a little early."

"Did you tell him what it's about?"

"No." Mike put his empty glass on the counter. He lowered his voice to just above a whisper. "I kind of gave him the impression that it's a doctor's appointment."

"And he bought it?" I asked. "You know you're the worst liar in the world, don't you?"

"He didn't seem to doubt me." He poured himself another half glass of pop and drank it all at once. "I didn't want him trying to talk me out of it."

"Do you really have to do this?" I asked.

"Yeah," he answered, covering a silent burp with his fist. "Unless you have any other ideas."

"Canada's only a few hours away."

He raised his eyebrows and made a humming sound. "I'm not sure that's a great option."

"What did Mom say?"

Shrugging, he walked around the counter, checking the ketchup bottles from the tables to see which needed refilling. He carried the half-full ones back to the counter in the crook of his arm.

"You told her, didn't you?" I asked. "Please tell me you did."

"Not exactly." He lined the bottles up on the counter.

"What do you mean by 'not exactly'?"

He cringed. "Not at all."

"Golly, Mike," I said, hoping it didn't sound too much like a scold. "You should have asked her about it. She might have had some ideas."

"I'm almost twenty, Annie. I'm an adult," he said, making his voice deeper. "It doesn't matter anyway. They're sending me whether I like it or not. I might as well just volunteer and at least have some say over things."

"I guess."

"She's going to be furious, though. I know she will be." He moved behind the counter again and wiped the bottles down with a wet rag. "I don't know how I'll tell Joel."

In the thirteen years since our baby brother was born, Joel loved no one as much as he did Mike. If he ever tired of such undying admiration, Mike rarely let on. He took to the role of big brother near perfectly.

"Why haven't you told him?" I asked.

"Gee, I don't know," Mike answered, uncapping the ketchup bottles. "I tried. I just didn't have the heart."

"You aren't abandoning him, if that's what you're worried about."

"Maybe that's it."

"Still, you have to tell them sometime."

"I will," he said. "Don't worry."

"The sooner the better," I said.

"I'll know more about what's going to happen after my meeting with the recruiter." He sighed. "It's a pickle, that's for sure."

"Maybe they won't want you."

"Come on, buddy, you're going to hurt my feelings."

"Oh, get out of here."

"Soon enough, sis." He turned toward the kitchen. "Soon enough I'll get out of here all the way to Vietnam."

If there was any consolation to be had for missing out on summer, it was that Bernie let me read during the lulls of the day, provided I had all my silverware wrapped and tables clean. I'd just settled onto the stool behind the cash register with book in hand when the bell over the door jingled with the arrival of someone. Regretfully, I shut the book and put it back on the counter. Scout Finch would just have to wait a little bit longer.

My mother stood just inside the door, purse hanging from her bent arm, and looking every bit the lady in her red blouse and tweed skirt. She'd worn her hair down that day with the ends in upturned curls.

She'd never been one to lie about her age. In fact, I'd heard her more than once brag about being over forty. "Just over," she'd say. The conversation inevitably turned to how she looked so young.

"My secret?" she'd say with a conspiratorial wink. "A hairdresser who can keep my secrets and a strong girdle."

My mother, Gloria Jacobson, ever the charmer who turned heads anywhere she went. And me, her beanpole of a daughter who hardly took the time to twist a braid into her hair most mornings. It was a wonder she never tried to give me beauty tips, as much as I sorely needed them. Then again, I'd never asked. Never much cared to, either.

"I can't stay long," Mom said, making her way to the counter. "I have a few other errands to run before going back to work."

"Late lunch?" I asked, checking my watch.

She rolled her eyes. "Mrs. Channing was in for a checkup today, and you know how she can go on."

She lifted her hand, making a puppet out of her fingers, opening and closing them like a mouth.

"Did she ask again about you and the doctor?"

Mom sighed. "Of course she did."

After Frank left us, Mom found herself in need of a job for the first time in her life. She'd put on her most professional-looking dress and walked over to Dr. Bill DeVries's office to ask him to hire her. She'd said he owed her. For what, I'd never had the courage to ask. The doctor, though, just happened to have a position open at his office. She'd worked as his receptionist ever since.

If rumor could be believed, the good doctor had held a torch for my mother since they were young. He'd even invited her to prom, but a day late. She'd already accepted Frank's invitation.

Most of the women in town waited for a romance to bud between Mom and Dr. DeVries. They'd waited more than twelve years with no sign of giving up hope. I wasn't sure if theirs was an act of sheer determination or utter stubbornness.

Either way, Mom could outlast anyone, even the old biddies of Fort Colson.

"I told her that I'm still married and, as far as I know, that won't change anytime soon," Mom said, instinctively touching the gold wedding band on her left ring finger.

When I'd asked her years before why she still wore it, she told me it was to "discourage any interested parties." I wondered if it was also to keep certain chatterbox busybodies from speculation.

A small town like Fort Colson was fertile soil for gossip to take seed.

"Is Bernie here?" Mom asked.

"He's in the office," I answered. "It's bookkeeping day."

She reached into her purse, searching for something. "I'm sure it's putting him in a foul mood."

"Well, no more than usual," I whispered.

"He's not being grumpy to you, is he?" She arched one of her eyebrows. "You don't have to put up with his moods, you know."

"He's my boss."

"And he's my cousin."

"Second cousin, Mom." I rolled my eyes. "Everyone around here is your second cousin."

"Still." She went back to digging through her purse. "You don't have to take it from him. You'd get treated better working in an office somewhere."

"You know I'd hate that." I leaned my elbows on the counter. "I'm horrible at typing."

"You'd learn. Besides, there's more money in it." She tilted her head. "Or you could go to college."

"I don't mind his moods," I said. "Besides, I can't afford college."

"We could work something out." Her hands stilled and she looked up into my eyes. "I could work more hours. Maybe get a second job."

"You don't have to do that." I slid my book off the counter. "I wouldn't want to go anyway."

She gave me a sharp look—eyes narrowed and mouth puckered—that told me she didn't believe a word of it. The look didn't last long, just enough so that I'd see it. Then she turned her attention back to her purse.

"If you say so. Ah," she said, pulling an envelope from the depths of her handbag. "This came today."

Red and blue stripes colored the edge of the wrinkled envelope and a darker blue rectangle with white letters that read "BY AIR PAR AVION." It was addressed to me, the sender was Walter Vanderlaan, Private First Class.

"Any idea why he'd be writing you?" she asked, tapping his name with her long, red fingernail.

"No." I shrugged one shoulder. "I haven't a clue."

"You're sure?" She turned her head, giving me the side-eye.

I picked up the envelope, tapping a corner of it against the counter. Walt and his parents had been our neighbors when I was small. Our folks would play cards some Friday evenings, letting us kids stay up late to swim in the shallows of Old Chip or watch *Ozzie and Harriet* on television.

Walt had been my friend even though he was Mike's age. When he knocked on the door to ask for a playmate, he sought me. When we picked teams for a game of tag, he'd call my name first. More than once I'd overheard our mothers talk about writing up papers for an arranged marriage.

He was my very first friend and I was his.

But after Frank left and we moved, we didn't talk much anymore. And the older we got, the more Walt hated me. At least that was how I interpreted his name-calling and dirty looks.

I tried my hardest not to grimace, looking at my name on the envelope written in Walt's handwriting. "He's hardly spoken two words to me since we were little."

"Well, apparently he wants to talk to you now."

"I can't imagine why." I pushed up my glasses. "I'd think he has plenty of other people he could write."

"People change. Being at war can make a boy get ideas." Her eyes widened, she nodded once. "It makes them take notice of things they might otherwise overlook."

"Mom, no. He wouldn't—"

"Annie, you aren't getting any younger. You're eighteen, after all. And I know you are probably in a hurry to get married." She leaned over the counter toward me. "I'm sure you think he's a nice boy, but . . ."

"He's not nice," I interrupted. "I already know that. I've always known that. Besides, I'm not in a hurry to get married."

"Honey, he's at war. I'm sure he's lonely." She sighed. "I guess I just want you to be careful."

"Careful of what?"

"I don't want you getting your heart broken."

"Mom, I harbor no secret affections for Walt Vanderlaan. I promise. Besides, he's been engaged to Caroline Mann for ages." I stuffed the letter in between the pages of my book. "Don't worry. I won't write him back, if that's what you want."

"You can if you would like." She let out a breath and leaned her elbows on the counter. "Just don't keep any secrets from me. Can you promise me that?"

I nodded, squinting at her, trying to figure out what she was up to. She never sighed that way unless she had something up her sleeve. Then, her blue eyes sharpened, as if she was trying to see through me. I'd never in all my life held up under her X-ray gaze.

"Is there anything that you'd like to tell me?" she asked. "Any secrets about Michael?"

"What do you mean?"

"I know he's keeping something from me."

"Gosh, Mom, why would you think that?" I widened my eyes, hoping to look puzzled instead of guilty.

"What's this appointment of his?"

"How do you know about that?"

"Mothers always find out," she answered. "What's this appointment?"

The door to the diner opened, letting in a handful of girls who wandered to the window booth, whispering to each other about this or that. I let them know that I'd be right with them, and they nodded as if they were in no hurry.

"You know, don't you?" Mom asked. "Is he in some kind of trouble?"

"Mom."

"It's not about a girl, is it?" She touched my hand. "Please tell me it isn't."

"Mother."

"I understand, times are different than when I was his age." She stood upright, smoothing her blouse. "With the music and the movies now, I know that it can all be so confusing . . ."

"Mom, I swear to you it has nothing to do with a girl," I said, trying to stop her from saying something that would make me blush.

"All right," she said, putting her hands up in surrender. "I'm just worried is all."

"It would be better if he told you."

"Okay." She snapped her purse shut. "I should get back to work anyway."

I nodded.

She touched my cheek with her fingertips. "You're getting so grown up."

"If only I looked it." I pushed up my glasses. "I'm tired of people thinking I'm twelve."

"Someday you'll be glad you look younger." She winked at me.

"Maybe."

"Trust me, you will." She turned her attention to the pastry case, where we kept the desserts from the Dutch bakery down the road. "See if Bernie will let you bring home some leftover *banket* for dessert. Tell him I'll pay him back next week, all right?"

"Sure."

"And your *oma* is coming for supper. She might like it if you walked with her."

She picked up her purse, putting it back over her arm, and walked out of the diner, hips swaying with each step.

Mike reminded her of Frank. She never said it in so many words; still I knew. The way his brown eyes were unable to hide his mood, how his dark hair curled when he let it get long, his deep voice, his dimple-cheeked smile. All of Mike was all of Frank.

The girls at the booth ordered a glass of Coke each and a plate of french fries to share. The whole time they stayed, they watched everyone walk past on the other side of the window, giggling and gossiping.

While they ate, I sat behind the counter, my book unopened with the envelope peeking out, begging me to find out what was inside. I told myself I'd toss it in the mailbox at the end of the street with a big "RETURN TO SENDER" scrawled across it.

But stuffing the book into my purse, I knew I'd do no such thing.

Dear Annie,

I'll bet I was the last one you expected to get a letter from. I hope it was a good surprise, seeing my name on the envelope. No doubt the only reason you opened it was to find out why in the world I would be writing you.

Anyway, I found this feather on the ground over here in Vietnam and thought I'd send it to you. I hope you still like birds. Don't worry, I cleaned it really well. Isn't it pretty?

Wish you could see the birds here. They're like nothing at home. I tried taking a picture of one of them for you, but the darn thing flew away just as I snapped the shot.

Do you remember when we were kids and we'd watch the hummingbirds flit around the feeder in my front yard? You said they were magic and I wouldn't believe you. You cried, remember, when we found the one that died after it flew into the window. I think about that sometimes, you know. I felt bad that you cried that day. It was so small—impossibly small—and weighed almost nothing at all.

I never told you, but I buried it under my mother's hydrangea tree and marked the grave with a fieldstone. It's still there. When I get home, I can show you if you want.

Your friend,
Walt Vanderlaan

PS: You can write back to me if you'd like. I hope you will.

Susie Finkbeiner is the CBA bestselling author of *All Manner of Things*, which was selected as a 2020 Michigan Notable Book, as well as *Stories That Bind Us*, *The Nature of Small Birds*, and other novels. Susie and her husband have three children and live in West Michigan. Learn more at www.susiefinkbeiner.com.

Rediscover the Power of Story

to Open the Doors of Our Hearts

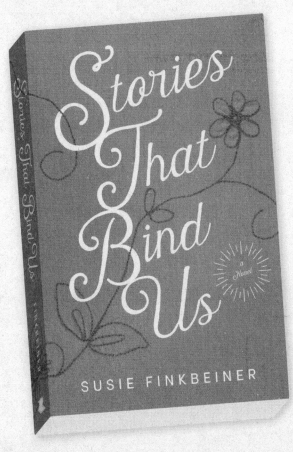

Betty Sweet is still recovering from the loss of her husband when she becomes the temporary guardian of a five-year-old nephew she never knew she had. As they struggle to move forward, they build a relationship upon the foundation of storytelling and its special kind of magic.

"A beautiful story about the intricacies of family and the power of love. Most definitely a must-read novel."

–HEIDI CHIAVAROLI,
Carol Award-winning author of *Freedom's Ring* and *The Orchard House*

When Mindy announces that she is returning to Vietnam to find her birth mother, it inspires her father, mother, and sister to recall the events of her adoption at the end of the Vietnam War during Operation Baby Lift. Told through three strong voices in three compelling timelines, this beautiful time-slip story explores the meaning of family far beyond genetic code.

Meet Susie

SusieFinkbeiner.com

LET'S
TALK
ABOUT
BOOKS

- Share or mention the book on your social media platforms. Use the hashtag **#TheAllAmerican**.

- Write a book review on your blog or on a retailer site.

- Pick up a copy for friends, family, or anyone who you think would enjoy and be challenged by its message!

- Share this message on Twitter, Facebook, or Instagram: **I loved #TheAllAmerican by @SusieFinkbeiner // @RevellBooks**

- Recommend this book for your church, workplace, book club, or small group.

- Follow Revell on social media and tell us what you like.

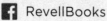 RevellBooks

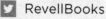 RevellBooks

 RevellBooks

 pinterest.com/RevellBooks